A REAL BASKET CASE

A REAL BASKET CASE

MYSTERY
BETH GROUNDWATER

FIVE STAR

An imprint of Thomson Gale, a part of The Thomson Corporation

THOMSON
™
GALE

Detroit • New York • San Francisco • New Haven, Conn. • Waterville, Maine • London

THOMSON
★
GALE

LIBRARY OF CONGRESS CATALOGING-IN-PUBLICATION DATA

Groundwater, Beth.
  A real basket case / Beth Groundwater. — 1st ed.
    p. cm.
  ISBN-13: 978-1-59414-547-6 (hardcover : alk. paper)
  ISBN-10: 1-59414-547-4 (hardcover : alk. paper)
  1. Gift baskets—Fiction. 2. Murder—Investigation—Fiction. 3. Drug dealers—Fiction. I. Title.
  PS3607.R677R43 2007
  813'.6—dc22   2006034798

First Edition. First Printing: March 2007.

Published in 2007 in conjunction with Tekno Books and Ed Gorman.

Printed in the United States of America on permanent paper
10 9 8 7 6 5 4 3 2 1

ACKNOWLEDGMENTS

An old African proverb states that "it takes a village to raise a child." The same can be said for a novel. I have a whole village of supportive writer friends to thank. First, my critique partners over the years: Charlie R, Drue D, Debby L, Dave C (RiP), Ann B, John B, Jim R, Susan R, Donnell B, Pat M, Keith M, Susan M, Jane M, Joni F, Julia A, MB P, Chris M, Bruce M, Vic C, Kirsten A, Annette K, Shawn R, Barb N, Maria F, and, especially, long-patient Bill M and Bob S. Second, published writers who gave me sound advice and encouragement: Jimmie B, Laura H, Pam M, Deb S, Kathy B, Linda B, Ann P, Maggie M, Pat C, and Chris G. Lastly, the writing communities I've joined: Pikes Peak Writers, Rocky Mountain Fiction Writers, Pikes Peak Romance Writers, and the Guppies chapter of Sisters In Crime.

I'd also like to thank my agent, Barret Neville, for his faith in my talents and his contract acumen, and my editor, Denise Dietz, for polishing my prose until it gleamed. To all the staff at Tekno Books and Five Star Publishing, thank you for your professionalism and for producing such a great-looking product. Many thanks to the volunteer instructors of the El Paso County Sheriff's Academy for educating me about crime, jails, and police procedure.

My husband, Neil, and two children, Anne and John, deserve super kudos for putting up with my long sojourns in my basement writing den, while laundry moldered in the washing machine and dinner preparations were forgotten. You kept the faith during the seven years it took me to get published. I have my parents to thank for my ambition, my values, and my self-confidence. And to all my other supportive extended family, especially my eager aunts, here it is, finally, the culmination of my dreams. Now, on to the next book . . .

CHAPTER 1
DEATH

Claire gripped the toilet bowl with white-knuckled hands. Her stomach heaved again. This time nothing came up. Laying her cheek against the hard porcelain rim, she let the comforting cold seep into her skin. She waited then wiped her mouth with a tissue. She scrubbed at the rust-colored stains around the rim—bloody fingerprints.

My fingerprints. Enrique's blood. Oh, God.

All her wiping managed to do was smear the stains. She stared at the damning evidence. Enrique was dead because of her.

Tears threatened again. She squeezed her eyes shut, willed the tears away, and took a deep breath. She balled up the tissue, threw it in the toilet, and flushed. After pushing herself to her feet, she leaned against the wall to clear her head and settle her lurching stomach.

Her robe gaped open, exposing her bloodstained thighs, the sticky streaks cracking where they had dried. She yanked her robe shut and cinched the belt tight. She felt an overwhelming urge to shower, to stand under burning hot water and scrub and scrub and scrub until her skin was raw. But no amount of scrubbing could wash away the guilt.

And the police detective was waiting.

She lifted her chin and squared her shoulders. "I think I can talk now."

Detective Wilson stood in the middle of her master bathroom, an authority figure awkwardly out of place among the mirrors, marbled green tile, plants, glass-enclosed shower, and whirlpool bathtub. He leaned over the sink and wrung out a washcloth, then handed it to her. "Wipe your face with this. It'll help you feel better."

The cool cloth on her sweat-drenched forehead did feel good. Washing her face and hands in the sink felt even better. Claire stared at the red-stained water that whirlpooled around and around the basin before being sucked down the drain. The coppery, new-penny smell was overpowering. She grabbed the knob to turn off the faucet.

She gulped down the bile rising in her throat again. She couldn't give in to the hysteria that tugged at the edge of her sanity—not yet. She faced Wilson as she dried her hands. "Sorry about that."

He shook his head. "Don't be. It's a common reaction to shock."

His even, quiet tone calmed her somewhat. He was tall, large-boned, with a heavily lined face, black hair flecked with gray, and solemn, knowing gray eyes to match. He held a small notebook in one of his slim-fingered large hands and stood waiting patiently for her. This man obviously had seen death many times before. But how could the murder of a human being ever be routine?

He studied her face. "You feel okay to talk?"

Hell, no. "I think so."

He led her to the vanity chair. "Water?"

"No, thanks." Claire felt compelled to glance through the open bathroom doorway to the master bedroom. The forensic technician stood with her back to them, bent over the king-sized bed. Enrique's body had been removed, but the vivid image of his gaping wound burned in Claire's mind. She shuddered and hugged her robe close.

Wilson's gaze followed hers. He shut the door, then perched

on the edge of the Jacuzzi tub, opened the notebook, and took a pen out of his pocket. "I know this has been a big shock, Mrs. Hanover, but I need you to tell me everything that happened, with as many details as you can remember. First of all, this Enrique Romero wasn't assaulting you, was he?"

Claire's cheeks flushed. "No, he wasn't."

"How do you know him?"

"We met three days ago."

Wilson's eyes widened before he could mask his expression.

With a resigned sigh, Claire said, "I'll tell you the whole story . . ."

CHAPTER 2
SEDUCTION

Enrique's muscles flexed and stretched in rhythm with his steady thrusts. His bronzed skin glistened. Long ridges and furrows defined the perfect sculpted form of his Adonis thighs.

Claire couldn't help but stare at those testaments to virility as she strained to match his tempo—in, out, in, out. Her breaths came in quick gasps. She swiped at a bead of sweat on her brow. She couldn't keep up this pace for long.

". . . three, two, one," Enrique said.

Good. He's counting down.

"Excellent. Now onto your backs."

Claire flopped down on the floor with a sigh that was matched by a long exhale on her left from her best friend. Ellen's perfect lavender-and-aqua-clad body had barely broken a sweat, while Claire's old black leotard clung to her damp skin like mutant plastic wrap. "I'm gonna kill you for this, Ellen. Our ten years of friendship will not save you from my wrath."

Ellen winked. "You'll survive."

"But you won't. And your death will be slow and painful, just like this class."

With a laugh, Ellen shoved her hips in the air. "Only ten more minutes until cool-down. You're not going to quit on me, are you?"

"Hell, no." Determined to finish her first aerobics class even if she had to crawl to the showers, Claire concentrated on her pelvic thrusts. Up, down, up, down. Unsure how long she could continue the agonizing squeezes, she glanced to her right at her second best friend, Jill, Ellen's co-conspirator in coercing Claire into this torture room.

Jill's round belly bobbed in rhythm with Claire's. Weighing about the same as Claire, but four inches shorter, Jill's pounds-per-inch ratio was higher. Sweat trickled down her face, but she cracked a smile without breaking her pace.

No sympathy there, either. If Jill could do it, Claire wasn't about to surrender. With gritted teeth, she watched herself in one of the mirrors covering three walls of the harshly lit room. A scan of the four rows of middle-aged women panting and pushing on the floor encouraged her. Many were in worse shape than she was. Much worse.

The instructor, Enrique, prowled among the women with quiet steps, correcting form and dispensing compliments as needed. Claire sensed his presence before his shadow fell over her.

He knelt beside her. "Not that way. Tilt your pelvis more." His hand hovered over her stomach. "May I?"

Claire swallowed and nodded. Her nostrils sucked in his musky man scent. Unbidden, her gaze trailed down the washboard abdominal muscles outlined by the damp tank top clinging to his chest.

He placed one hand on her stomach and one behind her butt, then eased her pelvis into the correct tilt. "Press against my hand."

Closing her eyes to concentrate on her form, not his, Claire thrust her hips upward. The impression of his hand seared through her leotard. *Oh, God.* Her eyes snapped open.

"Perfect. Now do twenty more like that." He rose.

A bead of sweat rolled off his perfect, patrician nose and plopped on Claire's chest. The drop slid between her breasts.

Clearly oblivious, he moved along the rows of grunting house-wives.

Ellen chuckled. "Overpowering, isn't he?" A sly grin played on her collagen-enhanced lips.

Claire rolled her eyes, but her heart was thumping, and not just from the exercise. Her body's reaction to Enrique secretly terrified her.

During the cool-down stretches, she noticed many women's gazes flicked to Enrique's masculine thighs bulging beneath nylon shorts, then slid away, as if the women didn't want to be caught looking. Their gazes always returned, drawn as seductively as suicidal moths to a bug zapper on a steamy summer night. Other women, uncaring, stared brazenly.

Somehow, Claire made it through the rest of the aerobics class and limped after Ellen and Jill into the changing room. Locker doors slammed and women chattered as they peeled off damp clothes and migrated to the showers.

"Well?" Ellen planted her hands on her hips. "Think you'll live?"

Claire collapsed on a bench. "Losing this holiday weight isn't going to be easy."

"No one said it would be." Ellen took a bottle of shampoo out of her locker. "But having eye-candy to watch while you sweat the pounds off makes it more interesting."

Jill toweled off her red face and snorted. "That's about all he's good for, the egotistical moron. Speaking of candy . . ." She dropped the towel, fished a bite-sized chocolate out of her gym bag, and popped the morsel into her mouth with delicate fingers.

Claire gaped. "How could you—right after exercising?"

Jill frowned, then shrugged and mumbled around the chocolate, "That's when I need the boost the most. Besides, I earned it."

Claire realized she might have hurt Jill's feelings. "Sorry, I just meant I'd probably get nauseous if I ate anything now."

Jill's lips curled. "Chocolate never makes me nauseous. Can't stay, girls, got errands to run." She scurried out of the locker room.

With her brunette hair held high in a ponytail, and her small, tapered fingers and feet, Jill looked like a chubby star scrawled by a kindergartner. Claire doubted any amount of aerobics classes would change Jill's shape, especially if she kept rewarding herself with chocolate, but Claire applauded her for trying.

After grabbing her towel, Claire followed Ellen to the showers. "Why does Jill dislike Enrique so much?"

"Don't worry about it." Ellen leaned back to wet her hair under the shower spray. "She'll get over it."

Get over what?

"This class is good for her, though. I don't know what results she's gotten, but I've lost three inches so far. Not bad for five months." Ellen patted her flat stomach.

At forty-eight, Ellen still had a figure to be proud of, but her expression was hard and lined, even with Botox injections smoothing out her forehead wrinkles. Ellen's husband had left her two years ago for an attractive young lawyer at his practice, and the rejection had taken its toll.

Lathering the gym's coconut-scented liquid soap on her own poochy stomach, Claire wondered if Roger would ever do such a thing. No, her husband wasn't interested in another woman. His career was his mistress. Claire barely saw him anymore. When he did come home, he spent hours on the computer, poring over ledgers and corporate accounts before falling exhausted into bed long after she'd turned out the light.

She had hoped that when their two children left home, she and Roger would rekindle the close relationship they'd shared before parenthood had engulfed them. But no such luck. She even suggested counseling. Roger had said nothing was wrong and he didn't have time.

Claire stepped from the shower to dry off. Here she was, forty-six and bored out of her gourd. The home-based gift-basket business she started when her nest emptied only required twelve to sixteen hours a week. She spent too many evenings in front of the TV with a bowl of canned soup, waiting for Roger. Her restlessness had inspired her to accept Ellen's offer to join the three-times-a-week exercise class. And if she trimmed a few inches, maybe Roger would notice.

Ellen stood next to her in front of the sinks as they dried their hair. She shut off her blow dryer and pointed to the part in Claire's chin-length bob. "Your roots are showing."

Claire peered in the wide mirror. Each time her dyed-blond hair grew out, more gray showed. She sighed. "Yeah, I'll have to make an appointment."

Tilting her head, Ellen studied Claire's reflection. "Why not let it grow out?"

"No way." Claire unplugged her hair dryer and headed for her locker.

Ellen trailed behind her. "If you streak it, the gray would look good on you. Roger might like the change."

"My hair was this color when I met Roger. I won't change it until it's all coming out white."

"Come to think of it, Dave didn't go for my redhead look. Not even a new set of boobs kept him off that bitch." Cradling her gel-filled breasts, newly minted two years ago when the trouble with Dave started, Ellen laughed. That cruel laugh was new, too. "I like them, though. And what makes you think Roger cares what color your hair is? He hardly notices you anymore."

Normally Claire found Ellen's blunt honesty refreshing, but this struck too close. She sat on a bench to tug on her shoes. "I like my hair blond, too."

"Good." With a firm yank, Ellen zipped her gym bag shut.

"As long as you do it for yourself, that's all right. But don't do anything for a man. They aren't worth it."

Mulling over this new vehemence in her formerly easygoing friend, Claire nearly bumped into Ellen when she stopped abruptly outside the locker room door.

The aerobics instructor, black hair damp from his shower and smelling faintly of the coconut soap, smiled at Claire. His deep brown-eyed gaze bored into her. "Ellen, are you going to introduce me to your lovely companion?"

Ellen shot him a not-so-friendly glance then plastered a smile on her face. "Sure. This is Claire Hanover." She swept a deprecating hand toward the instructor. "Claire, meet Enrique Romero, the Romeo of Graham's Gym."

"Thank you for sharing your friend with me. And Claire . . ." He took her hand and stared into her eyes until she looked away. "I hope you will return to my class on Wednesday."

"I . . . I plan to." Claire slid her hand from his grasp, but not before he gave it a playful squeeze.

A stately brunette in her late thirties brushed past on her way out of the locker room. She turned to Enrique. "See you soon?"

"Yes. At the usual place." Enrique winked at her then refocused on Claire. "I look forward to seeing you again."

As she walked out of the gym, Claire felt his gaze on her back. She zipped up her coat against both his scrutiny and the brisk winter breeze schussing down the snow-laden slopes of Pikes Peak into Colorado Springs.

"Who was that woman?" Claire asked Ellen.

"Brenda Johnston. An architect. I don't know her well. She keeps to herself." Ellen stopped Claire with a touch on her arm. "Enrique's interested in you, you know."

Claire's face flushed. "What?"

"He has a thing for older women."

"Who're you calling an older woman?" Claire had never attached that label to herself before.

Ellen grinned. "Older than he is, that is. If you want a little excitement, all you have to do is say yes."

"I'm married, remember? I couldn't do that to Roger."

Ellen shrugged. "Wake up and smell the cappuccino. You're no more important to him than a piece of furniture."

The words stung, but Claire had to admit her friend probably was right. The hugs and hand-holding of years past had given way to quick pecks on the cheek. Guiltily, she realized that mixed with her shock was pleasure that she had attracted Enrique's attention—that she could attract any man's attention.

"Roger will never find out," Ellen said. "Does he even know you're here today?"

"No."

"See? And he probably doesn't care, either." She peered at Claire. "C'mon. A little fling will do wonders for your attitude, let alone your sex life. Think about it."

With a disturbing premonition that Enrique signaled trouble—deep trouble—Claire shook her head and rubbed the hand he had grasped.

Claire glanced at her watch that night—nine-thirty. *When is Roger coming home?* As she rose from the family room sofa, her stiff joints cracked. She stretched and made a note to take another ibuprofen, the candy of the middle-aged, before bed.

The TV sitcom had been one long string of sexual innuendoes and worn-out, demeaning jokes. Why did she sit through the tiresome show until the end? Because she had nothing better to do—like talk to her husband. She'd finished a basket order late that afternoon and couldn't work up the enthusiasm to start another one.

She glanced at two of her large Colorado Collection gift baskets, which sat on the side table, ready for their Thursday delivery to a local real estate agent. Decorated with leather strips, beads, and turkey feathers, they brimmed with southwestern food products—wildflower honey, blue cornbread mix, and the requisite hot sauces and salsa mouth-burners with names like Pure Hell, Durango Red, and Scorned Woman.

Claire's lips curled. *Scorned Woman, that's what I feel like.*

She scooped up the remains of another soup-and-crackers dinner, stomped into the kitchen, and dumped the dishes in the sink. She picked up the phone then slammed it back down again. Where would it get her to yell at him?

She paced the floor and took a couple of deep, calming breaths, then called Roger at his office. "Do you know what time it is?"

"Jeez, I didn't realize it was so late. I've got my staff hustling to get ready for our investors' briefing Friday."

"That's four days from now. Why are you working late tonight?"

"Because I have a goddamn mountain of work to do." Roger paused, then resumed in a more conciliatory tone. "Sorry. I didn't mean to take out my stress on you. I'll be tied up on this all week. I can't force my staff to stay and not stay myself. The dry run's Thursday, and I have to get the books in order by then."

Claire drummed her fingers on the counter. "Does that mean I'll be eating alone every night until Friday?"

"I'm afraid so. I can't let Ned down on this one."

Since being promoted to the position of chief financial officer a year ago, Roger had been diligent in doing whatever Ned Peters, president of the mid-sized technology company, asked. Excessively diligent.

"But you can let your wife down," she said.

"Dammit, Claire, that's not fair. You know this is an important step in my career. If I perform well as CFO for Ned's private company, I can move on to a large public firm. Then the bucks'll really flow."

"But I don't want more money. I want you." God, that sounded pathetic. But she was sick of playing second best to Ned and his infernal chips and bits.

Roger exhaled loudly. "You know it's not just the money. I've told you before. It's the prestige. CFOs are part of the elite, the movers and shakers of the corporate world."

Again, Roger hadn't understood her point. Frustration welled up in her throat. "You act like you value your career more than our marriage. Can't you delegate some of this work so you can come home at a decent hour once in awhile?"

"It's my responsibility to make sure this briefing is right. I can't delegate that."

"But—"

"I'll take you out to dinner Friday when this is all over. You pick the place. In the meantime, why don't you get out more on your own? Do something with your girlfriends."

Could she count on Ellen or Jill to kiss her goodnight, hold her in their arms, make love to her? *Hell, no.* Roger wasn't going to either, hadn't for what, weeks now?

Claire slapped the refrigerator then stared at her reddened palm. He still didn't see what he was doing to their marriage. But from the irritation in his voice, she knew the time had come to back off. "I started an exercise class today."

"See, that's what I'm talking about. Make new friends in the class, organize a ski trip with them, whatever."

She remembered their family ski trips, when the kids were young enough to put up with their parents' companionship and Roger could escape from his work long enough to actually have some fun. Back then, Claire and Roger had looked forward to traveling more when the kids were grown, and they had planned imaginary trips to romantic, faraway places like Tuscany,

Bangkok, and Cancun. Nowadays, Claire rarely ventured farther than the factory outlet shops in Castle Rock.

"I'd rather ski with you," she said.

"I already told you. You can't depend on me to fill your time. Not when I'm building a reputation here."

"You promised we'd go to Breckenridge one weekend this month."

"There's not a chance in hell that's going to happen now."

Claire simmered. "So a promise to your wife means nothing anymore."

"Honey, that's not . . . wait a minute." Roger covered the receiver to talk to someone in his office, then returned. "Gotta go. We'll talk about this later. Don't wait up for me."

"Roger—" Claire realized she was talking to a dead line.

On Wednesday, Claire took the ten a.m. aerobics class again. She had trouble keeping her eyes off Enrique and concentrating on the exercises. He seemed to watch her more than the other women, or was that her overactive imagination? She caught herself sucking in her stomach and comparing her profile to others in the mirrors. Not as bad as the Bartlett pear in the back row, but no comparison to willowy Brenda. Claire's form was more like a sturdy oak.

Afterward, Claire's sore muscles complained about being strained again so soon. In the locker room, she popped an ibuprofen into her mouth while she changed into street clothes. She chatted briefly with Jill, who raved about a new almond coffee cookie recipe before leaving to attend a PTO meeting at her son's high school.

After a quick shower, Ellen had rushed to a massage appointment. Claire wished she had a massage appointment. She rubbed her neck with one hand while she walked down the corridor toward the front door of the gym.

"Feeling a little sore?" Enrique stepped in front of her, his grin showing dazzling white teeth.

Surprised, she sucked in a breath. A whiff of his musky after-shave stirred up a little quiver in the pit of her stomach. "I guess I'm not used to this yet."

"Let me." He eased her around and kneaded her shoulders expertly, forcing taut muscles to loosen.

Face flushing, Claire protested, "No, no, I'm fine. Aren't we in the way here?"

Enrique continued the massage. "You are too tight, and others can walk around us. No problem."

She gave up and tried to relax. His hands on her felt good—too good. As his thumbs worked up the back of her neck, she closed her eyes and let her head loll. When he stopped and turned her around to face him, she couldn't help feeling disappointed.

"Better?"

Claire rolled her shoulders. "Better."

He cupped her elbow. "Now we will have a drink together, some juice, perhaps, and discuss your exercise program."

"But—"

"No buts." Enrique steered her into the gym's health food bar and toward a booth in the rear.

The chatter of conversations and the roar of blenders devouring ice assaulted Claire's ears. The place smelled like a farm market—grass, probably wheat grass, and carrots, lemons, and cucumbers. Bewildered, she sat in the booth.

Enrique slid in across from her. "Carrot-apple juice with protein powder will restore your electrolytes. Okay?"

Claire knew nothing about electrolytes. "Okay."

He ordered two from the waitress. Then he rubbed his hands together. "It has been a while since you exercised, yes?"

"I walked some in the summer and fall, but I quit when the

cold weather moved in. Then I got busy over the holidays."

"Typical. We must get you limber and fit again." He grabbed one of the drinks the waitress delivered and took a couple of gulps. "You need to start a weight-lifting program to build your strength and bones."

A vision of herself pinned by a dropped weight bar, sprawled on her back like a flipped turtle with arms and legs flailing, almost made Claire spit out her drink.

He poked a thumb at his chest. "I will be your personal trainer."

"What do you charge?"

"Nothing for you."

"Why would you do that for me?"

Enrique patted her hand. "You are a beautiful woman, Claire. I will make you even more beautiful."

She pulled her hands into her lap. It had been a long time since someone had called her beautiful.

Enrique gazed into her eyes. "I am serious. You have a very nice body, just a little soft. But your face, ah, your face. Your eyes are large and blue, blue like our Colorado sky. They are mirrors to your soul."

Claire felt her cheeks redden.

He smiled. "Right now, you are a little embarrassed."

"A little." She leaned back. He was getting too close. "I'm not sure I like where this conversation is going."

Enrique drank some juice and studied her. "I think you do like it. Very much."

She picked up her glass and took a nervous sip of the grainy, sweet juice. Was he flirting or just stating what was obviously written all over her face?

He grinned at her. "You see?"

She tried unsuccessfully to stifle a smile. "I'm a terrible liar."

He leaned forward. "What are you doing tomorrow morning?"

"I . . . nothing."

He finished his juice and stood. "Meet me here at ten. We will go through the weight machines. Then you will be very sore. You will need a massage. All over." He winked and strode off.

Claire's chin dropped. A massage? She stared at his retreating form. *He has great buns. Oh, God.*

Then she noticed the check. She pulled out her wallet, dropped some money on the table, and picked up her gym bag. *I have to call Ellen.*

Claire paced across her Mexican-tiled kitchen, phone clutched tight against her ear. She stared out the window. Her house nestled among scrub oak and ponderosa pine in the foothills of Colorado Springs. Patches of snow dotted the yard where shadows hid them from the February sun. A squirrel scampered along the rail of the redwood deck. The creature seemed to know what direction to take—unlike herself.

When Ellen answered the phone, Claire said, "I'm in trouble. Big trouble. Enrique plans to guide me through the weight machines tomorrow, and he said something about massaging me all over."

"See, I told you he was interested. Here's your chance for a little fling."

Claire twisted the phone cord. "I don't want a fling." Her chest and cheeks flushed, either from a premenopausal hot flash or the thought of a fling with Enrique. She couldn't tell. She picked up a magazine and fanned her face.

"Nothing like a little action on the side to liven up a marriage. I should know. The best sex I ever had with Dave was after he started seeing that slut."

"C'mon, Ellen, I'm not looking for a divorce."

"Of course not. You won't have a serious relationship with Enrique. Just a little fun. That's all he wants."

Claire felt her eyes narrow. "How do you know?"

"He won't tell you, but some women in the class have been with him. They can't resist bragging in the locker room."

"Yuck." Claire remembered that woman, Brenda, arranging to meet with Enrique.

Ellen laughed. "You don't have to tell a soul. In fact, I advise you not to. An opportunity like this doesn't come along very often. Not with a hunk like Enrique."

Claire sucked in air between her teeth. She still loved Roger, even if he never gave her a chance to show it. But lately, she'd begun to wonder if he still loved her. "I can't sneak around behind Roger's back, no matter how troubled our marriage is. Maybe I should just quit the class."

"Not after I finally convinced you to start exercising. You need this class."

"I do need to lose a few pounds." Claire pinched the skin over her abdomen. More than an inch for sure.

"And Enrique's right. Aerobics won't do it alone. You need to lift weights, too." Ellen paused. "You should meet him tomorrow."

"I told you. I'm not going to cheat on Roger."

"I know, I know, though I'm disappointed in you. Just tell Enrique you're not interested in fooling around. He'll shrug it off, and you'll still get the weight-training you need."

Nibbling at her lip, Claire said, "But no massage."

"If you don't get a massage after that session, you'll ache all weekend. And he gives a *great* massage."

Claire's hands turned ice-cold at the thought of a strange man placing his hands on her not-so-firm-anymore body. "I would feel too self-conscious. I'll just soak in the tub and take some ibuprofen."

"Are you sure?"

"I'm sure."

Ellen sighed. "Sometimes you need to be nudged in the direction that's best for you."

Claire managed a sheepish laugh. "Like when you talked me into starting my basket business?"

"Exactly. You were blind to all the compliments you got on ones you made as gifts for your friends. Someone had to force you to see how good you were at it."

"I'm glad you did. Creating them keeps me from missing the kids so much."

"Back to Enrique. Just remember, there's no harm in looking, and he's definitely an eyeful." Ellen hung up.

Claire stared at the phone. The thought of spending the next morning with Enrique sent a shiver down her spine that settled in the pit of her stomach. *Oh, God.*

CHAPTER 3
BODYWORK

Claire shoved her bag into a locker. Nervous sweat dampened her hands as she took off her coat and checked her reflection in the mirror—oversized T-shirt and leggings, slouched socks, and sneakers. If only she'd shopped the day before for a coordinated exercise outfit like Ellen's.

Sucking in her stomach, Claire took a last glance and patted down her hair. She gritted her teeth and stepped out of the locker room.

Enrique stood by the door to the weight room, reading a fitness magazine. His skimpy shorts and tank top left little to the imagination. When he saw her, he smiled and returned the magazine to the rack. He pushed his arms up in a mock-lift that made his biceps bulge. "Ready to build those muscles?"

Claire squared her shoulders. "As ready as I'll ever be."

"Good. Let us begin." He waved his hand toward the rows of weight machines. "We will start with a circuit of eight machines."

She groaned.

For the next forty-five minutes, Enrique patiently explained each machine. He helped her find ideal seat positions and selected weights that made her work, but not too hard. Moving from machine to machine, he recorded the positions and weights on a clipboard chart.

Distracted by his nearness, Claire struggled to listen to his instructions. She gradually lost her nervousness while Enrique pointed out—on her—the muscles each machine worked. Straining against the machines gave her a sense of power. She could learn to like this.

At the end of the circuit, Enrique studied her chart before sliding it into a file cabinet drawer. "You did very well for your first day. Are you surprised by how much weight you can lift?"

Claire rolled her stiff shoulders. Her leg muscles complained, too. "I may not be able to lift much tomorrow."

Enrique laughed, then leaned in close and lowered his voice. "That is why you must continue to lift, to keep those muscles from freezing."

As his breath caressed her cheek, heat rushed into Claire's face.

"A massage helps, too." He pulled an envelope out of his shorts pocket and handed it to her.

Puzzled, Claire opened the envelope. She pulled out a gift certificate for a massage made out to her and signed by Ellen.

"Ellen told me you were interested in a massage today." Enrique winked.

Claire felt boxed in, the decision already made for her. Wasting Ellen's money by refusing would be awkward. She gulped and nodded. "But nothing else."

"That is fine with me." Enrique tilted her chin up so she had to look directly into his eyes. "Until you decide you are ready for more."

She stared, tongue-tied.

Enrique dropped his hand. "Now you must change. I will meet you in the lobby, then we will go to your house."

"My house?" *No way.*

"Where else?"

"Doesn't the gym have massage rooms?"

"I am a freelance therapist and cannot use those rooms."

She tried to hand the certificate back to him. "I don't feel comfortable with—"

"Massage therapists make house calls all the time." He patted her shoulder. "Many clients prefer to relax in the privacy of their own homes." With a confident stride, he headed down the hall, toward the men's locker room.

Weak-kneed, Claire wobbled into the women's locker room, as the implications of taking Enrique home sank in. She had to make sure he knew this was just a massage, a professional relationship and nothing more. She rushed through her shower, quickly changed into stretch jeans and a sky-blue Nordic ski sweater, then worked on her hair. Twenty minutes after leaving the weight room, she stepped into the lobby.

Enrique sat on a bench, looking casually elegant in black jeans, pearl-buttoned Western shirt, and a fleece-lined leather jacket. All he lacked for the urban cowboy ensemble was a ten-gallon hat. Rising, he looked her up and down and flashed a thumbs-up.

He steered her to the take-out counter of the health food bar. "Let us order a juice to go. You need to replenish your fluids." He ordered two.

"Enrique, this is awkward, but I want to make sure we're clear on something."

The young man behind the counter brought the juices, and Enrique snapped his fingers. "I forgot the massage oil. I will meet you in the parking lot." He headed for the men's locker room.

The young man said, "Seven-fifty, please."

Claire felt a wisp of annoyance over being stuck with the check again. Was this a habit of Enrique's? But she could easily afford it, and he probably didn't earn much as a fitness instructor. She paid the man and slipped on her coat before picking up the plastic cups.

In the parking lot, she squinted against the sun's glare, but with full hands, she couldn't retrieve her sunglasses from the purse dangling on her shoulder. Nor could she button her coat against the chill. She was debating where to put the cups when Enrique sauntered out a side door, carrying his gym bag.

Claire caught herself scanning the lot for anyone she knew. *Cut it out. I'm not doing anything wrong.* Still, she couldn't help feeling relieved that the lot was empty except for the two of them.

Enrique waved, then approached and took his drink. "Where is your car?"

"Right there." She indicated the late-model blue BMW sedan at the end of the row. She itched to get them in their respective cars and out of public view. "Do you want to follow me in your car?"

"Mine is in the shop." He pointed to the auto shop on the corner. "Maybe you could return me here after?"

Another favor. But Claire could tell from his winsome smile that he didn't realize what he was asking. And it wasn't like she had pressing business that afternoon, or that giving him a ride could be viewed as immoral. She nodded. When they reached her car, she pressed her key fob and unlocked the doors. After tossing her gym bag on the back seat, she slid behind the wheel.

Enrique sat in the gray leather seat beside her and dropped his bag next to hers. He placed his drink in the cup holder and glanced around. "Nice car. Your husband must have a good job."

Poised to turn the ignition key, Claire's hand dropped to her lap. *What am I doing?* Fear stabbed her chest as she envisioned the risk of Enrique pressing himself on her, of her being swept up with desire. *No!*

"I can't do this."

Enrique laid his hand on hers. "If you don't get a massage, you will hurt tonight and not be good company for your husband. I want to make you feel good, that's all."

"That's all." She slid her hand out from under his and stared him down. "Nothing but a professional massage. And I'll never be ready for more."

He held up his hands, palms out, and grinned. "Okay. Only a massage. How do you say it? Boy Scout promise?"

Ellen did say Enrique would shrug it off if I said I wasn't interested. Placated, Claire started the engine and pulled out of the parking space. She didn't tell Enrique that being good company that night would make no difference because Roger wouldn't be there.

Enrique settled in the seat and picked up his juice. "So, tell me about your home. Is it southwestern style?"

He's good. Every woman likes to talk about her home. She described how she'd shopped for Navajo and Pueblo Indian crafts and blankets to complement her house's stucco and tile-roofed architecture. After moving to Colorado from the East Coast twelve years earlier, she had enjoyed learning the history and culture of her new environs.

Enrique seemed genuinely interested and asked several questions as she guided the car up the steep, winding canyon roads of her upscale neighborhood. When a white-tailed red fox scampered across the road, causing her to brake hard, he asked, "Do you see many wild animals here in the foothills?"

"Lots of birds, squirrels, and mule deer. Roger hates the deer. He calls them giant rats because they eat our flowers and strip the bark off the aspens. He chases them out of the yard whenever he sees them." Claire pursed her lips. "I wish he wouldn't do that."

Enrique laughed. "You feel sorry for the deer?"

She shook her head. "The stags can be dangerous, especially in fall rutting season. The neighbor's dog got gored when it cornered one last year."

"Yes, one has to watch out for stags during mating season."

Claire glanced at Enrique. What did he mean by that? She decided to ignore the comment's sexual undertone. "We also hear coyotes howling on the ridge but never see them. Occasionally, we'll smell a skunk when we have the windows open in the summer."

"No air-conditioning?"

"Don't need it." Claire pulled the BMW into her long driveway. She glanced around but saw no one on the street. Then she caught herself. *Why am I worried?*

She pressed the garage door opener and drove into the third bay. As the door slid down behind them, she cut the ignition and let out the breath she'd been holding.

Enrique stepped out of the car and reached in to retrieve the two gym bags from the back seat. "Lead the way."

"You can leave your bag in the car," Claire said.

He hefted his bag and smiled. "The massage oil is in here."

A nervous flutter tickled Claire's throat, and she cleared it before saying, "Fine." She preceded him into the kitchen and took her gym bag into the adjoining laundry room.

Enrique shucked off his jacket and looked around, as if wondering where to put it and his gym bag.

"I'll take those," she said.

"I will need the bag later, but here." He handed her his jacket and put the bag on the floor.

Claire hung Enrique's jacket along with her own in the hall closet. Through the glass beside the front door, she spied a UPS package on the porch. She unlocked the door, dropped the package on the front bench, then returned to the kitchen.

Enrique had found the wine rack and was scanning labels. "How about some wine? It would be relaxing."

Claire glanced down at her hands, clasped in a tight knot before her. Yes, wine was a good idea. "Pick one you like. I'll fix us some cheese and crackers for lunch." She handed him a corkscrew and glasses then opened the refrigerator.

With a practiced pull, Enrique deftly extracted the cork from a bottle of Australian Shiraz. He filled their glasses with the plum-colored wine and carried them to the counter where she had laid out a tray with Brie and Jarlsburg cheeses, crackers, and grapes. He smiled, handed her a glass and lifted his. "A toast . . . to an excellent hostess."

Claire drank two quick gulps. The slow burn down her throat to her stomach felt good.

Enrique settled on a stool and pointed at a family portrait on the wall. "Tell me about your children."

"My son, Michael, graduated from the Colorado School of Mines last year and works as an engineer for Electronic Data Systems in Boston."

"He must be very intelligent. What about your daughter?"

"Judy's a junior at the University of Colorado, currently in France on a semester study program."

"Will she be an engineer too?"

"No, but she had us wondering. Michael knew his junior year in high school that he wanted to be an engineer. Judy didn't pick her major until the last possible minute. Then she decided to make it a double. Art and French. In spite of her stubborn independence, she chose the same major as her fuddy-duddy mom."

Enrique raised a brow. "Art and French. *Très chic.*" In a mock salute, he kissed his fingertips and spread them wide.

Claire laughed. "I didn't do much with the major besides teach art in elementary schools before the kids were born."

"So your nest is empty now. Do you miss them?"

"Yes, terribly." Claire stared at the portrait, at Roger's handsome squared jaw and the clear blue eyes that made her heart thrill when he looked at her with desire, which hadn't happened since forever. She focused on the images of her children, and guilt washed over her. What would Michael and Judy think of their mom sharing wine with another man, alone, in their home?

She put down her glass. "Enrique, I'm—"

"Feeling a little awkward? I promise I will do no more than you want. You shouldn't waste Ellen's gift."

Her back muscles were already stiffening. A massage made sense, and he did say he would respect her wishes. "I don't want to disappoint Ellen."

Enrique squeezed her hand. "Of course not. But now, let us eat. I am famished." He slid a cracker into his mouth.

The light remark dispelled some of her tension. She clinked her glass against his and took the last sip.

Enrique refilled her glass. He maintained a steady flow of conversation as he plied her with cheese and more wine.

Soon she felt a warm buzz and laughed as Enrique tossed grapes in the air and caught them in his mouth. Before she knew it, the wine bottle lay in the sink, empty.

He stood. "Where is your bedroom?"

Claire's eyes widened. Then she realized he hadn't brought a massage table. "Oh no, not my bedroom." Her gaze lit on the kitchen table. "How about there? I could spread some towels."

He glanced at the table and shook his head. "The surface must be soft, like a bed."

"Maybe one of my kid's bedrooms, then."

"Let us check them out. Come." He took her hand, pulled her off the stool, and steered her into the hall. Once there, he dropped his gym bag on the floor and removed the bottle of massage oil and a CD.

She preceded him upstairs, gripping the rail to steady herself, then led the way into her daughter's room.

Enrique glanced at the bed, pursed his lips, then checked her son's bedroom. Before she could stop him, he walked into the master bedroom suite. "Perfect."

She trotted after him. "Wait."

Enrique walked around the large room, furnished with two bulky walnut dressers, a sitting area, oil paintings of snow-capped mountains, and a raised king-sized bed, its side facing the door. "Nice, very nice."

He moved to the other side of the bed and pressed a hand on the mattress. "This is just the right softness, and I won't have to bend over much."

The image of him leaning over her while she lay on the bed she shared with Roger made Claire's throat tighten.

Enrique pointed at the compact stereo system on the headboard. "May I play my CD? The music will help you relax."

The freight train pushing her down the track of least resistance roared in her ears. "Sure."

"Now, bring some towels. While I prepare, you may change out of your clothes."

"Out of my clothes?" Claire instinctively clasped her arms across her chest, as if already covering her nakedness.

Enrique laughed and raised the bottle of massage oil. "You cannot receive a massage wearing jeans and a sweater. Leave your underthings on if you wish."

She gulped. She would definitely leave them on.

He waved his hands toward the master bath suite. "Go."

Claire returned with the towels. Enrique had pulled back the bedclothes. The soft strains of a Navajo flute floated from the speakers. She walked back into the bathroom and closed the door. Staring in the mirror, she debated her reflection.

Should I?

C'mon, it's just a massage.

But what if Roger finds out?

How could he? He probably wouldn't care anyway. He did say I couldn't depend on him to fill my time. Maybe he hates being with me. Maybe he doesn't love me anymore.

She swallowed the lump in her throat. Decision made, she turned away from the mirror. Once she had stripped down to her plain white bra and panties, she grabbed her thick, terry-cloth robe and threw it on before she caught a glimpse of her middle-aged body and lost her nerve. She closed her eyes, counted to ten, and stepped into the bedroom.

Enrique smiled and clasped her hand. "No need to be nervous. I've done this many times before."

Done what?

He led her to the bed and untied the belt of her robe. Easing it off her shoulders, he let it slip to the floor.

Claire cringed. Other than Roger and her doctor, no man had seen this much of her since she'd birthed her two children. *Who had left their marks.*

"You are a beautiful woman, Claire. Do not let anyone tell you different." He paused, then pointed at the bed. "Lie on your stomach on these towels."

Claire did as she was told.

Enrique moved to stand beside her, then unfastened her bra.

She tensed and lay nervous and stiff, arms tight against her sides. She wondered what would happen next and if she should allow it. When his warm hands, slick with sandalwood-and-rose-scented oil, touched her back, she shivered.

His palms slid down, up, and down again, pressing deep into her flesh and willing her to relax.

The muscles in her back loosened one-by-one under his firm touch. Her brain, already fuzzy from the wine, loosened too. His soothing strokes and the calming flute music pushed her remaining worries aside.

He must have felt the difference, because he began kneading her shoulders.

She finally yielded to the bliss with a sigh.

"Yes, just relax. I will do all the work, and you will feel

wonderful. You *do* feel wonderful," Enrique said with a laugh. All Claire could muster was a murmured assent.

Enrique worked on her neck, back, and shoulders, then massaged her arms and legs, freeing cramped muscles and releasing the accompanying pain and tension.

Claire had never felt so relaxed—like warm gelatin. When Enrique refastened her bra and asked her to roll over, she mumbled, "I don't think I can."

He eased his hands under her and helped her roll onto her back. His hands lingered on her waist a moment too long before he drew them away to pour more of the fragrant oil into them. Then he began massaging her thighs.

A warm tingle spread over Claire's body. She closed her eyes. Enrique's hands froze. "You—"

BLAM!

Claire's whole body jerked. Her eyes snapped open. She sought the source of the loud noise reverberating through the room.

Past the other side of the bed, a flash of metal glinted in the doorway. Then it disappeared.

Footsteps thudded down the stairs.

With a groan, Enrique fell face-forward across her hips.

Hot, sticky fluid seeped onto her belly. She propped herself up on her elbows and stared down the length of her body with dawning comprehension—and horror.

A red pool oozed over her, the towels, and the bed. A ragged, bloody hole gaped in Enrique's back and shirt where the bullet had exited.

Overwhelmed with whirling, frantic fear and revulsion, Claire screamed. And screamed again.

A raw, animal instinct for survival seized her. Scrambling, she pushed herself out from under Enrique's dead weight. She leapt off the bed and swiped at blood dripping down her legs. Feeling dizzy, she grasped the headboard to steady herself.

Will the shooter come after me next? She crouched beside the bed and listened.

Nothing.

Only the sound of her heart pounding against her ribcage, with the accompanying rush of blood in her ears. *Think, Claire. Now what?* She forced herself to feel Enrique's neck for a pulse. Her trembling fingers found none.

She picked up the phone and dialed 9-1-1, smearing blood on the receiver. When the operator answered, Claire shouted, "A man's been shot! Send an ambulance!"

"Please calm down, ma'am. I need to confirm your address."

Claire realized she was panting, almost hyperventilating. She took a deep, slow breath and listened to the operator recite her address. "Yes, that's it."

"You said a man's been shot," the operator said. "Are you in danger?"

"I don't know. Someone was here, but I don't see anyone now. He or they might still be in the house."

"The police and ambulance are on their way. Do you hear any noises in the house?"

"No."

"Which room are you in?"

"The upstairs master bedroom, to the left of the stairs."

"It's probably best for you to stay where you are. What's the status of the victim?"

Claire looked at Enrique's body, slumped over the bed, leaking blood all over the linens. He was so young, with so many years left to live. Why would someone shoot him? She squeezed her eyes shut. Tears ran down her cheeks.

"I think he's dead. He was shot in the chest." She swiped at her runny nose.

"Does he have a pulse?"

"I didn't feel—"

"Claire?" Roger's voice sounded from downstairs.

Without thinking, Claire yelled, "Oh, God."

What was Roger doing home?

She glanced down at her nearly naked body smeared with blood. She dropped the phone, grabbed her robe, and threw it on.

Roger stumbled into the room, holding a handgun. He gaped at Enrique's body.

Claire stared at her husband. As far as she knew, he'd never fired a gun before in his life.

Did he kill Enrique?

The emergency operator's voice floated out of the telephone receiver at Claire's feet. "Hello? What's going on?"

Roger looked at the telephone, then at her. Taking in her blood-smeared, semi-clothed state, his eyes burned with rage.

Claire backed up against the wall, sure she would be his next victim. She screamed.

Roger jumped, and the gun went off, firing a slug into the floor. He dropped the gun. With a puzzled glance at her, he approached Enrique's body and pressed his fingers against the neck. His hand came away smeared with blood. "This man's dead."

Claire nodded, mute.

The operator shouted, "Ma'am, are you all right?"

Roger stepped toward Claire. "Are you hurt? Did he attack you?"

Claire stared at his blood-red hand. *Oh, God.* She screamed again.

Roger opened his mouth to speak, but was silenced by the sound of heavy footsteps thundering up the stairs.

Two policemen barreled into the room with guns drawn. "Don't move."

Chapter 4
The Husband

"Then you arrived, while the policemen were talking to us separately." Claire glanced at Detective Wilson, whose face had remained impassive throughout her tale, then realized she'd twisted the towel in her hands into a knot. She laid it on the bathroom counter.

She hadn't seen her husband since the cops had handcuffed him. *What's he thinking?* Detective Wilson had told one of the patrolmen to keep her in the bathroom while he talked to Roger, then she'd overheard him send Roger away with the other cop. By the time Wilson walked into the bathroom, Claire was puking her guts out.

After choking out the story, Claire felt like a cheap trollop, even though nothing had happened between her and Enrique. *Or had it?* Deeply embarrassed, she felt grateful Wilson hadn't shown any emotion during her tale.

He looked up from his notes. "Just before he was shot, you said Mr. Romero started to speak. What did he say?"

"I only heard one word, 'you.' "

"You." Wilson thought for a moment. "Had he met your husband before?"

"No."

"Did he know what your husband looked like?"

Claire shook her head, then stopped. "He saw the family portrait downstairs."

Wilson made a note. "Can you demonstrate for me how your

husband held the gun?"

Her hands shook as she showed how Roger had shot a slug into the carpet. *A bullet meant for me?*

After Wilson finished his questions and closed his notebook, Claire said, "What will happen to Roger?"

"With the evidence we've found here, we have enough to charge him with manslaughter or murder."

Oh, God. Claire bit her lip.

Wilson handed her a tissue. "After we interview your husband, the D.A. will decide what the charge will be. Then your husband will go to Metro jail, where he'll be booked. He'll probably be arraigned tomorrow morning."

"What will happen at the arraignment?"

"The judge will inform Mr. Hanover of the charges against him, ask him to plead guilty or not guilty, determine if he can be released on bail, and set the amount. I suggest you call a lawyer."

Claire remembered Roger asking if Enrique had hurt her. "Roger may have thought I was being assaulted." He'd soon find out differently, though. "If that's so, would he still be charged?"

"I'm afraid so. Probably for manslaughter." Wilson gave her a weak, sympathetic smile, then closed his notebook. "But the timing is suspicious—him coming home exactly when Mr. Romero was here."

Claire clutched the soggy tissue. Suspicious indeed. If Roger found out about the massage, he'd be angry, jealous. Good God, what if he tried to kill her when he was released? But he'd dropped the gun when he had the chance before.

"When can I see him?"

Wilson checked the date on his watch. "It's an even day and your last name is in the first half of the alphabet, so you can visit him tonight between six-thirty and nine-fifteen."

Even days, alphabet? Claire's head pounded. Overwhelmed, she had no idea what to do first. She rubbed her forehead.

Wilson offered to get her some aspirin. When Claire accepted, he said, "Do you have someone you can call? To be with you?"

"My friend, Ellen Kessler."

Claire waited for word on Roger's charge, then used the kitchen phone to call Ellen at Stein Mart, where she sold discount-priced, high-fashion clothing two days a week. Claire blurted out the story before hysteria could start her weeping again. Since a few hours had passed, she wasn't still reeling from the shock of being dropped down a surreal rabbit hole, but like Alice, she knew doses of expanding and contracting reality were yet to come.

"How awful! Claire, I'm so sorry. I'll never forgive myself for buying that massage for you."

"It's not your fault, Ellen." *I shouldn't have accepted it.*

"Are the police sure Roger shot him?"

Claire nodded, then realized Ellen couldn't hear that over the phone. "He had the gun in his hand. What's worse is that the D.A. is charging him with murder, not manslaughter."

"So they think he did it in a fit of jealousy?"

Claire's throat constricted with guilt and fear as the image of Roger holding the gun flooded her memory. "I was afraid he'd shoot me, too, but when I screamed, he dropped the gun."

"Lost his nerve, huh? But what might he do to you when he gets out on bail? You have to protect yourself, Claire. The faster you slap a restraining order on him, the better."

Restraining order? Claire felt a jolt in the pit of her stomach. "I'm not ready to do anything like that. I'm still in shock."

"Of course you are. But think about it. He shouldn't be in the same house with you. In fact, the way he's been ignoring you, you haven't had much of a marriage for a long time."

"I don't want to talk about this. I just need to get through the next few hours. Oh, I should tell you that Dave called me after Roger contacted him."

"Dave? He's not going to be any help. You need to hire a *good* lawyer."

Claire couldn't help but smile at Ellen's reaction to the news that her ex-husband was involved. "Dave said he'll give me the name of a good criminal lawyer, but first he'll represent Roger at the arraignment tomorrow." She marveled at how easily the legal term tripped off her tongue, when a few hours ago she hadn't even known, in detail, what it meant.

"I hope Dave doesn't botch the arraignment. Sorry, you know how I feel about him. Just today I was talking to Jill about him, while we ate at the Broadmoor before my shift. Good God, that was probably when Enrique was shot. I shudder to think."

Claire did shudder.

"Anyway," Ellen said, "Jill wants to talk to a divorce lawyer and asked me about Dave—"

"Jill's getting a divorce?" Claire felt stunned. If anyone had asked, she would have said the Edstroms were a happy couple. What was this, a divorce epidemic among her friends?

"Not yet, but she thinks Paul's losing interest in her and suspects he's cheating on her. She's deathly afraid he'll ask for a divorce and wants to know what her options are."

"Why doesn't she talk to Paul?"

"You know Jill, the perfect little housewife. She'd rather dish up his favorite meal and hope that makes him notice her than have a serious discussion. No wonder she can't lose weight with the feasts she puts out for Paul and her son. But don't tell Jill I said anything to you about the divorce thing."

"I won't."

"Back to lawyers. I said, 'No way, honey, would I recommend Dave.' I gave her the name of my lawyer instead. She knows her

41

stuff and fleeced Dave good. She'd be good for you, too, when you're ready. But if you want me to, I'll call her to see who she recommends for Roger."

"I need to talk to Roger first. I can't make decisions now. I'm a total basket case."

"Do you want me to come over? I can take off early here if I tell them—"

"No, don't!"

"I was going to say, if I tell them I have a sick friend who needs me." Her tone indicated she felt miffed Claire would assume otherwise.

Claire glanced at her watch—four-thirty already. Outside her kitchen window, dusk had fallen. "I'm going to the jail soon."

"Do you need someone to go with you? Can you drive?"

Claire studied her hands. Amazingly, they were steady. Her stomach was turning cartwheels, though. "I can drive."

"What can I do? Have the police finished there?"

"Detective Wilson said they wouldn't need to come back." Claire grimaced and glanced at the kitchen ceiling, which lay directly below the master bedroom. "He gave me the card of a company that cleans up after crime scenes. Could you call them?"

"Sure. Give me the number."

Claire hesitated. For the umpteenth time, she wished she still lived next door to Ellen instead of a twenty-minute drive away. The resale home near the five-star Broadmoor Hotel had been perfect for socializing with her friends. But since moving into the showy custom home that Roger had insisted on building in Coyote Hills, Claire had to schedule outings with Ellen and Jill in advance. The favor Claire wanted to ask was big, but she knew Ellen would do it, no matter how much it inconvenienced her.

"Would you be willing to meet the cleaners here if they can

come while I'm gone? You still have the key I gave you, right?"

"Yes, and I'd be glad to come. It'll be better for you if you don't have to go into your bedroom until it's, you know, back to normal."

The horrific, bloody scene flooded into Claire's mind. She took a shuddering breath. "You're right. I do *not* want to go in that room. I grabbed some clothes before the police left then showered in the kids' bathroom."

"Ugh. I don't plan to go in there either."

"Are you sure you can handle this?"

"What are friends for? Cripes, I still can't believe this happened. What the hell was Roger doing home in the middle of the day?"

Claire pulled into the parking lot of the Metro Detention Facility, across from the city courthouse, and caught a glimpse of herself in the rearview mirror. Her face looked blotchy and washed-out. She hadn't put on any makeup, because she couldn't bring herself to go into the master bedroom yet. Her hair hung in the limp strands it had dried into after her shower. Instinctively, she ran a comb through her hair, then threw the comb in her purse in disgust. Now was not the time to worry about her appearance.

When she reached the front desk, she filled out a form requesting a visit with Roger, then sat on the edge of a plastic chair to wait. She glanced around with a mixture of curiosity and apprehension. The waiting area, with its dull gray linoleum floor, well-worn puke-green chairs, and vending machines dispensing peanuts and pork rinds, could have been a bus station. A faulty fluorescent light buzzed by the entrance.

The room's inhabitants fit the bus-station theme—none looking forward to the long, tiring journey ahead, but waiting patiently nonetheless. A frazzled young mother with wrinkled clothes toted a baby on one hip and shushed the fidgety toddler next to her. A silently weeping, rotund Hispanic woman sat in the far corner, clutching a shredded tissue. A wizened old man in a wrinkled trench coat, seemingly dozing in a chair, opened a bleary eye to peer at her.

Claire felt like a piece of flotsam in a sea of discarded humanity. Did any of them know her husband had just murdered a man in her bedroom? Imagining accusing eyes, she drew her coat tightly around her.

When the desk sergeant finally called her name, she followed an attendant up the hollow-sounding concrete stairs and through a door unlocked by an unseen watcher who could observe Claire through a TV camera. Claire walked into a visitation hallway lined with four small closed Plexiglas windows on one side, separated by short partitions that stuck out a few feet into the hall. A uniformed sheriff's deputy, whose belt bristled with a Taser, pepper spray, and expandable baton, but no gun, stood at the end of the room.

As Claire passed the first window, she glimpsed the Hispanic woman standing in front, talking to a grim-faced man on the other side. The attendant led Claire to the third stall. A scratched Plexiglas window faced a wide hallway on the other side, similar to the one in which she stood.

"Wait here," the attendant said.

An opening under the window, covered with sturdy steel mesh, carried his words into the other hallway. A large, bearded prisoner waiting to speak to a visitor squinted at her and scratched at a snake tattoo on his forearm, then frowned and looked away.

After the attendant left, Claire looked around. She found no chair, and no place to set her purse. The institutional gray walls and ceiling reminded her of heavy rain clouds. She glanced up, half expecting a drop to leak on her.

Feeling depressed and unnerved, she pulled tissues out of her coat pocket and fingered them. The sound of a door creaking issued from the mesh opening and made her start. She peered through the window.

In the hallway on the other side of the glass, a uniformed man held the door open and pointed to the window where she stood. Roger shuffled in slowly, keeping his eyes trained on the floor while he made his way to the window.

Good God, he's wearing handcuffs. Claire brought her hand to her mouth.

Roger seemed to have aged years in the few hours since she'd last seen him, an old man at forty-nine. Baggy orange overalls had replaced his business suit. The garish color made his pale face look like death. His glasses were askew, and the circlet of gray hair around his bald pate was mussed.

Claire wondered if he'd been running his fingers through his hair, a habit when he felt stressed, a habit she'd always found endearing. A sudden realization jolted her. Even though Roger had killed Enrique, she still loved her husband.

A memory flashed of the last time she'd seen him in orange— wearing a Denver Broncos team jersey when they attended a football game at Mile High Stadium one cold, blustery afternoon several years ago. He'd snuggled close to warm her while they sipped hot chocolate and laughed like teenagers. His eyes had danced when he looked at her, and their lovemaking had been passionate that night.

She longed to reach out and hug him now, but could only place a hand on the cool window. She stood immobilized, staring at what Roger had become. Her throat constricted as she drowned in her own guilt. If she hadn't brought Enrique home, Roger wouldn't be here. *What have I done?*

Roger stopped at the window with a sigh, pushed his glasses up on the bridge of his nose by raising both hands, then dropped the handcuffed pair in front of him. "Dave contacted me. My arraignment is tomorrow at ten-thirty."

Claire lowered her hand from her mouth and swallowed hard. "I'll be there. Roger, I'm so sorry. It's because of me that you're here."

Roger glanced at her with red-rimmed eyes then stared at his hands. "I missed the dry run of the investor's briefing. I need someone to explain why to the office. Could you call them?"

Claire felt amazement, then a surge of anger. *He's been arrested for killing someone, and all he can think of is work?* She opened her mouth to speak, then clamped it shut. *Wait.*

This had always been his way of coping with anxious situations—to focus first on concrete actions. His self-restraint had subdued her own panic when they'd taken trips to the emergency room with their kids—toddler Judy with a spiking fever and eleven-year-old Michael with a broken arm. After the danger had passed, he'd held her while she trembled in relief.

The danger hadn't passed this time, and they couldn't hold each other. She was responsible for his plight. The least she could do was try to make things right at his office.

"I'll call them first thing tomorrow. I know that dry run was important to you." *But if the dry run was so important—* "Why did you come home, Roger? You never come home for lunch."

His head jerked up. "Because you asked me to."

"What?"

"My secretary gave me a phone message that you called, said it was an emergency, and you needed me to come home right away."

"I never called."

He peered at her as if wondering whether to believe her. "Then whoever did call set me up."

"Oh, my God." *Does he believe I planned this to get rid of him?* She shook her head. "You can't think I—"

"I don't know what to think. I don't seem to know you anymore." Roger's jaw worked, before he managed to grind out any words. "Who was he?"

Claire realized the police had probably insinuated she was having an affair during their questioning of Roger. She tensed. "An aerobics instructor at Graham's Gym. I met him a few days ago."

Roger's eyes widened. Expressions of surprise, irony, then resignation passed over his face.

The resignation hurt Claire the most. "No, it's not . . . how do I explain?" Hot shame flamed in her cheeks. She choked out the whole deplorable story.

His expression grew stonier with each word. Finally, he blurted, "How could you let him touch you? You're my wife!"

He slammed his fists on the Plexiglas, then glanced at the now-alert officer on his side of the wall. When the guard took a step forward, Roger dropped his hands and pursed his lips, obviously struggling to contain the rest of his outburst.

Claire swiped angrily at tears dribbling down her cheeks. "Yes, I am your wife, but I haven't felt like a wife for years. You barely know I'm around. You ignore me. You're never home." She leaned over to whisper, "You hardly touch me anymore."

"But to have an affair with a gigolo half your age."

Fury bubbled up inside Claire. "First of all, he's not a gigolo. I told you we weren't having an affair—"

"How am I supposed to believe you? I know what I saw. How can I trust you?" Roger glared at her.

"How can I trust *you?*" She clenched her hands. "You shot a man. I feel like I don't know *you* anymore."

"I didn't shoot him."

Claire felt like she'd been slapped. "What?"

"I didn't shoot him."

"But you had the gun in your hand."

"It was lying on the floor in the downstairs hall, next to an open gym bag. I was so surprised to see it, I left the front door open. Then I heard your voice in the bedroom, so I called you."

"I remember."

"When you yelled 'Oh, God,' I thought you were in trouble. I grabbed the gun and ran upstairs."

Claire stared at him with her mouth hanging open.

Roger stared right back. "Imagine my surprise to find a strange man bleeding all over my bed and you cowering in the corner. I assumed he assaulted you, and you somehow killed him."

"You thought *I* killed him?"

He nodded. "Then you screamed."

"I was afraid you were going to shoot me next."

"What? Oh, Claire."

"That's why I screamed. God, I've never been so scared."

"You should know I'd never hurt you," he whispered.

From his crestfallen expression, Claire realized Roger spoke the truth, and felt deeply hurt she would think otherwise. She unclenched her hands. If they released him on bail, she'd be safe.

"And I didn't kill that guy, either." Roger combed the fingers of one hand through his hair, while the handcuffs dragged the other hand along.

The clumsy attempt at a familiar habit made Claire's gut lurch.

"From the way the police manhandled me when they hauled me off, they obviously thought differently. That scared me. I refused to talk to them and called Dave."

Claire peered at him. His story made sense, but she had trouble accepting it. Her mind whirled with questions. She pointed her chin at the uniformed officer, then leaned forward to whisper, "You're not lying to me because of him, are you?"

Roger slammed his hands on the glass again. "Dammit. I'm not lying." He slumped against his arm, defeat lining his face. "What have you gotten me into?"

CHAPTER 5
PHONE MESSAGES

As Claire pulled her car into her driveway, she noticed Ellen's red Volvo parked in the pullout to the side. She checked her watch while she waited for the garage door to open. Eight o'clock. Ellen was still there, and she'd worked all day, too. *What a friend.*

After climbing out of the car, Claire trudged to the door leading from the garage into the kitchen. She felt bone-tired, and her heart was as dead and cold as the icy wind that blasted under the lowering garage door. When Ellen opened the door to the house, flooding Claire with warmth and light, Claire fell into her open arms. She had never needed a hug more.

Ellen patted her back. "You've had a horrible day. Go ahead and cry if you want."

Claire drew back. "That's all I've done today. I'm all cried out. Or just numb."

Ellen led her to a stool. "Sit here. I'll warm some soup for you. Tomato okay?"

An image of blood-red soup formed in Claire's mind. She grimaced and shook her head.

Ellen gasped. "Oops. Bad choice. Chicken, that'll do. Let's see, rice or noodle?"

As Ellen rummaged in the pantry, Claire noticed her friend had her sleeves rolled up and hair tied back. She remembered why Ellen was there and shuddered. "Did you, I mean, what about . . ." Claire's voice trailed off as she glanced at the ceiling.

"You wanted to redecorate that room anyway, didn't you? The police took the linens, and I had the cleaning company throw out the mattress pad. I remade your bed with some sheets I found in your linen closet."

Shocked, Claire stared at Ellen. How could she talk about mattress pads and sheets so banally when someone they both knew had just been killed?

Ellen wrinkled her nose while she dumped a single serving can of soup into a bowl. "Good thing your pad was extra thick. The mattress is okay. The cleaners also managed to get the stains out of the carpet. They finished about half an hour ago. Not a spot left." She waved her hand cheerily in the air, as if belittling the enormity of the favor she had performed.

Artificially so, Claire thought. Maybe Ellen was trying to comfort her by making the horrific seem commonplace. "How could you stand it?"

A clouded look passed over Ellen's face before she frowned. "When I showed them upstairs, I blocked out any thought of it being Enrique's blood." She shivered, then punched buttons on the microwave.

Claire studied her friend. Ellen looked as if she'd survived the ordeal all right, better than Claire would have by far. When Ellen placed the steaming chicken noodle soup in front of her, Claire realized she was famished. She took off her coat, grabbed a spoon and began to eat.

Ellen sat and watched Claire until she'd finished. "Did you see Roger?"

"Yes. He said he didn't shoot Enrique."

Ellen's eyebrows rose. "Really?"

"He said he found the gun in the hall and picked it up before coming upstairs. That's why he was holding it when I saw him."

"Sorry, but that sounds awfully lame."

Claire toyed with her spoon. "I know. I know."

"What do you think?"

Claire replayed the scene with Roger in her mind. "He seemed sincere, but . . . I'm not sure what to think."

Ellen laid a hand on Claire's arm. "Maybe you need to think about whether you two still belong together."

"We've been through so much. I'd feel lost without him."

"I hope you're not going to give me that schmaltz that he 'completes' you."

"No. Instead of compensating for some lack in me, because of his support I'm stronger than I ever dreamed I could be. And I think I did the same for him. Whenever one of us felt overwhelmed, the other would provide the right encouragement to push on."

She remembered Roger holding her while she wept on his shoulder and raged that life wasn't fair. She was in the throes of postpartum sleep-deprivation six weeks after Judy was born and dealing with three-year-old Michael's jealous tantrums. Roger volunteered to do night feedings for a week so she could catch up on her rest, even though she was an at-home mom and he was working ten-hour days.

"You made a great couple years ago, but you've grown apart," Ellen said. "And now this. Why hold on just for old times' sake?"

A dried bouquet of roses hanging above the kitchen cabinets caught Claire's eye. Her gaze was drawn to first one rose, then the next one, then the next—twenty-six in all, one for each wedding anniversary and all in pink, the sweetheart color. Roger never forgot. How could she abandon her Rock of Gibraltar when he needed her most? When she needed him the most.

"It's more than old times' sake, Ellen. It's life itself. I'm sticking by him, if he'll have me." A stifling yawn overtook her.

"Okay, I can see you're tired. I'll stop, but I need to tell you one last thing. A reporter called while you were gone. I told him you couldn't come to the phone and hung up."

Claire dropped her head in her hands. Her stomach flopped, and she glanced at Ellen. "Reporters. I didn't think about them. This will be in the morning papers, won't it?"

Ellen nodded solemnly. "And on TV. They already reported it on the evening news, though they didn't have any names yet."

"Everyone will know Enrique was killed in my bedroom. What will my friends think? Oh, God, what will the kids think? I haven't called them yet." She shook with the horror of it all.

"Call them now. All you can tell them is the truth. That a man was murdered in your home and the police accused Roger, but he says he didn't do it."

Claire reached for the phone. She felt lower than dirt. She ground her teeth as she dialed Judy's number. Her dry mouth felt like it was already full of the gritty grains of black soil she wanted to bury her head in. She woke her daughter from a sound sleep eight hours ahead in France and had to keep repeating herself because Judy couldn't believe what she was hearing.

Twenty tissues and an hour later, Claire put down the phone, worn out from explaining everything again to Michael. Her children's shock and disapproval was palpable, even over the long-distance lines. Both insisted on coming home, but she told them to wait until she knew when their father would be released.

Ellen brought a glass of water and rubbed Claire's shoulders while she drank. "Any other relatives you need to call tonight?"

Claire thought about her mother, ensconced in the Liberty Heights retirement facility ever since her father had passed away a few years ago. In the semi-twilight of mid-stage Alzheimer's, her mother rarely read the newspaper and only watched soap operas and game shows on TV. Telling her could wait, maybe forever. She'd just forget it all the next day anyway.

Lately, it seemed when Claire visited that her mother often didn't recognize her. Oh, she hid it well. She'd make polite conversation with the unknown visitor until Claire dropped broad hints to help her mother make the connection. The probability that she had inherited her mother's susceptibility to the disease terrified Claire every time she misplaced her car keys.

Claire's brother and his wife were on their annual winter getaway in Mexico for another two weeks, so she could put off calling them. Roger's parents had passed away years ago, thank God. But not his sister.

Claire groaned. "Roger's sister, Regina, in Iowa."

She dialed the number, but no one picked up. She left a message on the answering machine asking Regina to call back, then turned to Ellen. "She belongs to a quilting group. I think they meet on Thursdays. If she gets home late, I may not hear from her until tomorrow."

"You probably shouldn't be alone tonight. Want to sleep at my house?"

Claire shook her head.

"How about if I spend the night here, then?"

"No, you have to work tomorrow. And I'm so exhausted, I'm sure I'll fall asleep as soon as my head hits the pillow—the one on Judy's bed, that is. I can't go in my bedroom yet."

"You sure you don't want me to stay?"

"I'm sure."

Hesitantly, Ellen picked up her coat. "Call me if you need me. Even if it's the middle of the night."

Claire hugged her friend. "Thanks. I don't know what I'd do without you." She stood in the doorway and watched Ellen walk to her car and drive away.

As Claire slipped between the cool sheets of her daughter's narrow single bed, she reviewed her conversation with her husband. Something nagged at the edges of her sleepy consciousness—the phone message that was supposedly from her. *I'll have to call Roger's secretary tomorrow.*

Claire sat bolt upright. That thought meant she believed he

was innocent. And the killer was still on the loose! What if he thought she saw him? She clambered out of bed to check the door locks, then returned to the room and stood transfixed, shivering in the dark.

If Roger didn't kill Enrique, who did? And why?

The next morning, Claire hunched over the newspaper spread on the kitchen table, her temples throbbing as if she'd overindulged in cheap red wine the night before. She stared at the headline: LOCAL BUSINESSMAN CHARGED WITH MURDER. Below the story was a picture of her house, apparently taken with a telephoto lens from the street.

She pushed aside her breakfast—grapefruit with brown sugar and a soft fried egg on whole-wheat toast. She had hoped the routine of making her typical morning repast would provide some comfort, but one glance at the paper took her appetite away.

She reread the story, wincing when Roger's name appeared as the suspect. She still felt an eerie sense of unreality, as if she was caught up in a horrible nightmare where she had no control over the events swirling around her. But she couldn't deny it. She was wide-awake.

Enrique's name hadn't been released, pending notification of next-of-kin. Claire felt a pang of sympathy for whomever that next-of-kin might be, especially if it was his mother, assuming she was still alive. Claire tried to imagine how she would feel if her son Michael was killed. Her throat closed up. God, what that woman would go through. Claire massaged her head.

The *Gazette* reporter, Marvin Bradshaw, had labeled her Coyote Hills neighborhood "exclusive" and quoted the median price of homes. Claire envisioned the reporter rubbing his hands, itching to ferret out and divulge more sordid details.

She gulped extra-strong coffee and stared out her kitchen

window. With no apparent awareness of the excitement the day before, ground squirrels foraged in the drifts of dried scrub oak leaves. The whirling lights of the police cruisers and people tromping through the yard hadn't bothered the creatures. She, however, had barely slept a wink.

The phone rang.

Claire let the answering machine, which already held nine messages, take the call. The thin, reedy voice of nosy Mrs. Saunders drifted from the machine, asking what was going on and if Claire needed anything.

Yeah, right. Mrs. Saunders would have to get her answers from the morning paper. Claire would not give satisfaction to the old snoop today. Dreading what she'd find, Claire punched the replay button on the answering machine. The first two were from Marvin Bradshaw.

Fat chance he'd get a call back. The next was Mrs. Saunders again, followed by two other neighbors, then an ominous single word message, "Bitch," followed by a hang-up. And another hang-up. *Ouch.* The last message played.

"Claire, this is Rita Wilaby calling. Weren't you supposed to deliver my two gift baskets yesterday? Anyway, I'll be in my office doing paperwork most of today, so you can just bring them by without calling first."

Claire smacked her hand against her forehead, causing it to throb even more. *Damn.* At least, it sounded as if the real estate agent hadn't heard about the murder. Claire carried the heavy baskets from the bench into the garage and stuffed them into the trunk of her car, so she wouldn't leave the house without them.

As she reentered the kitchen, the phone rang again. *I've got to get out of here.*

Claire threw on some sweats, athletic shoes, and a jacket, and drove to the north parking lot of the Garden of the Gods Park.

She got out, pocketed her cell phone, and took a deep breath of the cool, crisp air. A walk among the towering sandstone slabs of the park, uplifted and tilted on their sides, never failed to clear her head. The weather would help, too—piercing blue skies without a wisp of a cloud, the rising sun shooting spear points of light between the rocks, and a temperature in the high thirties. A perfect Colorado February day.

She stopped at Jaycee Plaza, where a plaque explained how Charles Perkins, head of the Burlington Railroad, had donated the land to the city founded by his good friend General Palmer. Palmer had urged Perkins to build a home in the garden, similar to his own castle in picturesque Glen Eyrie canyon, but Perkins had kept the estate natural. Like most of Colorado Springs' residents and visitors, Claire was grateful he had.

She watched cliff swallows flitting in and out of their nests in tiny holes high in the cliffs and remembered them doing the same during a friend's second wedding ceremony here. But weddings were the last thing she needed to be reminded of when her own marriage was in jeopardy. She left the plaza and struck out on the Central Loop trail.

After maintaining a brisk pace for a while, she paused in front of the several-hundred-foot-high South Gateway rock to catch her breath. A trio of climbers roped together inched their way up the steep face. Claire felt a woozy tingle in her legs, as if she was there with them. *How can that possibly be fun?*

She checked her watch. Nine o'clock. Time to call Roger's office. She took out her cell phone and dialed his private line. After three rings, his secretary picked up.

"This is Claire. I called to explain why Roger missed the dry run of the investor briefing yesterday."

"Oh, Mrs. Hanover, Roger's lawyer called Mr. Peters last night. Mr. Peters told me when I came in this morning that the police arrested Roger for murder. How awful!"

Claire remembered Ned Peters as a tough, no-nonsense manager. Although president of the firm, he worked long hours and expected his staff to be just as dedicated. Their personal lives weren't supposed to interfere with deadlines—ever. She blanched as she imagined what his reaction might be. "Did Ned sound upset?"

The secretary paused. "He looked angry, said he had some major damage control to perform with the investors. He told me to find the briefing Roger prepared."

"Did you?" Claire watched the middle climber, who seemed to be less experienced and more tentative than the other two, search for a handhold.

"Yes, but I still can't believe Roger could have killed someone. What happened?"

Claire sighed in dismay. The woman's morbid curiosity undoubtedly would be echoed countless times over the next few days. "He's innocent. This all will be cleared up soon."

The climber's hand slipped and threw him off balance. He fell.

Claire gasped.

"What! What's the matter?" the secretary asked.

Frozen in terror, Claire watched the man plunge down, until the rope attached to his harness yanked him short. He swung from a piton anchored to the cliff between him and his mate below him. Stunned, he didn't move until the other two climbers shouted instructions at him.

Then he swung back and forth until he could scrabble a handhold. He pulled himself to the rock, found footholds, and clung to the cliff like a squashed spider, his chest heaving.

Claire refocused on the phone in her hands. "Sorry I scared you. I'm at the Garden of the Gods and just saw a climber fall."

"Is he hurt?"

"No, he was smart. His rope saved him. He was climbing in a

group and had gear." *Unlike the handful of tourists who managed to kill themselves each summer scrambling up the rock with no ropes, hardware, or brains.* "Back to what we were talking about. Tell Mr. Peters that Roger's arraignment is this morning, so he should be released on bail today. I'm sure Roger will contact him right away."

"But—"

"Roger said you gave him a message that I called yesterday. Do you have a record of it?"

"It should be in my message book, on the carbon copy." The phone carried the sound of pages flipping. "It's not here. Oh, I remember. Our new receptionist took the message and gave it to me."

"Could you forward me to her?" Claire sat down on the knee-high rock wall next to the trail.

"I guess so." The secretary said it reluctantly, as if the last thing she wanted was to give up the chance to question Claire some more.

A moment later, a girlish voice said, "Hello?"

"This is Claire Hanover. I understand you took a phone message yesterday for my husband that supposedly came from me."

After a delay, during which Claire heard paper rustling, the girl said, "I took the message at eleven-fifteen and gave it to Mr. Hanover's secretary a few minutes later."

"What did the woman say?"

"It wasn't you?"

"No." Claire drummed her fingers on the ice-cold rock next to her.

"Goodness. I just assumed it was you, since you, I mean the caller, said 'This is Mrs. Hanover.'" The receptionist paused. "You . . . she said she needed Roger at home, it was an emergency, and he should be there by noon. I had a little trouble understanding you . . . her. She may have been on a cell phone."

"Do you remember what she sounded like?"

"I couldn't tell much with the static. The voice was definitely an older woman's voice. Older than me, I mean. I know that much for sure, but something was different from the way you sound now."

Heart beating faster, with the prospect of freeing Roger with this new information, Claire struggled to remain patient with the girl. "What? How was the voice different from mine?"

"The woman had an accent, like she was from Mexico or South America. Does this have something to do with—"

"Thanks for your help." Claire hung up.

As she rose and headed back to the car, she wondered who had called Roger, and why. Someone had wanted him to find her with Enrique, but did that someone do it to hurt Roger, Claire, or Enrique? In any case, she had succeeded on all three counts. And Roger's life was hanging in the balance just like that climber's.

But now Claire had hope; new information to give the police. Maybe Enrique had told someone about his appointment with her, a woman perhaps . . . with a Hispanic accent.

CHAPTER 6
GUILTY OR NOT GUILTY?

Claire reached the city courthouse at ten-fifteen and found the courtroom a few minutes later. She slipped through the door and searched for Dave Kessler, Roger's interim attorney and Ellen's ex-husband. The cavernous room smelled of dark oak, lots of it, polished with lemon-scented wax. The somber hush made her slow her steps so her heels wouldn't click on the hard floor. She'd ditched her usual jeans and athletic shoes for a skirt and low-heeled pumps, hoping the image of a respectful wife might help Roger.

Up front, a rail separated rows of audience benches from the raised judge's dais, two tables, and an empty juror's box. A tall, orange-suited young man, with a swastika razored into his close-cropped hair, stood defiantly before the judge while his lawyer droned.

Claire spied Dave sitting near the front. He had put on a few pounds since she last saw him, but he still had his full head of wavy salt-and-pepper hair.

She slid onto the bench beside him and whispered a nervous hello.

He placed a finger against his lips then wrote on the legal pad in his lap: "Roger's up next."

Claire nodded and scanned the courtroom. The dozen or so other occupants of the benches seemed to be primarily pinstripe-suited lawyers, waiting patiently for their cases. Toward the rear of the courtroom, a short, middle-aged man with wispy brown hair caught her eye and gave a short wave. She studied his features, then looked away and frowned. She could have sworn she'd never seen him before.

Trying to get a sense of how Roger would fare, Claire focused on the proceedings before her, straining to hear every word.

The judge was a stout, white-haired black woman. She carefully explained the consequences of each type of plea—guilty, not guilty, and not guilty by reason of insanity, then waited for the young neo-Nazi to confer in whispered tones with his attorney. When he entered a plea of not guilty, the judge set bail, explained the reason for the amount, and scheduled a preliminary hearing.

The judge seemed both efficient and fair. Claire slowly exhaled the breath she'd been holding and unclenched her hands. Maybe the judge would be lenient with Roger.

As Swastika Scalp was led away, the bailiff announced Roger's case. Dave stood and moved past Claire to the front of the courtroom.

She leaned forward and grasped the back of the bench before her.

A door opened in the left wall, beyond the railing. Accompanied by a uniformed guard, Roger shuffled through the door. He still wore the jail's orange jumpsuit and ankle and wrist shackles. Dark shadows under his eyes suggested he'd had a sleepless night.

So intent on studying her husband for signs of strain or anger or anguish, Claire realized she'd missed the first few exchanges with the judge, and she moved her gaze away from Roger.

"I see you already have an attorney. You also have the right to confront and cross-examine witnesses . . ." The judge continued to list Roger's rights, finishing with, "Do you understand these rights?"

Roger raised his chin. "Yes, your honor."

Hearing his soft-spoken words made Claire's throat ache.

"How do you plead?" the judge asked.

Roger straightened, looked directly at her, and spoke the words clearly, "Not guilty."

Claire felt a jolt, as the words, *unlike me*, popped into her head. Her damp hands slipped on the bench back, and she gripped it harder.

The judge said, "Next is the issue of bail."

The prosecuting attorney stepped forward. "Your honor, the accused has the resources to flee the country. He has a sizeable investment portfolio, owns luxury automobiles, and holds considerable equity in his home. The people request this man be remanded without bail."

Claire hadn't realized Roger might have to stay in jail until his case was tried. She bit her lower lip. That would be awful, not just for him, but for her, too. Knocking around the large house by herself during the day was bad enough, but at night, every noise made her flinch. What if he was convicted? Then she'd be alone for years—her worst fear. She had thought she wouldn't have to face it until she became an old widow like her mother, but now the possibility loomed near. And what would prison do to Roger? She felt faint.

Dave stepped forward. "Roger Hanover won't be leaving Colorado Springs, let alone the country. He's an upstanding citizen of this city who gives generously to local charities, and he's never been arrested before. He is deeply attached to both his family and his career. As you can see, his wife is in the courtroom." He pointed toward Claire and motioned for her to stand.

Claire flushed and rubbed her clammy hands on her skirt, her skin crawling from the stares of many eyes. She rose briefly and nodded before returning to her seat.

Dave turned back to the judge. "Mr. Hanover intends to stay

and fight the charges since, as he stated so firmly, he is innocent."

The judge peered over her reading glasses at Roger. "Mr. Hanover, do you have anything to add?"

Roger squared his shoulders. "I plan to return to my work and family and clear my name. I have no intention of leaving town."

His voice was clear and strong. Claire marveled at how self-assured he sounded. *God, I love that man.* But the pride she felt for him only made her berate herself even more for putting him in this position. If not for her stupidity, he wouldn't be here, defending his life.

After examining the papers before her, the judge said, "Bail is set at five hundred thousand dollars. Also, Mr. Hanover, you must relinquish your passport to the court, and you may not leave the city limits without this court's permission."

Stunned, Claire recoiled in her seat. *Half a million!* Where could she come up with that amount of money?

Dave returned, tapped her on the shoulder, and motioned for her to follow him to the rear of the courtroom.

She stood and moved to the end of the bench. As Roger was led out of the side door by the guard, she tried to catch her husband's attention, but he kept his gaze trained on the clumsy ankle shackles. Wishing she had a chance to hug him, she watched the door close behind him.

When Claire walked down the aisle, the wispy-haired man stood and caught her elbow. "Mrs. Hanover, my name is Marvin Bradshaw. I'm a reporter with the *Gazette*. I have a few questions for you."

Claire's mouth fell open. He was the same reporter who had written the story under the damning headline in the morning paper. She trembled with fury at the audacity of the man.

Dave backtracked, shoved an arm between Claire and Bradshaw, and pulled Claire away. "No comment."

Bradshaw raised a hand. "But—"

"I said, no comment. Now leave us alone." He glared at the reporter until the man stepped back. Then he ushered Claire through the courtroom doors. Once in the corridor, he wheeled on Claire. "Don't talk to any reporters, ever, without my say-so or the say-so of Roger's criminal lawyer. Understand?"

"Yes."

"This is very important, Claire. You could divulge something inadvertently that would undermine Roger's case."

She bristled. "I'm not stupid. I've already been avoiding reporters, and I certainly don't intend to talk to that man."

"Good. Sorry about that. He caught me off guard." Dave wiped his brow then opened his briefcase. "I've alerted a high-stakes bail bondsman I know. He'll put up the five hundred thousand, given your assets."

He handed her a piece of paper. "We need these documents. How soon can you gather them?"

Claire scanned the list. Roger's passport was stored in the safe deposit box. The brokerage and mortgage statements she could find at home. "About an hour and a half. Why do you need all this?"

"As the judge said, Roger has to relinquish his passport. The statements are for the bondsman. You also need to get a cashier's check made out for thirty-five thousand to the bondsman."

She couldn't believe she heard him right. "Thirty-five-thousand dollars?"

"Be glad it's only that. He's willing to take seven percent instead of his usual ten, given evidence of your net worth."

"Do we get the money back when Roger appears in court?"

"No." He placed his hand on her shoulder. "Being accused of a crime, especially murder, is expensive."

"I never dreamed—"

"Nobody does." He flipped a page over on his legal pad and scanned a sheet covered with handwriting that Claire recognized as Roger's. "Roger listed a money market account that has enough in it to cover the check."

Her throat tightened. One more brick in what used to be her well-organized world had just crashed to the ground. "That's Judy's college account."

Dave glanced up and, upon seeing her face, his features softened a bit. "Yeah, well for now, it's Roger's freedom account."

"Of course." Claire flushed, feeling foolish under Dave's scrutiny. "We'll figure out Judy's finances later."

"I need to see Roger." Dave placed a business card in her hand. "Once you've got the documents, meet me at this address. It's right around the corner."

Dave led her out of the courthouse. With a curt wave, he sent her on her errands then strode toward the jail.

With the documents and cashier's check in a folder on the car seat next to her, Claire drove back downtown. She passed Acacia Park, its stately elm and oak trees bare, and its benches empty except for a couple of homeless men with greasy mismatched clothing sitting slumped on separate benches. Claire figured they'd probably been booted out of the city shelter, as they were every morning, to spend the day looking for work. These two must have chosen to nap in the sunshine before manning a local street corner with an open palm and a hand-lettered cardboard sign proclaiming something like "Veteran, Please Help." Instead of giving them handouts, Claire chose to donate money to the shelter, which offered job and substance abuse counseling to clients who wanted it.

She drove by a group of teenagers, probably between classes at Palmer High School, situated next to the park. They were passing something among them, most likely a joint. One boy with hair moussed into long black spikes glanced sharply at her as she drove by. The boy needn't have worried. Claire had more important things to do than turn them in.

As she turned down Nevada Avenue, she remembered quite different summer scenes at the park. City workers lunching out of brown bags or take-out containers while listening to jazz or classical concerts in the band shell. White-haired men competing on the shuffleboard courts. The aromas of roasting chilis and kettle corn from the weekly farmers' market. Children screeching and leaping with delight in the capricious waterspouts of Uncle Wilbur's fountain under the plaster eyes of the whimsical tuba player. *Oh, to be young and worry-free.*

Just before twelve-thirty, Claire parked her car in the lot facing a brown brick two-story office building near the courthouse. She entered through the glass doorway and glanced around the lobby, empty except for a statue of a blindfolded woman holding a set of scales. The stately quiet of the place enveloped her like an ominous cloud. She shuddered.

After taking the stairs to the second floor, she found the bondsman's office and entered.

A bored-looking receptionist sat filing her nails behind a small black lacquer desk. She didn't bother to glance up when Claire entered.

On the other side of the room, Dave sat on the edge of a leather loveseat. When he saw her, he stood and dropped the magazine he'd been reading onto the glass-topped coffee table. "Got everything?"

Claire held up the folder in her hands.

He ushered her into the back office, where a gray-suited man with slicked-down black hair sat behind a huge walnut desk scattered with papers. Smoke curled from a cigar that lay in an overflowing ashtray. The man held out his fat, tobacco-stained hand for the manila envelope Claire clutched to her chest.

"Wait," Claire said, her nose wrinkling from the cigar fumes. "This is all moving too fast for me."

The bondsman frowned and crooked an eyebrow at Dave.

Dave grabbed her arm and glared at her. "We haven't got all day. You don't want Roger to spend another night in jail, do you?"

From Dave's angry expression, Claire realized he blamed her for Roger's situation. "No, I don't." She handed over the documents.

A whirlwind twenty minutes later, Claire had relinquished the cashier's check for the bondsman's fee and signed over the equity in their house and the contents of their investment account as collateral for the bond. Nervous sweat trailed down her spine, because she didn't fully understand all the papers she signed. She had to trust that Dave was looking out for Roger's interests.

Dave took Roger's passport and one of three copies of the agreement the bondsman had handed her. "Let's go." He strode out of the office without looking back.

Claire trotted after him, glad to escape outside into the clear, cold air. She followed Dave down the block and across the street into the courthouse.

Without a word to her, he worked through the process to release Roger, handing over the passport and bond agreement.

Relieved to be free of the confusing paperwork, Claire focused on Roger's homecoming. She would fix his favorite meal of lamb chops and baked potatoes. Maybe she could find some asparagus at the market, and a chocolate cake. Open a bottle of the French Pinot Noir they had been saving for special occasions. Then she would beg his forgiveness.

Dave escorted her down a corridor and into another room. While she sat and waited, he paced, his dress shoes clicking on the linoleum floor.

A uniformed officer led Roger through the door. Roger's eyes looked gaunt, and he needed a shave. He wore the same suit he'd had on when he was arrested, now wrinkled and limp.

Claire rushed to give him a hug but stopped short when he held up a hand.

His jaw was set in a hard line. "I need time alone to think, Claire."

Her heart sank. "But I need to talk to you. I have so much to explain."

"I'm not in the mood to hear it right now." Roger glanced at his watch, then at Dave. "If you drive me home so I can change, I'll make it to the office in time to convince Ned I should speak at the investor conference."

What? He was thinking about work? Claire's blood began to boil, but she stifled her immediate reaction. She needed to salvage her marriage. "I can drive you home."

Roger refused to meet her eyes. "I'd rather have Dave drive me. I'll be taking some of my things, too."

Claire's insides twisted. She clutched herself in a tight hug that she desperately wished came from him.

"I've accepted Dave's offer to stay at his place for a few days." Roger ran his fingers through his gray fringe. "Then I'll decide what to do next."

Claire stepped closer. "Roger," she whispered, "give me a chance. Please."

"I don't have time to deal with this now." He turned away. "C'mon, Dave, I can't afford to be late."

Roger shoved his balled fists into his pockets and walked toward the door. Grim-faced, he turned back to Claire. "I've got serious problems to solve at the office. This fiasco could cost me my career." Then he strode out of the room, followed by Dave.

Oh, God. With a sob, Claire dropped into a chair and let her tears flow.

CHAPTER 7
THE GIRLFRIEND

Dazed with grief, Claire followed a policeman through the narrow hallway of the downtown police station into a large room filled with a dozen desks. She had called ahead from the courthouse to request a meeting with Detective Wilson. Half a dozen detectives sat at the desks, talking on telephones, working at computers or reading case files. Two men scribbled something on a large whiteboard then passed her on their way out.

When he saw her approach, Detective Wilson removed a stack of files from the chair next to his desk and offered it to her.

Claire slumped into the chair.

After a glance at her tear-streaked face, Wilson said, "I'll be right back." He walked away and returned with a glass of water. "Here, drink this." He slid a box of tissues toward her. "And feel free to use these."

He settled into his chair and waited while she gulped some water and blew her nose. "Tough day?"

Claire shredded a tissue. "You don't know how much I wish I could live yesterday over again. If I hadn't agreed to a massage, Enrique Romero would be alive and Roger would . . . Roger would still be living with me."

Wilson frowned. "I heard he made bail. But he's not returning home? Where's he staying?"

"At Dave Kessler's place." Seeing the detective's puzzled expression, Claire said, "His lawyer."

He nodded and asked for Kessler's address and phone

number. After writing those down, he leaned back in his chair and peered at Claire. "Now, what can I do for you?"

With Roger's rejection of her, convincing the police that someone was out to frame him became even more important. If she got them to drop the charges, maybe Roger would talk to her. Maybe she could convince him to return home. She licked her lips and groped for the right words.

"Roger said he got a message at work yesterday that I called and needed him to come home. But I didn't call him. When I talked to his receptionist today, she said she had assumed it was me, because the caller said so, but the caller spoke with a Hispanic accent."

Wilson shrugged. "Someone who knew about your liaison with Romero wanted your husband to find out. Doesn't matter much who, because I've got to tell you, Mrs. Hanover, it still places your husband at the scene with the murder weapon in his hand."

He plucked a piece of paper off one of the piles on his desk. "The lab sent a fingerprint report this morning. Only Mr. Romero's and your husband's fingerprints are on the gun. Your husband's were on top. And he had GSR on his hand."

"What's GSR?"

"Sorry. Gunshot residue. Shows the gun was in his hand when it was fired."

Claire fought to suppress her rising panic that the detective already had his mind made up. What happened to being innocent until proven guilty? "But I told you. When I screamed, Roger jumped and fired the gun by mistake."

"There's no way to prove whether he fired the gun once or twice. We only know he did fire it. Tell me about the gun. A nine-millimeter semiautomatic is not your typical household-protection handgun. How long have you owned it?"

Confused, she said, "Owned it? Do you mean the gun Roger

held in his hands?"

Wilson peered at her. "Ye-es."

"We don't own a gun. I won't allow them in the house. I've never seen it before. Roger said he never saw the gun before, either."

"Where'd he get it?"

"He said he found it lying on the hall floor."

Wilson pursed his lips. "Told me the same story."

Claire's eyes narrowed. Was the detective trying to trip her up? Did he think she planned this murder with Roger? "Then why did you ask me?"

"Thought he might tell you something different." Wilson made a note. "I'll have the gun traced. Anything else?"

Claire grabbed another tissue and dabbed at her nose to give herself time to think. Detective Wilson seemed uninterested in what she had told him so far, except for trying to catch Roger in a lie through her. She suspected he wouldn't show much interest in what she had to say next either, but she had to try. "Roger said he didn't do it. Didn't shoot Enrique."

Wilson raised an eyebrow. "Do you believe him?"

She couldn't lie, much as she wanted to. "I'm not a hundred percent sure, but I think I'd know if he were lying to me. He sounded so certain."

"Most of the people we lock up claim they didn't commit the crime they're accused of. Maybe some can't even admit to themselves that they're capable of committing a crime. Later, many of them admit their guilt. But the others . . ." He shook his head. "The prisons are crammed with guys who still claim they're innocent after they've been tried and convicted."

He leaned forward and clasped his hands on the desk. "I also have the ballistics results. The bullet that killed Enrique Romero came from that gun. You saw the gun in your husband's hand, and, as I told you, only his fingerprints and Romero's are on it.

This is a cut-and-dried case."

A whirlpool of panic sucked at Claire's feet. A cut-and-dried case? No, it couldn't be. Not when there were still unanswered questions. "But what about the gun? Where did it come from? Aren't you supposed to tie up all the loose ends in a case?"

"I said I'd trace the gun, but tying up that loose end won't change the conclusion." He swept a hand over the stacks of case files on his desk. "With this many active cases, I can't afford to chase rainbows on one I consider closed. I'd have to see something a lot more substantial to change my mind."

Claire drove home late Friday afternoon in a dejected daze. First thing, she checked the answering machine in the kitchen. Regina had returned Claire's call. With dread, but before she could back out, Claire picked up the phone. She explained the situation to Roger's sister, who grew more agitated by the minute. Finally, Regina cut her off and asked how she could get hold of Roger. Glad to pass off the burden of calming the woman, Claire gave her Dave's phone number.

Returning to the hall, she opened the closet to hang up her coat, then stopped with her hand in mid-air and stared. Stuffed in among the coats and ski jackets, Enrique's leather jacket still hung on a hanger.

She had forgotten to tell Detective Wilson about it, and the police probably assumed it was Roger's.

Her despair changed to hope. Maybe the jacket could offer the "something a lot more substantial" the detective had talked about. She reached for the jacket, then shuddered and drew back.

C'mon, it's just a jacket. He wasn't even wearing it when—no, don't think about that. Pick it up. Now.

Before she changed her mind, she grabbed the jacket and thrust her hand into a pocket. After finding the outside pockets empty except for a pair of gloves, she checked an inside pocket and pulled out a letter. Enrique's name appeared in the top left corner, above an address in Colorado Springs.

The envelope was addressed to a Lucia Romero in Nogales, Mexico. His mother? Or a sister? Guilt knotted Claire's gut. Had the police found this Lucia and notified her of her son or brother's death? Was the woman grieving even now as Claire held the last letter to her from Enrique?

She dropped the letter as if it burned her hand, then took a deep breath. *C'mon, Claire, if this can help Roger, you need to use it.* She forced herself to retrieve it.

Carrying the jacket and letter, she walked into the kitchen and picked up a pad of paper from the telephone desk. After she had written down both addresses from the envelope, she tried the other inside jacket pocket. She found a scrap of paper containing a name, Leon, and a phone number. These, too, she added to her pad.

Then she opened her phone book to Romero. Enrique's name appeared halfway down the page. The address matched the one from the letter. Claire wrote his phone number on the pad. On impulse, she picked up the phone and punched in the number.

After the third ring, a young-sounding woman said, *"Bueno?"*

Claire slammed down the receiver. Trembling, she stared at the phone. Did Enrique have a wife? A live-in girlfriend? Maybe she was the Hispanic woman who had called Roger's office. But how would she have found out where Roger worked?

Claire paced the kitchen. She had something, but not enough to impress Detective Wilson. She imagined his voice dripping with sarcasm. *So Romero had a Hispanic girlfriend. What a surprise. Now that's a real case breaker.*

She shook her head. She couldn't call Wilson yet, but she had to do something with this information. She snapped her fingers. *Of course.*

She thumbed through her address book until she found the entry for her former college roommate, Deb Burch, a Ute Indian. After serving as a tribal police officer on the Southern Ute reservation in Ignacio, Colorado, Deb had become a private investigator in Denver. She would know what to do.

Claire called Deb and spent half an hour updating her on the situation.

"You believe Roger's innocent?" Deb asked.

"Yes."

"So do I. Roger's no killer. And it sounds like the cops won't help you." Deb paused. "Damn, I'm tied up on an investigation. I have to fly to L.A. tomorrow morning then zip back here in time to testify in court Thursday. Otherwise, I'd drive down to the Springs and do some digging."

"What should I do?" Claire couldn't keep the edge of desperation out of her voice.

"First, examine the envelope. How thick is it?"

Claire picked up the envelope and shook it. Something inside slid back and forth. "Not very." She held the envelope up to the light. "It appears to be a check. No letter."

"He's probably sending *dinero* home to mama. Write down the address. We might need to interview her later. The next step I would take isn't tough . . . for me, that is. Maybe you could do it. In fact, it makes more sense for you to do it."

"Me?" The word came out as a squeak.

"Yeah, you, Minnie Mouse. Go to Romero's address tomorrow. When the woman answers the door, give her the impression you work at the gym and knew him. Worm your way into the house."

"Why?"

"So you can find out more about this Romero guy."

Claire's mouth went dry. "I don't think I can do that, Deb. You know I'm terrible at lying."

Deb laughed. "Remember that time you tried to lie your way out of taking an art history exam you hadn't studied for? By the time you finished, your dear departed Great Aunt Maude had died of liver failure with complications of psoriasis and typhoid fever."

"And I was stammering so bad, it took me three tries to say 'psoriasis.' That professor could see through me like a pane of glass that had just been Windexed."

"Do you want to wait until I return?"

"I can't sit and do nothing for a week." *Oh, God, what am I getting into?*

"Then you'll just have to screw up your courage and do it. Here's what you say . . ."

At ten-thirty the next morning, Saturday, Claire sat in her car across the street from the two-story brick apartment building where Enrique had lived. She clenched the steering wheel, licked her dry lips, and peered out the window.

The faded sign in front proclaimed "One-Bedroom and Efficiency Units for Rent, with Cable TV." Even though the building sat end-on to the street, from Claire's vantage point she could count fourteen apartments, seven on each floor. Metal stairs led to a balcony in front of the second-story units. Since Enrique's apartment number started with two, Claire guessed his must be located upstairs.

A biting cold wind blew tattered newspapers, a balled-up McDonalds bag, and a Tecaté beer can skittering down the street. The can bounced off pockmarks in the worn asphalt. The pavement cracks mirrored crooked lines left by flaking paint on the sides of the small, dilapidated houses lining her side of the street.

Claire wondered if her BMW would be safe while she made her visit. Maybe calculating eyes already peered from behind frayed curtains or stained blinds at the expensive automobile, estimating what could be gotten for the wheels or the car itself. For the umpteenth time, she wished Roger hadn't bought her the showy car. She would've been happy with a Toyota.

Move, Claire. She flipped up her coat collar and stepped out of the car. In one shaky hand she held a shopping bag containing Enrique's jacket. She was glad she thought to bring the jacket. Since it wasn't on his body, it couldn't be evidence. Beside, using its return as an excuse to visit made her lie more plausible.

After locking the car and setting the alarm, she resolutely turned her back on the small haven of security and marched across the street. She climbed the stairs to the second-floor balcony. Scanning door numbers, she walked along the metal railing until she found Enrique's apartment—second from the rear. After taking a deep breath, she knocked.

"*Quién es?*"

Oh, God. Claire hadn't figured on speaking Spanish. Maybe this woman also knew English. "Hello?"

A deadbolt slid sideways, the door opened a few inches, and a dark-haired young woman peered out. Her bleary eyes and the robe she clutched at her throat told Claire she may have come too early and roused this woman out of bed.

Already, Claire was starting off on the wrong foot. "I'm sorry. Did I wake you?"

The woman opened the door a little wider and looked up and down the walkway. Apparently satisfied Claire was alone, she said, "No, I was reading the newspaper. What do you want?"

Claire felt a surge of relief that she wouldn't have to rely on her rusty high school Spanish. "I'm from the gym where Enrique worked."

"You're not a cop?"

"No, I'm not."

"Good. I want no more questions about Enrique."

Heartened by the news that the police had done that, at least, Claire held up the shopping bag. "I have something for you. May I come in?"

The woman held the door open.

Claire stepped into the dimly lit room. She noted the shabby furnishings—a couch covered in an ancient plaid fabric, a recliner with a torn vinyl seat, a TV perched on a bookcase overflowing with Spanish scandal sheets and magazines, and a scuffed pine kitchen table and chairs. An open newspaper and a coffee cup sat on the table.

As Deb had instructed, Claire took off her coat, draped it on the back of one of the kitchen chairs, and sat, as if she planned to stay awhile. She clutched her hands under the table, to hide their shaking. "That coffee smells good."

The woman didn't take the hint. She sat at the table across from Claire and stared at her. "You worked with Enrique?"

Claire adopted the ditzy persona Deb said would work best. "Everyone at the gym is just horrified about what happened. You poor dear. We feel awful about the whole thing." She reached over to pat the woman's hand.

The woman withdrew her hand into her lap. Her dark eyes flashed. "I bet the ladies in his class miss him the most."

Damn right. Claire feigned innocence. "Oh, yes, I'm sure they do. Enrique was an excellent instructor."

"*Excelente,* yes. A little too *excelente.*" The woman laughed dryly. She picked up her cup, then slammed it down without drinking any coffee. Brown liquid sloshed on the table. "They should have kept their hands off him."

Claire strained to keep her voice light. Maintaining her ruse was becoming difficult, but thank goodness the woman seemed distracted. "What do you mean?"

The young woman waved her hand as if to brush aside the

topic. "Never mind."

"I'm sorry for your loss. Had you two been married long?"

The woman looked confused and shook her head. "Not married. Just, you know, girlfriend and boyfriend."

"My mistake. And I'm so rude. My name's Cathy. What's yours?" Surreptitiously, Claire rubbed the dampness off her hand onto her jeans then held it out.

The woman tentatively shook Claire's hand. "Condoleza."

"Condoleza. What a lovely name. But your last name must not be Romero."

"Martinez."

What was the next question? Oh, yeah. "Is your family from around here?"

Condoleza shook her head. "Mexico." Obviously tiring of Claire's chatter, she pointed to the shopping bag. "What is in the sack?"

"Oh, dear, I almost forgot why I came." Claire pulled Enrique's leather jacket out of the bag. "He left this. It's such a nice jacket. I thought you might want to have it, to remember him." She passed it to Condoleza.

Condoleza gathered it up and inhaled deeply. She glanced at Claire. "*Sí,* it's Enrique's. Thank you." Though Condoleza hugged the jacket, her eyes remained dry.

Surprising, for the girlfriend of a man who'd been murdered two days ago. Claire tried to form another question but a noise interrupted her thoughts.

A pale, lanky young man with shoulder-length brown hair and a droopy mustache stepped into the short hallway behind Condoleza. He wore only sweatpants and looked drowsy, eyes unfocused. "Who the hell's that? Another cop?"

Condoleza spun around to face him. "Someone from Enrique's gym, Travis. Go back to bed."

He walked to the table, rubbing the sleep from his face. As

he approached, a glint of silver at his chest drew Claire's eye. A small ring pierced the flesh around his left nipple. *God, why do young men think that's attractive?* The only thought it brought to her mind was pain.

He poked the jacket. "What's this?"

"Enrique's coat," Condoleza said. "She brought it to me."

The young man snatched the jacket from Condoleza's arms and held it out in front of him. "Nice. Might fit me."

He shrugged it on. Without a second glance at Claire, he walked down the hallway. "Get rid of her."

Condoleza's eyes conveyed regret. Whether regret that the man took Enrique's jacket, for his rudeness, or for her own situation, Claire couldn't tell. She felt sorry for the woman and helpless because she could do nothing for her. She'd already messed up this woman's life enough by causing Enrique's death. The thought jolted her. *Did I cause his death?*

Condoleza stood and pulled her frayed robe tighter around her. "I'm sorry. You have to go now."

Claire rose. "I understand." She picked up her coat and walked out, repeating the man's name in her mind. *Travis, Travis. How does he fit in the picture?*

The apartment had only one bedroom. Had Condoleza been seeing two men at the same time? Maybe she was tired of Enrique and wanted to get rid of him. But why did she clutch the jacket and sniff it, as though she missed the scent of him? Could Travis be a relative, come to comfort her? No, he wasn't Hispanic. Maybe a friend. But how much of a friend?

The visit raised more questions than it answered. Claire shuddered. At least she'd pulled off her ruse without being discovered. She hurried to her car, anxious to leave the seedy neighborhood. In her haste, instead of the unlock button on her key fob, she pushed the trunk release. The trunk lid popped up.

When she went to push it down, she stopped with her hand on the lid.

The two gift baskets still sat in the trunk.

She leaned her head against the trunk lid, shut her eyes, and cursed herself thoroughly under her breath. She'd never been late with a delivery—never. And she'd missed this one twice. Along with being pissed at her, Rita Wilaby had probably heard about the murders by now.

Claire slammed the trunk shut and slid into the car. She drove directly to Rita's office, only to find it closed, with a note tacked to the door that the real estate agent would be out showing homes to a customer all day.

Chapter 8
On Her Own

Wrapped in her thick purple bathrobe, Claire retrieved the Sunday morning newspaper from her driveway and entered the kitchen. She blew on her hands to warm them, then pulled the paper out of its blue plastic bag, threw it on the table, and turned to make coffee. She whirled back.

A large photo of Roger and her, blown up from a group shot at a charity function last month, stared out from the front page. She slumped into a chair to read the article accompanying the headline: MORE ON LOCAL MURDER. That Bradshaw reporter had not only listed their names, but named Roger's firm, and had dug up information on their charity activities.

And the kids.

Claire closed her eyes and clutched her throbbing forehead. *Why did he have to drag my children into it?*

In morbid fascination, she read on. Bradshaw quoted unnamed neighbors, who said the typical things.

I can't believe this happened in our neighborhood.

Can't blame him, can you?

Roger Hanover seemed so quiet, maybe too quiet.

Claire tried to imagine who would have said each thing. The neighbors' comments about her were worse.

I'm shocked, truly shocked.

This isn't the Claire I know.

Couldn't she have gone to a motel or something?

Claire's stomach churned with anger. They all assumed the

worst—that she'd cheated on Roger. How could they? But then she had put herself in a compromising position. If Enrique had lived, would she have gone further?

She tossed the paper aside. Maybe she deserved the negative comments. *Claire Hanover, you are lower than dirt.*

The phone rang.

She stared at it. Who was calling now? The reporter again? A nosy neighbor? She let the answering machine pick up.

After her greeting and the beep, she heard, "Mom? If you're there, pick up."

Claire grabbed the phone. "Hello, Michael."

"I read the story from your paper on the Internet. What's going on? Is Dad still in jail?"

"He's out on bail."

"Can I talk to him?"

She winced. "He's not here. He's at Dave Kessler's house."

"Is Dave representing him?"

"For now, but Dave's a corporate lawyer. We'll have to get a criminal lawyer soon." Claire sighed. "To tell you the truth, your father's not just meeting with Dave. He's staying there."

"Oh." Michael cleared his throat as if he couldn't decide what to say next.

"This is temporary. I love your father and hope to convince him to come home soon." Her voice caught. "Right now, it's hard for him."

"How are you handling all this, Mom?"

Claire forced her voice to be even. "I'll be all right. It's your dad I'm worried about."

Michael sounded unconvinced. "Maybe I should catch a flight home. I'll ask for a couple of days off."

"I don't think now is the right time. Your father and I have to sort this out on our own. But he needs your support. Call him." She gave Michael Dave's number and her love then hung up.

Almost immediately the phone rang again. Claire reached for it, then stopped and waited for the machine to pick up. Maybe this time a reporter or nosy neighbor would be on the line.

Right the second time. Nosy neighbor.

Disgusted, Claire threw the front-page section of the paper in the recycling bag. She decided she needed to get her hands busy. Maybe tying bows on that unfinished baby basket would get her mind off her troubles. Trying to construct a pleasing, ordered arrangement out of a random pile of gift items often helped Claire organize her thoughts. *And God knows, they're in chaos now.* She marched downstairs toward her workshop, rolling up her sleeves.

She flipped on the light as she entered the room and ran her hand across the scratched and marred surface of the large oak dining table she'd found at a church yard sale. It was well worn, like herself, but did its duty as a work surface. The basket she'd selected for the baby gift sat in the middle, with a pile of purchased infant clothes, teethers, receiving blankets, and diapering products next to it. Wide pink and blue ribbons had already been woven around the bottom.

Claire turned to the plastic shelves on two walls that contained baskets, packing and wrapping materials such as Spanish moss and colored cellophane, fabric remnants, and clear boxes labeled "Ribbons," "Tags/cards," "Plastic/dried flowers," and "Trinkets." She opened the box of ribbons, found thin ribbons that matched the colors of the wide ones, and set to work tying bows on the basket handle and around the edge.

When disturbing memories of Enrique's body pushed into her mind, breaking her concentration, she pawed through the shoebox of Enya, Yanni, and other soothing CDs, and popped one in the boom box on the table. She finished the bows, but when she started arranging the gifts in the basket, using small empty boxes to give the items varying heights, she ran into trouble.

As she stacked and restacked gifts, attempting to make a coherent whole out of the pieces, she tried to fit together a story of Enrique's murder that made sense.

If someone besides Roger had killed Enrique, like Condoleza or Travis, how did the killer know Enrique was at her house? Did Enrique call someone from the gym? Condoleza? Okay, maybe Condoleza knew, but how would she know where Roger worked, to call him and leave the message for him to come home? Enrique could have known where Roger worked from asking Ellen, maybe, but why would he tell Condoleza?

Then, even if Condoleza did leave the message for Roger, why would she come over and kill Enrique or, more likely, have Travis kill Enrique, knowing Roger could show up any minute? Wasn't setting up an embarrassing discovery enough? And if Travis did it, how did he get in?

Duh. Claire tapped her forehead. She'd left the front door unlocked after picking up the package outside.

But if Travis left the same way, why didn't Roger see him?

No scenario seemed to work, in either the basket or her mind. Frustrated, Claire pulled everything out of the basket and left the room to clear her mind.

The basement family room looked gloomy—too gloomy. *Time to shed some light on things.* She walked over to the sliding glass door then noticed the vertical blinds at the end were twisted. *Curious.* She reset the blinds and opened them. Bright winter sunlight blazed through the glass. Hungry for a breath of fresh air, she reached for the lock to open the door to the backyard.

Her hand froze.

The door was unlocked.

How did that happen? Sometimes when the kids were young and running in and out, they would forget to lock the door, but she and Roger never left it unlocked. She spun and looked at the steps behind her that led to the main hall, where Roger had said he found the gun.

She turned back to the door and stared at the lock. All it took to unlock the door was a simple flick of a finger. Anyone could do it, even someone who'd never set foot in the house before. If the killer had checked out the house from the outside, he would have seen there was an exit from the basement.

Her head buzzed. Roger was right. Here was the evidence that someone else was in the house and had escaped out the back door when he heard Roger coming. That would explain the twisted blinds, too. The killer shoved them aside while running out the door.

Why didn't the police find this? Claire recalled how thoroughly they had searched the rooms, stairs, and hallway on the top two floors where she, Roger, and Enrique had been. Then she remembered one cop asking Detective Wilson if they should look for evidence in the basement. He had said not to bother, that none of the "players" had been down there.

Claire rushed upstairs. She searched through her kitchen desk until she found Detective Wilson's card and called the number. The man who answered said Detective Wilson was out, but he took Claire's message to call her as soon as possible.

Too jittery to concentrate on arranging the basket, Claire walked into the laundry room. A pile of new, unwashed linens lay on the dryer. In a frenzy of shopping to keep her turbid emotions at bay, she had bought new bedding after visiting Condoleza the day before, then added matching throw pillows and a valance.

She threw the sheets in the washer and started the machine. Physical activity was the solution. She would keep busy with housework and ignore the phone, unless Roger or Detective Wilson called.

Claire spent the rest of the morning laundering the new linens and hanging valances in the master bedroom windows. She threw open the blinds and cracked the south-facing window to let the cleansing sun and crisp winter breeze wash the room of all remaining traces of Enrique's death. To banish the jagged memories, she tuned the radio to an oldies station and cranked the volume up.

When she finished making the master bed, she stood back to survey her handiwork. A rich gold and jewel-tone bedspread in a floral scroll print covered the bed. The valance echoed the antique print, and striped and floral pillow shams and throw pillows sat artfully arranged on the thick spread.

Claire ran her fingertips along the pillows. Could she sleep here tonight? An involuntary shudder rippling across her shoulders made her grip her arms tight. *Not alone.* With Roger, maybe. She hoped he would accept the new décor—and her.

Roger. She checked her watch. She hadn't called him the day before, though she'd been tempted many times. She wanted to give him the space he had said he needed, and she hoped he might call her. It was two o'clock. She couldn't wait any longer.

When Dave Kessler answered his phone, she asked for Roger. Dave seemed hesitant but didn't say no.

Moments later, Roger picked up the phone. "Hello, Claire." His tone was flat, dead.

Her throat caught at the sound of him. God, she missed him. "Did Regina call?"

"Yeah. You sure got her spun up."

"You know your sister. She does that all on her own. I had to tell her. You wouldn't want her to find out from the newspapers or TV."

He blew out a breath. "No, but she took a lot of calming down. And Michael called. He sounded upset, wanted to come home. Damn, I hate what this is doing to the kids."

Oh, God. "What did you say to him?"

"I don't want him to get mixed up in this. I told him to stay in Boston."

At least they agreed on that. Anxious to keep Roger talking, Claire chose a topic she knew he would respond to. "How did the investor conference go?"

"Ned wouldn't let me participate."

"Oh, Roger, I'm sorry. You worked so hard on it."

"Ned had me brief Joe so he could present the numbers instead."

Claire winced. Joe was Roger's deputy financial officer. Roger would view this step by Joe as a threat. "Why wouldn't Ned let you make the presentation?"

Roger's voice dripped sarcasm. "He said the CFO being accused of murder just might make the investors nervous."

Ouch. She said the first dumb thing that popped into her mind. "I guess that makes sense."

"Trouble is, someone already pulled the story off the news-wire and asked Ned about it during the conference. That pissed him off. He told me he had to backpedal to cover for me. Didn't like it one bit."

"I'm sure you can get back in his good graces next week."

"I won't have that chance." Roger's voice dropped in tone. "He told me to take administrative leave for a week."

Oh, dear. That was a major blow. No wonder Roger sounded angry and depressed. And it was her fault. "I'm sorry, honey."

"I'm afraid that at the end of the week, he'll put Joe in charge and tell me to take leave until the trial's over. Even if I'm found innocent, which isn't bloody likely, after being out of the loop so long, I might as well not come back at all."

Claire gasped. "How can Ned do that? You've done everything he asked, and more." *Much more.*

"He can do whatever the hell he wants to. It's his company."

"But if you'd been in the conference, you could have responded to the question by telling them the accusation is a mistake, that you're innocent."

"Ned doesn't get that logic." Roger paused, and his voice changed to a softer timbre. "Do you believe I'm innocent?"

Now was not the time for Claire to voice any lingering doubts. "Of course I do. And I discovered something that should help convince the police. The basement sliding glass door was unlocked. The killer probably escaped that way."

"Are you sure you didn't just leave it unlocked sometime?"

"You know how careful I am about that door. Besides, the vertical blinds were twisted, as if someone had shoved them aside."

"But you have no proof the door was unlocked Thursday. The police will think you made up the story to help me."

"I plan to tell Detective Wilson anyway. I left a message for him."

"*Did* you make it up?"

"No!"

"But you would have, wouldn't you, if you'd thought of it?"

"No. Yes. I don't know." She swept her hair back in exasperation. "If I did make it up, Detective Wilson would figure it out. You know what a bad liar I am."

"The point is, you would have, and that's what he'll think."

Claire refused to let his pessimism rub off on her. "Okay, even if that doesn't help, I've got something else that should."

She told Roger of her visit to Condoleza Martinez. "Enrique probably told her he was giving me a massage. Maybe she was furious with Enrique, thinking he was starting another affair, or she wanted to ditch him for this Travis. So she made that call to you, because she wanted you to discover us."

"How the hell would she know where I work?"

"Ellen talked to Enrique about me. She could have told him

where you work, and he could have told Condoleza."

"Why would she tell him that? Besides, how does this information help me?" Roger sounded peeved. "That story still puts my finger on the trigger."

"Condoleza could have done it. She didn't seem heartbroken about his death. Or that Travis guy could have shot Enrique. Or someone else, someone in Enrique's life we know nothing about."

"You're clutching at straws."

Roger sounded like he was giving up, but she wasn't, not on him or their marriage. "Tell Dave everything I told you. I intend to give this information to Detective Wilson, too. Maybe it will convince him to search further."

"It won't do any good. The police think they have their killer already. Me. Dave says their case is strong, even though they can't use your statement that you saw me holding the gun. Damn, that was real helpful." Roger's tone dripped sarcasm.

"I told the truth. Did you expect me to lie? What if they caught me in the lie? Then it would look even worse for you." Claire heard her voice rising and glanced at her clenched fist. She caught herself. Her anger wouldn't get Roger back. She raced through a quick count to ten. "Honey, I'm trying to help."

"Some help. Because of your little fling, my next career could be as a prison inmate."

That hurt. She wanted to shout that she didn't have a fling, that he was being too pessimistic, that . . . No, those words would not bring Roger home. "I want to talk to you, face-to-face. I want to fix what I broke. Please give me a chance."

Roger groaned.

Claire plunged on. "I just finished replacing all the linens in the master bedroom. Come see it. Tell me if you like it. Then we can talk."

"How can you think of redecorating at a time like this?"

Claire gritted her teeth. "I had to. The police took the linens."

She hadn't found the nerve to sleep in the master bed yet. Maybe with Roger beside her, she would.

"Please come home." Claire almost whispered it. "I love you."

"I'll think about it." He hung up.

At eight-thirty Monday morning, Claire walked into the busy detective bullpen area of the downtown police station. She felt as if she was stepping onto hostile turf, even though Detective Wilson had been courteous to her last time. But the overwhelming evidence had convinced him he held the guilty party. She knew changing that conviction would be an uphill battle. She spied him and approached his desk.

He looked up in surprise. "Mrs. Hanover. You didn't need to come to the station. I just saw your message and was going to call you soon."

"I couldn't wait." Claire sat in the visitor's chair next to the desk and unbuttoned her coat. After having fidgeted in her car for half an hour while mustering the courage to see him, she would not leave until she said her piece.

"Over the weekend I found the basement door unlocked. That's why I called you. Roger and I are always very careful to lock it. I think the real killer heard Roger come in, dropped the gun in a panic, ran downstairs, and escaped out that door. The vertical blinds were twisted, too." Hopeful he'd have to do something with this information, she leaned back and waited for his reaction.

"Nice try." Wilson shook his head and crossed his arms over his chest. "How long did it take you to dream up that story?"

She made her voice firm. "I don't dream up stories."

"Can you prove one of you didn't leave it unlocked, or that you're not making up the whole thing?"

Claire glared at the smug man. "This is just how Roger

said you'd react."

Wilson raised an eyebrow. "So you plotted with him over the weekend, and this is the best you could come up with?"

"No!" Claire's frustration mounted. "Aren't you going to check it out?"

"Did you touch the door or the blinds?"

"I untwisted the blinds so I could open them. That was before I saw the door was unlocked. I didn't touch the door, but I pushed the lock down. I wasn't going to leave the door unlocked. I'm sleeping in that house alone, remember?"

Wilson spread his hands wide. "You disturbed the supposed crime scene."

Claire gritted her teeth. "If your team had searched the whole house Thursday, you would have found the unlocked door, and we wouldn't have this problem."

"What reason did we have to go in the basement? Your husband, the man holding the smoking gun, had come in the front door and left it wide open. Not only did that provide easy entry for our patrolmen, but substantiation of his statement. We didn't find any prints on the door other than yours and his."

"Will you check the basement now?"

Wilson twisted his head to study a schedule board on the wall then refocused on Claire. "My technician's got a full day, but I can send her over this evening. You'll be there to let her in?"

Thank God he'd decided to do that at least. "Yes."

"Okay. Now, as much as I enjoy your little visits, Mrs. Hanover, I hope you'll leave the investigative work to us from now on. We *are* the professionals. I'll call you if anything important comes up." He made a move to stand, as if to escort her out of the office.

"I've got something else."

Wilson sighed and settled in his chair. "Yes?"

Although irritated by his condescending attitude, Claire vowed to stick to business. "I found out who called Roger, claiming to be me. Roger's receptionist said the woman had a Hispanic accent. It must have been Condoleza Martinez, Enrique's girlfriend."

"How do you know Miss Martinez?"

"I don't. I went to Enrique's apartment yesterday and found her there."

Wilson grinned. "So you know Mr. Romero better than you let on, enough to have been to his apartment."

Claire felt her cheeks redden, and she glanced around the room to check if any of the other detectives were listening. "I found his address on an envelope."

"What envelope?"

"The one in his jacket pocket."

Wilson leaned forward, his smile gone. "What jacket?"

"Enrique left his jacket in my closet." A niggling worry wormed its way into her mind. Did she do something wrong?

"What the hell? Why didn't you tell me about the jacket before?"

With obvious interest, two nearby detectives watched the interplay between Claire and Wilson.

"I forgot it was in the closet until I saw it over the weekend." Claire rubbed her damp hands on her jeans. "Enrique wasn't wearing the jacket when he was shot, so I assumed it wasn't important. Returning it gave me an excuse to visit Condoleza. I didn't think the reason Deb gave me was good enough."

"Who's Deb?"

"A friend of mine who's a private investigator."

"A private investigator? Did you hire a P.I. to snoop around on the case?" Wilson scowled at her, then the two detectives.

They turned away, but not before one cracked a wry smile.

Claire squirmed in her seat. This conversation was not going the way she planned. "I just called her for advice."

"I hate private investigators interfering in police business."

Claire wondered if she'd broken some law. "Was giving the jacket to Condoleza all right?"

"No, but it's useless to us now, with your and Martinez's fingerprints all over it. What did you do with the envelope?"

"I, uh, mailed it."

"Christ!" He buried his head in his hands.

"It only had a check in it and was addressed to a Lucia Romero. I assumed he was sending money to his mother or something. I thought I did the right thing." *Damn, I sound like a blithering idiot.*

Wilson raised his head and stared at her. "Do you remember the address?"

She'd done that right, at least. Claire rummaged in her purse. "I wrote it down. Here." She handed him a copy of her original notes.

Wilson peered at the paper. "Who's this Leon?"

Claire shrugged. "I don't know. The name and phone number were in one of the jacket pockets."

"Did you find anything else?"

"No."

"Mrs. Hanover, I appreciate what you're trying to do." Wilson laid the paper on his desk and smoothed it out with deliberate strokes. "You're feeling guilty about your little fling and want to worm your way back into your husband's good graces by proving his innocence."

Claire flinched. An indelicate way to put it, but not far off the mark.

"It's not gonna happen. As I said before, it doesn't matter who called your husband. He still pulled the trigger." He pointed an accusing finger at Claire. "But your mucking around in this case is only causing trouble for both of us."

"But—"

"No buts. I don't want to hear you've been off talking to people on your own. That's my job, get it?"

She hated to antagonize him any more, but she had to ask. "Are you going to talk to Miss Martinez?"

"We already have!"

A bead of sweat trickled down her chest. But this wasn't one of her hot flashes, this was pure anxiety. "I mean about the phone call."

"Of course. Now, if you have nothing further . . ." He waved his hand toward the door.

Claire stood to leave and glanced around the room. Her cheeks burned as she realized she'd gathered quite an audience. The two detectives from before stared at her. When her gaze fell on a man at a nearby desk, he hastily reached for a phone and knocked it onto the floor. As he bent to retrieve it, a uniformed policeman standing by his desk snorted down a laugh and elbowed the woman next to him.

A man approached Detective Wilson's desk and handed him a message slip.

Wilson read it, and his lips curled. "This is the trace on the gun. It belonged to Romero."

He tossed the message on his desk, on top of Claire's note, then glared at Claire. "Not some mysterious gunman. If Romero carried that gun in his jacket pocket, and your husband removed it from there, the jacket is evidence."

"But I hung the jacket in the closet when Enrique and I arrived, and it didn't feel heavy enough to have a gun in the pocket."

"Then Romero carried the gun in his gym bag, which was sitting wide open in the hall. That part of your husband's story could be true. The gun slipped out of the bag onto the floor, where he found it."

Wilson slowly rose and leaned his knuckles on his desk. "Regardless, tampering with evidence is a serious offense. You keep meddling in this case, Mrs. Hanover, and I may be forced to charge you. Go home and let the professionals do their work."

Claire had had enough. She spit out the words. "First of all, I did not have a *little fling,* and second, you *professionals* seem to be focused on proving Roger did it. I expected more objectivity."

She shouldered her purse, turned, and marched out of the room. Her back crawled as she felt the gaze of the other detectives follow her exit. She would not stop meddling, as he called it, as long as Roger, and their marriage, had a chance.

CHAPTER 9
THE BOSS

Stomach burning, Claire fumed on the way to the gym from the police station. If she hadn't planned to attend aerobics class to find out more about Enrique, she would have driven home. She felt like slamming pillows into walls and stomping around the living room.

Looking forward to working off her anger and frustration in another way, Claire shoved open the door to the women's locker room at the gym. The buzz of multiple conversations along the rows of lockers surrounded her as she walked in. She nodded to two women she recognized from Enrique's class, but they turned their backs on her. When she entered a row of lockers and dropped her gym bag on a bench, the woman standing on the other side of the bench walked away without a word. The conversations died down, replaced by whispers.

Claire picked up her gym bag to go change in the privacy of a toilet stall then stopped. *No, I refuse to be intimidated.* Even angrier now, she jerked open the locker door, hung up her coat, and peeled off her jeans.

The other women acted as if they couldn't wait to remove themselves from her presence. Lockers slammed shut, and the locker room door squeaked open several times in quick succession. The quiet in the room deepened.

Claire tugged her T-shirt down over her head with a quick yank and opened her eyes. The same tall brunette who had talked to Enrique Monday stood at the end of the bench, studying her.

"What?" Claire snapped.

"Sorry, I didn't mean to stare." The brunette smiled and extended her hand. "I'm Brenda Johnston."

Remembering the name, Claire shook her hand, hoping she'd found a possible ally, but wary that the woman had other motives for approaching her. "I'm—"

"Claire Hanover. I know." Brenda sat on the bench and stretched out her long legs. "Feel like you're getting the cold shoulder?"

"I don't just feel it. I know it."

Brenda laughed. "You may want to switch to the ten o'clock Tuesday and Thursday class. I take it, too. Enrique didn't teach that one."

"You're dedicated." Claire tugged a pair of leggings over her calves. "But I think I'll stick this one out. I'm mad, actually. Just because they want me out, I'll stay."

"Good for you." Brenda made a sweeping motion with her hand, indicating the rest of the locker room. "Half these women are upset because they no longer have Enrique Romero to drool over in class, and the other half are insanely jealous."

Claire sat next to her new acquaintance. "Jealous?"

"Yes, because Enrique dumped them in the past, and his latest interest obviously was you."

Half the class? Ellen said a few. "Tell me more."

Brenda peered at her. "Sounds like you didn't know what you were getting into. Here it is in a teacup. Enrique traded his sexual favors with women in the class for money, loans, gifts, whatever he could get from them."

"God, that makes me feel cheap." Claire remembered the times she picked up the bill for their juices.

"Most of the women he seduced knew what he was doing.

They figured it was worth it, to get their hands on him. Who knows? Some may have seduced him." Brenda's eyes were unfocused, as if remembering something. "Problem was, a lot of them wanted to keep him, but Enrique never stayed with one for long. He always moved on."

"Brenda, did you—"

"Hi, Claire." Ellen breezed into the row and squeezed past them to reach a locker. Brow furrowed, she glanced at Brenda.

Brenda pursed her lips as if she wanted to say more, then shook her head and left.

After the door had squeaked closed, Ellen sat beside Claire. "What were you talking to Brenda about?"

Claire's throat tightened. "Enrique Romero slept with half the women in the class."

Ellen laughed. "I think that's an exaggeration. But even if it's true, so what? The point is he was fun to be with, at least until he got knocked off."

Horrified, Claire stared at her friend.

With a nudge, Ellen said, "Joke. Just trying to lighten your mood a little. Sorry, I guess it's too soon for you to laugh about it."

"Brenda said Enrique did it for money. Twice he left me to pay for our juices. He was already sponging off me." Claire's eyes stung. She felt like she would cry from shame any minute.

Ellen gave her a big hug. "Claire, baby, don't take life so seriously. And I wouldn't take Brenda too seriously, either. She has her own reasons for being upset by Enrique's death."

And for making sure I felt scummy for associating with him? "Did she have an affair with him?"

Ellen stood and closed her locker. "He was her supplier."

"Supplier?" Claire's eyes grew wide.

"Cocaine."

"Ohmigod. He sold drugs, too?"

"Not in the way you might think. You had to ask him for it. If anyone into coke asked around, they soon found out he could get it for them, sort of doing them a favor."

Claire's mood lifted. "This information might help Roger. If Enrique was selling drugs, someone could've wanted him dead."

Guilt flooded in as a realization hit her. "God, by allowing Enrique into my home, I provided the killer with the perfect setup so he or she could frame Roger for the crime."

"For your sake, I hope you're right about Roger being innocent."

"You're a good friend." Claire stood and returned Ellen's hug. "I know you aren't convinced he's innocent, but I am, and I aim to prove it."

"How?"

"I don't know yet, but I'm working on it."

Frowning, Ellen studied her. "Be careful. I'd hate to see you get hurt by this. Any more than you already are, that is."

Claire felt a lump growing in her throat. "Thanks. I'll be careful."

Ellen glanced at the clock on the wall. "Time for class. A sub is teaching. When I came in, I heard some of the women talking about you in the hall. Can you handle it?"

Claire put on a brave smile, even though her stomach was quivering. "I'm ready to face the masses."

As she followed Ellen to the door, she had an idea. "Did Enrique ever mention a name that you remember? You know, the person he got the cocaine from?"

Ellen thought for a moment. "I think I overheard him say the name 'Leon' once to Brenda. That he would get the stuff from Leon."

Claire sat in her BMW in the parking lot of Graham's Gym. Slowly, she rubbed the piece of paper with Leon's phone number. She mulled over her options. Deb was still on a case in Los Angeles and hadn't left a phone number. If Claire called Detective Wilson, he would just get angry with her again. She had to do this herself, even if it meant facing the detective's ire. And facing Leon. What if he killed Enrique? But why would he kill one of his own dealers?

She wished she knew more about illegal drugs. She'd never even smoked a joint, not even when she and Roger were college students in the seventies. The choice wasn't from a sense of righteousness. It was from plain fear. And that's what made her hands shake now—fear. But she had to do this. If she chose not to, Roger could be convicted.

Claire picked up her cell phone and quickly punched in the number. When a gravelly voiced man answered, she said, "Leon?"

"Who's this?"

"A friend of Enrique's."

"How'd you get this number?"

"I got it from Enrique." *Or his jacket, at least.*

"What d'ya want?"

"If you're Leon, I need to talk to you about his death." Face-to-face was the only option, no matter how afraid she was of him. She would have to gain his trust if she was going to get any useful information out of him. And people didn't tend to trust strangers who called them on the phone, especially people operating on the wrong side of the law.

"I don't know nothing about that. Even if I did, why would I talk to you?"

Claire clenched the phone. "Because I might make it worth your while."

The man laughed. "You offering money or yourself?"

"I'm offering to exchange information." Claire flushed. She needed to regain control of this conversation. Maybe she could pique his curiosity enough for him to agree to meet her. "I'm sure you're just as interested in finding out who really killed him as I am."

"The police think a jealous husband killed him."

"The police are wrong."

"What makes you say that?"

"I'll tell you when I see you. When and where can we meet?"

"You a cop or something?" The man sounded suspicious.

"No, just a friend." Claire held her breath.

Silence. Finally, he said, "Meet me in an hour in the liquor store parking lot at Hancock and Chester."

"Where is that?" As she asked, Claire heard a click followed by dead air.

She dug out a map and looked up one of the street names. She squinted to bring the small writing into focus and found the intersection, in a bad part of town. She shuddered. At least the meeting would be out in the open. She checked her wallet and counted eighty-three dollars in cash. She might need bribery money if her information wasn't enough to get Leon to talk. First stop would be an ATM.

An hour later, Claire drove into an empty parking lot crisscrossed with weed-encrusted cracks. Boards covered the liquor store's windows. Trash sat piled in the doorway. *Great, no help there.* Nervously, she glanced around. A gas station on the opposite corner was open for business, and an old man pumped gas into his rusty Chevrolet, his thin frame hunched against the cold. She doubted he'd rush to her aid if trouble ensued. Nonetheless, she parked her car as close to the street and the gas station as she could.

A few minutes later, a black limousine with heavily tinted windows drove by slowly. It was standard-sized, not the typical stretch model that took high schoolers to the prom. Halfway up the block, it backed into a driveway and returned. The limousine pulled into the lot and parked three spaces away from her.

The driver and front-seat passenger, both large men wearing sunglasses, got out and approached her car.

Oh, God. Claire's heart started racing for the nearest exit.

The black driver pocketed his keys with one hand and, with the other, flicked a half-smoked cigarette onto the concrete. The white passenger's bare arms hung out of his denim vest. His huge biceps sported intricate tattoos and his oiled shaved head gleamed in the winter sunlight. He seemed impervious to the frigid air.

The driver opened her car door. "Get out."

Claire cringed. She told herself to remain calm. They wouldn't shoot her in broad daylight. *Would they?* With sweaty palms, she eased out of the BMW.

The driver said, "Hands on the car."

"What are you going to do?" Claire swallowed the lump of fear clogging her throat.

The driver shrugged. "You wanna talk to the boss, you gotta be patted down."

Claire looked at his companion, who stared at her from behind his shades. Neither man budged. Claire realized she could back out now, and maybe nothing would happen. But she wouldn't learn anything, either. She faced the car and placed her hands on the roof.

The driver was quick but thorough. He checked each pocket of her winter coat then unzipped it. He ran his hands down her sides and back then along each leg. When Claire flinched as his hand grazed her crotch, he didn't seem to notice, continuing his search.

The driver stepped back. "Now the purse."

She handed him her red leather Aigner bag.

He opened the purse and rummaged around, then closed it and returned it to her. He nodded at his companion. Signaling her to follow him, he said, "You can see the boss now."

When Claire followed the driver, the other man fell in step behind her. A cold drop of sweat trickled down the back of her neck.

The driver opened the rear door of the limousine and motioned for her to get in.

Taking a step back, Claire said, "I'd rather talk out here."

"Not gonna happen," the driver replied.

Claire glanced in the gloomy interior, but could make out little in the dim light allowed in by the dark tinted windows. A man sat in the middle of the far rear seat, but his face was cloaked in shadow.

Claire climbed in and sat in the rear-facing seat by the door. She started when the driver slammed the door shut behind her. She looked out the window and saw him and his companion take up sentry positions on both sides of the car.

A deep chuckle sounded from the rear seat, followed by a ring of cigarette smoke blown toward the ceiling.

The acrid smell made Claire cough.

"You sure ain't no friend of Enrique's with that fancy-pants car. And you ain't no cop, neither. You're too jumpy."

The large black man across from her looked older than his underlings and sported a hefty paunch. As Claire's eyes adjusted, she could make out more details. He wore a large gold ring on both ring fingers and a heavy gold chain that hung halfway down his chest. He stretched his legs, exposing black cowboy boots, finely tooled.

And Claire recognized a Rolex watch when she saw one. His was pure gold. Obviously, peddling cocaine was more lucrative than she'd ever imagined, not that she'd ever imagined herself "dealing" with a cocaine dealer.

He blew out another smoke ring, apparently waiting for her to speak.

She stifled a cough. "Are you Leon?"

"Who else? Who are you?"

"I met Enrique at the gym."

He chuckled again. "Ah, one of his lady friends."

Claire squirmed in her seat. "Not exactly."

"Customer, then. You need some blow? Travis is handling Enrique's ladies now. Most days, he's in the auto shop next to the gym. I pay them off to let him hang around."

Travis. The guy with Condoleza. Claire's thoughts whirled, but she didn't have time to fully digest this new tidbit. "I don't need some blow. I want information."

Leon leaned forward and squinted at her. "What's your name?"

She considered lying but realized he probably already knew her name from the photo in the paper, and was testing her. He looked a lot more astute than Condoleza. Claire could already feel her cheeks blazing with embarrassment. "Claire. Claire Hanover."

Leon's eyes opened wide, his curiosity plainly aroused. "So why's the wife of the man who killed Enrique asking to see me?"

"Because Roger didn't kill Enrique, and I need to find out who did. The police won't help me. They're sure they've got their man."

Leon leaned back and blew out another smoke ring. "What makes you think they don't?"

"It's not just because I love Roger. It's because I know him. He's not a killer. He found Enrique's gun lying in the hall and picked it up. That's why he was holding it."

"Enrique was offed with his own gun?"

"That's what Detective Wilson says. He traced it."

"Interesting. I heard Wilson caught the case. What else did he say?"

"That I should stop snooping around and let the professionals do their job." Claire bristled at the memory.

Leon laughed. "And here you are, still snooping. You've got guts, lady."

This was a vital juncture. Now that she'd cracked the ice, Claire had to convince Leon that helping her was in his own best interests. She clutched the edge of her seat. "If Roger didn't kill Enrique, that means his killer is still at large. What if Enrique was killed for business reasons, instead?"

Leon raised an eyebrow. "Business reasons?"

"Did Enrique sell cocaine for you?"

"All I'll say is that he worked for me."

"Then the killer could be after you next."

"Maybe." Leon leaned forward. "Now, this is important. Did Wilson tell you he was gonna check out Enrique's contacts, you know, friends and neighbors?"

"He only said he'd talked to Condoleza, Enrique's girlfriend."

"Good. I don't want Wilson nosing around my business. I can handle Condoleza." Leon gazed out the window and smoked his cigarette, apparently plotting his next move.

Claire saw her opening and jumped in. "You've been asking most of the questions so far. I think it's my turn."

Leon bowed his head slightly. "Ask away."

She swallowed, hard. "Did Enrique do his job well? Were you disappointed in him in any way?"

Throwing his head back, Leon laughed. "Lady, you've sure got balls. You accusing *me* of knocking him off?"

Claire decided to be brave, since Leon admired bravery and seemed to be in a jovial mood. "If the shoe fits."

"Don't fit me any better than your husband. Enrique never disappointed me, as you put it."

He didn't appear to be lying, but Claire couldn't trust her instincts. "What about Travis? I saw him with Condoleza after

Enrique's death."

Leon's eyes widened. "You get around. Yeah, Enrique and Travis were banging the same girl. Now that Enrique's gone, Travis has moved in with her. That Condoleza's one hot number."

So Travis was more than a friend. Remembering Condoleza's expression of regret at the apartment, Claire wondered if the young woman was a willing partner to both men. Or was she being passed around among gang members?

Leon took another pull on his cigarette. "But Travis is smart. Too smart to be killing anyone. He bides his time. He knows waiting is the way to get what you want sometimes."

"Like Enrique's business. You said Travis was handling that now. Was he anxious to take over?"

Leon shook his head. "Nah. As I said, he's cool. He knows not to act without my say-so."

Oh, God. "Your say-so? You order killings?"

Leon's wide grin displayed even white teeth. "Who said that? I'm just running an honest business here."

Plunging ahead before fear could freeze her resolve, Claire asked, "What about someone else? You know, competition. Could a rival of yours have killed Enrique?"

"I'll do some of my own snooping, but I doubt it. I got a rep', you see. No one messes with my business." He stared down his long nose at her. "No one."

Claire shuddered. She'd caught the implication of what would happen to anyone who did mess with his business—including her.

Leon checked his watch. "Speaking of business, I'm a busy man." He rapped on the window. "You know, of course, we never met."

"Of course."

"Wouldn't want nothing to happen to you or that husband

you're so fond of."

Aghast, Claire stared at the man, but she couldn't read his expression.

The driver opened the limousine door. Claire had no recourse but to leave. She climbed out and watched Leon and his henchmen drive off, her thoughts churning. The meeting had unnerved her. On the drive home, visions of how it could have ended differently wormed their way into her mind. Her body, shot in the chest, dumped in Fountain Creek.

She shook her head. She was blowing things out of proportion. Leon, in his own way, seemed to be a reasonable man, though she knew getting on his bad side would be a terrible mistake. Unfortunately, she hadn't learned much from the meeting. The most likely suspect so far seemed to be Travis, but she had to figure out how to prove it.

Chapter 10
Drug-Buy Training

Claire's turkey-vegetable soup cooled as she stared unseeingly at yet another trite Monday night sitcom. Wilson's technician had left an hour ago, after spending forty-five minutes in the basement. When Claire had asked her if she'd found anything useful, she'd shrugged and suggested Claire "call Detective Wilson in a couple of days." Unwilling to wait idly, Claire's mind kept rehashing her meeting with Leon.

The telephone rang. After the answering machine's greeting, Rita Wilaby's voice came from the speaker. "Claire, I'm getting impatient. Where are those baskets? I went to closing with one of those two clients today and had nothing to give her."

Claire winced. The baskets were still in the trunk of her car, totally forgotten after the encounters with Detective Wilson, Leon, and her whole exercise class. The real estate agent was a new client Claire had hoped would become a regular. But now, her first order probably would be her last.

With trepidation, Claire picked up the phone. "Rita, I'm so sorry. I tried to deliver them Saturday, but—"

"Saturday? What happened to Friday? And Thursday?"

Claire could almost feel the hot steam of Rita's anger radiating from the receiver. Or was that her own guilt boiling to the surface? "Roger's hearing was Friday, and I—"

"Hearing? What hearing?"

How could the woman have missed the story? "An aerobics instructor was murdered at our—"

"Ohmigod. Was that you?"

"Yes." The woman couldn't interrupt that sentence at least. Claire waited. Rita seemed to be speechless for the moment. "As you can imagine, I've had a lot on my mind," Claire continued, "but I promise I'll bring them to you first thing tomorrow. Nine o'clock okay?"

"Sure. Yes. Okay."

"Thanks for your patience. I'll see you then." With a sigh of relief, Claire hung up.

When the phone rang again a moment later, she picked it up. "Rita?"

"No, Deb. Disappointed?"

Claire smiled. "On the contrary. I'm glad you called. Are you back from L.A.?"

"Sorry, I'm still stuck out here. How'd your visit with Romero's girlfriend go?"

Claire told Deb about her meetings with Condoleza Martinez, Detective Wilson, Brenda, and Leon.

"Whoo-ie. I'm amazed. You've grown yourself some guts, girl. I don't think I would have gotten in that limo with Leon."

Claire peered at her stomach. *Grown a gut, maybe, but not guts.* "I didn't feel brave at the time, just anxious to find something to help Roger."

"Maybe you should come work for me. I could use someone with your chutzpah."

Claire laughed. "I didn't know Utes knew about chutzpah."

"Sure we do. We just call it something else unintelligible."

"Does this Travis guy make a good suspect?"

"He's a definite possibility, with two motives, the drugs and the girl. Too bad I'm stuck here on the coast, or I'd chat him up for you."

Claire took a deep breath. "I could talk to him."

"You? Talk to a drug dealer? You already took a huge risk

meeting with his boss. Remember, somebody has killed once and won't hesitate to kill again if you get too close. You're not trained for this sort of thing."

"Then train me, like you did before I talked to Condoleza."

"Are you loco?"

"No. Desperate. Roger's staying at his lawyer's house. I called last night and practically begged him to come home. He refused."

"That sucks big time. I feel for you, Claire."

"That's not all. The president of Roger's company told him to take administrative leave this week. Roger's afraid he'll be told not to come back. He blames me, and rightfully so." She gripped the phone, panic tightening her throat. "I've got to prove he's innocent."

"All right. Let's see what we can do. Leon told you Travis hung out at the auto shop around noon most days, right?"

"Right. And I bet Brenda has already visited him."

"Do you know her well enough to ask her to go with you?"

"She doesn't even know that I know she uses cocaine."

"Your first step should be to buddy-up to her. Let it drop that you bought from Enrique, too, and need another source."

Claire's spirits sagged. "You know I'm no good at lying. I get red in the face and stutter. I lucked out with Condoleza because she was barely awake. I didn't dare lie to Leon."

"You're no good at lying because you haven't practiced. So practice. Start with me tonight. We'll map out your whole conversation with Brenda, then do the same with Travis."

Claire shuddered. "Lying to a woman at the gym is one thing, but lying to a drug dealer is totally different. He's more likely to do something violent if he decides he can't trust me. And I don't want to wind up with any cocaine. What would I do with it?"

"Got dandruff? Cocaine used to be sold as a scalp tonic.

Seriously, tell him you don't need any yet or you don't have the money on you. Say you want to meet him first because you're nervous, which you are."

"I guess I can say that. It's the truth."

"The good news is, you should be safe in the auto shop. He won't try anything with people around. Whatever you do, don't go anywhere with him. And don't get in his car, like you did with Leon."

Claire felt like a child being scolded. "Yes, mom."

She spent an hour on the phone as Deb coached her through the two conversations. She spent another hour in front of the mirror, practicing her lies.

Exhausted, she finally fell into her daughter's bed. Her sleep was disturbed by hot flashes and menacing dreams of being discovered, forced into cars, and killed in an assortment of ways—shot, stabbed, beaten. She tossed and fought the sheets all night.

The next morning, promptly at nine, Claire walked into Rita Wilaby's real estate office. Lugging one of the heavy gift baskets, she managed to wave at Rita, who was on the phone. Then Claire fetched the other basket. When she returned, she sat in a visitor's chair to catch her breath and wait for the agent to finish her call.

The woman's hair was so starched with hairspray that it didn't move when she turned her head, and she wore enough makeup to be labeled "scary" by Roger. Her bright red lips were outlined in maroon lip pencil. Claire wondered who had come up with the idea of having two-color lips. It wasn't natural. And Claire never used mascara in the daytime. If she did, she'd never have used as much as Rita had caked on her eyelashes.

In fact, at a makeup party Claire had attended, when the presenter said mascara should be replaced every six months,

Claire had blurted out, "That's a single-use applicator for me, then." All the women had laughed, but many, including the presenter, had looked at her funny. She'd never accepted a makeup party invitation again.

Rita hung up the phone and rose to inspect the baskets. "Nice, very nice, though late. I have one of the closings today, but I'll have to make an extra trip to deliver the other basket." Her two-tone lips pursed in dissatisfaction as she jammed her hands on her hips.

Claire realized she was close to losing this valuable client. She would have to make a generous appeasement offer and eat the expenditure. "I'll be happy to give you one of these for no cost, to compensate you for your trouble."

Rita harrumphed, but walked around her desk and pulled out her checkbook. As she wrote out the check, she said, "Let me give you some advice, Claire, from a woman who's been the proprietor of her own business for over twenty years. If you want to be successful, you have to deliver on time, regardless of your personal troubles."

Claire bit her cheek to keep her temper in check. "I'm terribly sorry. It won't happen again." The likelihood of Roger being accused of murdering a man in their bedroom again was damn slim.

Rita held out the check. "Though I grant you, your troubles are severe."

Claire reached for the check, but Rita wasn't ready to release it. "Do you plan to move?"

Floored, Claire stared at the woman. "What?"

Rita shrugged. "After a murder, many homeowners decide to move. I'd be happy to list the house for you. Though it would have to be at a considerable discount, given the circumstances." Almost as an afterthought, the woman smiled.

Face flushed, Claire stammered as a dozen angry retorts

fought for control of her tongue. Finally, reason won out. She stood, took the check, and walked to the door. With her hand on the knob, she turned. "No, I don't plan to move."

Claire pulled the door behind her. *And I don't plan to ever, ever associate with you again.*

Sometime later, Claire sat nervously fingering her purse in the reception area of the gym. For the third time since she'd arrived, she glanced at her watch. Five after eleven. Brenda's class had ended twenty minutes ago. Where was she?

Just then Jill left the juice bar with a carryout cup. When she saw Claire, she walked over. The navy A-line dress she wore slimmed her generous figure.

Claire tried to figure out some way to get rid of Jill before Brenda appeared. Stumped, Claire said the first thing that came to mind. "Hi, Jill. That dress looks good on you."

"Thanks. Ellen picked it out for me at Stein Mart." Jill sat next to Claire, running her hand over her skirt like a preening bird smoothing its feathers. "What are you doing here today? Did you switch classes? Ellen told me about the cold shoulder you got yesterday."

"I didn't switch classes. I'm meeting someone." *I hope.*

"Who?" Jill sipped her drink.

Claire didn't want to answer that question, so she tried distraction. Jill couldn't resist talking about food. Claire sniffed the smoothie. "Do I smell berries?"

"It's a mixed-berry smoothie, a weakness of mine. They use vanilla rice milk and put in a touch of honey, so it's really sweet." She held out the cup. "Want a sip?"

"No, thanks."

Jill placed her hand on Claire's arm. "I'm glad I saw you. I wanted to say how awful I feel about you having to go through all this."

Claire nodded, her eyes stinging. When would she reach the point where she could talk about this without crying?

"You're not taking Roger back, are you, after what he did to Enrique?"

"What do you mean?"

Jill's eyes widened, and she leaned closer. "He's a murderer, honey," she whispered. "Think what he might do to you." With a theatrical shudder, she took a generous slurp of her smoothie.

Flabbergasted that Jill's opinion of Roger could change so rapidly, Claire wondered why neither one of her best friends had any faith in his innocence. "Roger's not a murderer. He didn't do it."

"How can you believe that when he was caught with the gun in his hand?"

Claire stiffened. "Because I still love him and trust he's telling the truth."

"You still love him? I thought you two were having problems." Jill looked aghast.

"We could have worked them out eventually." Or at least Claire hoped they could have. "Maybe we still can."

"Oh, dear." Jill stared into her cup.

Her reaction surprised Claire. "Why the sad face?"

Jill raised her head, but her eyes were unfocused, as if concentrating on something far away. She blinked hard, then seemed to finally notice that Claire waited for a reply. "Just envy. Not everyone can work out their problems."

Claire assumed Jill meant her own marital problems, but she didn't have time to get into a long discussion. Brenda could appear any minute. She debated what to say.

"Nothing for you to worry about, though." Jill plucked at her skirt. "I've made some mistakes in my life, and now I've got to live with them."

"Everyone makes mistakes, Jill. I made a huge one bringing

Enrique home to give me a massage."

"How'd you get mixed up with Enrique, anyway?"

Embarrassed, Claire shifted her gaze from Jill. "He rubbed my neck, said I was beautiful, showed me how to use the weights. Ellen told me he was interested in me."

Jill snorted. "Interested in your money, you mean."

"Maybe so." Claire hunted for a tissue in her purse.

"Sorry, that wasn't a nice thing to say. But you're better off without him. Enrique had an ego a mile wide." Jill's mouth turned down, as if she'd tasted something foul.

Claire blew her nose. She glanced up the hall and saw Brenda come out the locker room door. Darn! "Can we talk about this later?"

"Sure." Jill took another sip of her smoothie. "Let's do lunch. How about tomorrow after class?"

"Tomorrow's fine." Claire stood and headed for the check-in desk, hoping Jill would take the hint and leave. "Bye, Jill."

Thankfully, Jill left just before Brenda entered the lobby from the hallway. Brenda wore a smart-looking black pantsuit and red silk blouse. She didn't need the added height the black-heeled boots gave her, but they completed the look.

Claire glanced down at her own jeans and lace-collared sweat-shirt. Even though they were both designer labels, on her they looked dumpy. Why did everyone in this place look better than she did?

Brenda glided across the lobby like a model on a runway and peered at Claire. "Are you thinking of switching to today's class like I suggested? You missed it, you know."

"I know. Actually, I wanted to talk to you." Claire pointed to the health food bar. "Can I buy you a carrot juice or something?"

Brenda glanced at her watch. "I guess so, but I only have twenty minutes. I have an appointment at noon."

Claire had a suspicion what that appointment was for. She

smiled her friendliest smile. "This won't take long." She preceded Brenda to a booth in the rear.

After they placed their orders, Claire picked up a salt shaker and twirled it between two fingers. She leaned forward and lowered her voice. "I need your advice. Enrique supplied me with some, um, stuff I use. I mentioned it to Ellen, and she said you got the same stuff from him. I wondered if you'd found a new source."

Brenda's eyes narrowed. "Ellen should mind her own business."

"She was just trying to help me. I'm kind of desperate."

The waitress arrived with the drinks.

Brenda picked up hers and took a long sip. She looked at Claire over the top of the glass, as if debating whether to trust her or not.

Claire tried to form her face in the right expression—slightly pleading. Actually, she *was* pleading. *Don't figure out I'm lying, please.*

Brenda put down her drink. "The new source is a guy named Travis. He's usually at the auto shop across the street from noon to one. He's young and has long hair and a mustache. You'll find him in the waiting area."

"How do I approach him?"

"Tell him you're a friend of Enrique's and need his advice about carpet. That's the signal. He'll take you out back, to his car. That's where he conducts his business."

Oh, God, not another car. "What do you know about him? Can I trust him?"

Brenda brushed a crumb off the table. "I just met him. We conduct our transactions and that's it. He's not as friendly as Enrique and didn't seem to be a friend of his, either."

"Why do you say that?"

"He said he felt glad to pick up Enrique's customers. The

way he said it, kind of cold and impersonal, makes me think Travis could care less that Enrique was killed."

Mulling over Brenda's revelation, Claire sipped her drink. She realized she didn't know if the money in her purse was enough if she was forced to buy some cocaine. She and Deb had discussed prices, but they could be steeper in Colorado Springs than the high-volume markets of Los Angeles and Denver that Deb was familiar with. "Does Travis charge the same as Enrique?"

"How much do you want to buy?"

Claire's face flushed. She couldn't remember what Deb had told her about amounts. *Damn these pre-menopausal memory lapses. Why didn't I write that stuff down?* "An ounce, I guess."

"You mean a gram?" Brenda leaned back and crossed her arms across her chest.

"Yes, that's it." Disconcerted by Brenda's stare, Claire picked up the salt shaker again. She twirled it furiously while she looked at the table, across the bar, anywhere but straight at Brenda.

Brenda reached over, snatched the salt shaker, and slammed it on the table. "You don't have the vaguest idea. What are you really up to? Why are you asking all these questions about Travis?"

Busted. Claire had no recourse but to throw herself on Brenda's mercy and tell the truth. "I'm sorry, Brenda. I'm not trying to hurt you in any way. I just wasn't sure I could trust you."

Face glowering, Brenda stood to leave.

Claire grabbed her arm. "Please, hear me out. I need your help."

Brenda hesitated, shook Claire's hand off her arm, then slowly resumed her seat. She folded her arms across her chest again. "I'm listening."

Claire sat up straight. "I'm trying to save my husband . . . and my marriage. Roger's innocent, but the police think they have a solid case and aren't looking for anyone else. I think Travis may have had reason to kill Enrique."

"But you acted like you didn't know who Travis was."

"I lied." With a sheepish grin, Claire shrugged. "I know he was a rival of Enrique's. Maybe he wanted to eliminate the competition. I have to talk to him, but I need to find out what he's like first. That's why I wanted to talk to you."

"If you go to the police about Travis, what's to prevent you from exposing me?"

"I'd never do that. Besides Ellen and Jill, you were the only one who befriended me in class. That means a lot to me. I couldn't repay your kindness with betrayal." Claire peered at Brenda. "Do you believe me?"

Brenda studied her then leaned back. "I believe you. You're a terrible liar, Claire. It's written all over your face when you do, but your face is clear now."

Claire breathed a sigh of relief. "What else can you tell me about Travis?"

"I can tell you everything I know, including how to buy coke from him, since that's your pretense for seeing him, I presume."

Chapter 11
The Rival

Claire watched Brenda walk across the street to the auto shop. While she finished her juice, Claire mentally rehearsed the questions she would ask Travis. After Brenda had returned to her car, Claire slipped on a pair of sunglasses, tied a scarf around her hair, and checked her reflection in a pocket mirror. She hoped Travis had been too sleepy to get a good look at her in Enrique and Condoleza's apartment.

She walked across the street, telling herself that if she stuck as close to the truth as possible, she might not give herself away. She stopped for a moment with her hand on the cold glass of the door to the auto shop then pushed her way in. The jangle of the entrance bell made her jump.

The check-in room was lined with sample tires and posters of various essential engine parts she knew nothing about. The pungent odors of fresh rubber, engine oil, and burned coffee assaulted her nose. When she located the door to the waiting room, she marched straight for it, both to prevent a question from the counter clerk and to keep herself from backing out.

A soap opera blared from the TV, totally ignored by the room's two occupants. An elderly man sat in a chair, sipping a cup of coffee and reading a book. Travis lounged in another chair in the corner. He was flipping through a magazine with a monster truck on the cover. Claire recognized the face behind the droopy mustache. He wore more clothing this time—loose cargo jeans, camouflage T-shirt, and Enrique's leather jacket.

He looked up and waited expectantly.

Claire squared her shoulders and approached him. "Are you Travis? I need some advice about a carpet."

He nodded and stood, slapping the magazine down on the chair beside him. "Let's step outside." He walked out without looking back and led the way to the employee parking lot behind the shop.

Claire hesitated, but she had no choice other than to leave the relative safety of the auto shop. The lot was blocked from the view of most pedestrians by the shop itself, an adjoining bar, now closed, and two large dumpsters along one side. She felt closed in and exposed at the same time.

Travis stopped beside a dirty white Mustang and faced her. "I've seen you somewhere."

A cold stab of fear knifed down Claire's spine. Using all her willpower, she kept her expression passive. "I go in the gym across the street a lot."

"I don't."

Claire tried a nonchalant-like shrug. "I've got a common face. People tell me I look like someone else all the time." That was true.

He peered at her. "You ain't done business with me before?"

"No, and I'm kind of nervous about it." Here she'd worried about lying, but she hadn't told a lie yet.

Travis opened the passenger door of the car. "Get in."

Claire drew back. "I just want to talk."

His eyes narrowed. He glanced around suspiciously. "You a cop? Ya got to answer, or it's entrapment."

"I'm not a cop. It's just, you see, I knew Enrique at the gym, but I don't know you."

"You want some blow or not?"

"I don't need any today." She twisted her hands together, feeling the knuckles crack under the tension. "I'm new at this, and I want to find out some things before I buy."

Travis closed the door and leaned against the car, thumbs in his jean pockets, hips thrust out. "Whadda you want to know?"

Claire recognized the stance, full of testosterone and youthful arrogance. Just like her son Michael in his youth, when he thought he was invincible. Suddenly, with a surge of relief, she knew how to deal with this young man. "Enrique obviously had more experience with this than you do. How do I know you'll be discreet?"

Travis reacted as if she doubted his manliness, precisely what she wanted. He shoved himself off the car and paced in front of her.

"Lady, I've been dealing as long as Enrique. He came into the business late. I grew up in it. I shuffled pot when I was fifteen." He stabbed a thumb at his chest. "I've stayed outta the cops' hands for five years."

"If you're so good, how come Enrique got our business? We gym ladies have a lot of money to spend."

Travis bristled and spat out his next words. "You ladies ain't such a big deal. Last month I moved as much product as Enrique did, and I didn't need you rich bitches to do it. Enrique just had an in, is all. His job as a fitness consultant." Travis waggled his fingers at the job title, as if to say "la dee da."

He stabbed a finger at Claire's face and sneered suggestively. "Now Enrique's gone, the boss sees he don't need no gym gigolo to service you ladies. I'm doing jus' fine."

He settled against the car and waved his arm around the barren parking lot. "My office here's more private than Enrique's juice bar ever was. Satisfied?"

"Maybe." Anxious to leave before her nervousness made her blow her cover, she decided to brave one more question. She needed to clarify Condoleza's relationship with Travis. "Enrique mentioned a Condoleza to me. I got the impression she was his girlfriend. Do you know her? How is she?"

Travis leapt off the car and grabbed her arm, squeezing hard. "Why would he tell you that?" He shoved his snarling face in front of hers.

The combination of his sour breath and pungent aftershave almost overpowered Claire. She stifled a gag, leaned back, and squirmed, trying to free her throbbing arm. "You're hurting me."

"Answer the question." Travis stared at her, his eyes narrowed with suspicion. Then realization dawned on his face. "You were one of his special ladies, right?"

He grabbed her other arm and yanked her close, slamming his body against hers. "Enrique was nothing compared to me. Even Condoleza says so." He ground his growing erection against her pelvis.

Claire's mind raced. She had to play this right. She gulped and smiled. "I can feel it."

Travis threw back his head and laughed, a laugh full of bravado and male pride.

Claire stepped back. "But I'm too old for you. You'd wear me out." She shook her arms and raised an eyebrow at Travis in an unspoken request to release her.

He let go of her and held up his hands, palms out. "I might at that."

Heart pounding, she resisted the urge to rub her aching arms where Travis had clutched her. She knew she would find bruises on them later. She wondered if this hotheaded young man had bruised Condoleza, too. "Were you seeing Condoleza at the same time as Enrique?"

A sly grin played on Travis's lips.

"Did Enrique ever find out?"

"Nah. He could be dense sometimes."

Time to stroke the lion's mane. Maybe something would slip

out with the bragging. "I'm glad to hear Condoleza is being taken care of. I worried about what would happen to her. You know, one woman to another."

Travis snorted. "She worried, too, about you ladies. But not the same way. Condoleza got jealous, man, even though she cheated on him. She wouldn't care about this woman-to-woman stuff."

"I still felt for her, knowing how Enrique treated her." That was a guess.

"Yeah, well, I treat her right. I know how to squire a lady."

Claire tilted her head, coyly she hoped. "You take her out sometimes?"

"She likes to dance, 'specially Wednesday nights at Rum Bay when the Soul Tones are playing." He shuffled a short dance step then leaned against his car again, arms folded across his chest. "So we doing some business today?"

Claire smiled. "Not today. But I'll return in a few days when I run out." She held out her hand.

"I'm your man." Travis shook her hand firmly, then held on. "You sure we never met before?"

"I'm sure." A trickle of nervous sweat ran down the back of her neck.

Travis released her hand and refolded his arms.

Claire turned her back on him and walked toward the front of the auto shop, feeling his gaze on her until she rounded the corner. Careful to keep her steps slow and steady, she maintained the same pace until she reached her car in the gym parking lot.

Not until she'd slid into the driver's seat and locked the door did she breathe a sigh of relief. She glanced west at Pikes Peak, the city's geographic icon and weather predictor. Billowing storm clouds piled up against the huge mountain's summit and spread gray fingers out across the sky—a harbinger of an approaching snowstorm. Buffeted by her own emotional tempest, Claire sensed that like the weather, for her, the worst was yet to come.

When Claire returned home, twelve messages waited on the answering machine. For a moment, she considered getting an unlisted number. She checked the messages. She deleted those from her neighbors and that nosy Bradshaw reporter. When she heard Detective Wilson's voice, she held her breath. But he said the only prints they'd found on the basement door were hers and Roger's. She released the breath with a muttered curse.

The last message was from Ellen. She wanted to know how Claire was holding up. Needing to hear a friendly voice, Claire picked up the phone and punched in the number for Stein Mart.

After someone had fetched Ellen, Claire said, "I'm sorry I keep calling you at the store. Were you with a client?"

"Was I ever, and I'm so glad you rescued me. The woman insisted on one of my color analyses, and when I told her she was winter, she huffed and said she always assumed she was spring."

"I thought you didn't believe in those."

"The four seasons thing is such a crock, but once I came up with a match, I couldn't back down. I convinced her that skin color changes with age and she needs to update her wardrobe. When I heard you were on the phone, I asked Susan to take over, in exchange for half the commission."

"Sorry I'm costing you money."

"You know I work here more for the discounts than the commissions," Ellen said. "You're the one who could make real money if you got serious about your business. With some targeted marketing, you could rake in enough basket orders to keep you employed full-time."

"I never intended it to be full-time. I wouldn't enjoy it if I had to rush. I like creating the baskets, but I hate the business part, the handling the money and the paperwork. Thank God Roger helped me set that all up." *Sharing that work with him had actually been fun.*

"He may not be around to do that anymore, and you may need the income. I called earlier because Dave told me Roger was staying with him. Does that mean you two are splitting up?" She sounded almost hopeful.

Claire cringed. "Oh, God, I hope not. I'm trying to convince Roger to come home, so we can talk. But he won't listen."

"Men. They're all the same. I say good riddance to the lot of them."

When will Ellen get over her divorce? "I want to work this out with Roger, but all he's concerned about is his job."

"See? What did I tell you?"

Frustrated, Claire blew out a breath. "You don't understand. Ned Peters, the president of Roger's company, is upset. He thinks the bad publicity will scare off investors. If the choice comes down to them or Roger, Roger will get the boot."

"Cripes. I didn't know things were that bad at his company."

"It's all my fault." Claire blinked back tears. "Roger has a right to be worried and mad at me. That's why I'm desperate to prove I still love him."

"How're you going to do that?"

"By finding some lead to give the police. By convincing Roger's boss that Roger's innocent."

"Find some lead? How?"

Claire told Ellen of her meetings with Leon and Travis.

"Those are dangerous people you're dealing with. Are you crazy?"

She felt darn close to insane, with the emotional roller coaster she'd been on the last few days. "Call me motivated. If I save

Roger from losing his job and going to prison, he'll understand I want to save our marriage too."

"He damn well better understand the risks you're taking for him. Before all this, the biggest risk you ever took was starting your business, and you won't even go all out on that. What makes you think you know what you're doing here?"

Claire resented Ellen's implication that she was a bumbling fool. "I'm not going into this blind. Deb Burch gave me some advice. You remember her? My P.I. friend in Denver?"

"Why isn't she the one talking to these people?"

"She's in L.A. and won't return until the end of the week. I can't wait. I have to take something to Detective Wilson before then. He's convinced Roger's guilty."

Ellen spoke deliberately, as if carefully choosing her words. "Claire, I know you care for Roger, but did you ever consider that your feelings could be clouding your judgment? The police are experts at this stuff, and you're an amateur. They just might be right."

"I can't accept that." Claire said it with firm conviction.

"I know you don't want to. I'm saying this as a friend. I hope you won't take it the wrong way, but you need to consider the possibility, for your own good."

"I appreciate you trying to help, but I've got to keep pushing. I need hope. And so does Roger." Claire fought back tears. "If he keeps on thinking he has no chance of being cleared, I don't know what he'll do."

"But what you've found out so far is no help."

Claire swallowed. "I know."

"Your opinion that these drug-dealing goons have motive is not enough. It's your word against theirs. They'll deny they ever met you."

Claire stood and paced, searching for an idea. "I need something tangible, some piece of physical evidence."

"The police already have the gun. What else is there?"

"I don't know." Then it hit her. Travis had said Condoleza liked to go dancing Wednesday nights. Tomorrow was Wednesday. Maybe no one would be in the apartment. Could she? Did she dare?

"Ellen . . ." *No, I won't say anything.* Ellen would just try to talk her out of it, or even inform the police to keep Claire out of danger.

"What?"

"Nothing. I need to go. I have some thinking to do."

"Keep in touch. I'm worried about you."

As soon as Claire hung up, the phone rang. Assuming it was Ellen, she picked it up. "You forget something, Ellen?"

A familiar deep, gravelly voice said, "Hello, Mrs. Hanover."

Leon! Claire's hand gripped the chair beside her. How had he gotten her number? She glanced at the phone directory on her desk. Dummy! The same way the reporters had. The same way he could have learned her address and sent a henchman to polish off Enrique. "Hello."

"Now don't you go hanging up on me, or I might need to make a personal visit. I know where you live."

The phone felt hot. Then Claire realized her hands had gone cold and clammy. "I understand."

"I'll get to the point. Travis told me an interesting story about a lady visitor he had this afternoon."

Claire gulped. "Did you tell him who I was?"

"Didn't see the need to."

Thank God.

Leon's voice turned stern. "I thought I told you he didn't do it."

"Yes, you did."

"I also told you I don't allow no one to mess with my business."

"I remember." Trembling, Claire wondered if Leon planned to harm her. *Or Roger.*

Leon exhaled in what was almost a sigh. "I admire your loyalty to your husband, Mrs. Hanover, but you gotta stop this now. Don't talk to Travis or Condoleza again."

Claire sank into her chair. "Yes, sir." Why did she say "sir"? She felt like an idiot.

"I'm glad we understand each other."

After he'd hung up, Claire stared at the phone. He hadn't said what he would do to her if she disobeyed him, but she sure didn't want to find out. She wiped her damp hands on her jeans. Her fledgling plan to search Condoleza's apartment the next night seemed like a bad idea.

But wait a minute.

Claire stood again and paced the kitchen. Leon had said not to talk to Travis or Condoleza. She wouldn't do that. So, technically, she would keep her promise. And if she succeeded in getting in and out of their apartment, Leon would never know. If she failed to find a way in, he would never know that either. If she got caught—

She shuddered. *I won't get caught.* She realized she'd already made her decision.

Claire pictured her previous visit to Enrique's apartment. She remembered hearing a deadbolt slide open before Condoleza cracked the door. Claire walked to her computer and accessed a website about how things worked that she had bookmarked for Judy's high school homework. Lock picking was a topic, along with a warning that breaking into private property was both illegal and unethical.

When she read about the tools required, she raced upstairs into the kids' bathroom. She rummaged through a couple of drawers until she found the dental pick Judy had used to replace medicated strips when her wisdom teeth were removed and one socket refused to heal. Clutching the pick, Claire entered the garage next and grabbed Roger's smallest flathead screwdriver.

After printing the directions for picking a pin-and-tumbler lock, she grabbed her keys and coat, ran out on the deck, and dead-bolted the kitchen door behind her. As winds from the approaching storm whipped her hair, she inserted the tools into the keyhole and turned the screwdriver. Biting her tongue, she worked the pick, feeling and listening for each pin to drop.

The first try took twenty frustrating minutes. Her frozen ears felt like they would fall off, and she crammed her stiff fingers under her armpits to warm them. But each attempt went faster until, on her seventh, she opened the door in three minutes. Exhausted and numb with cold, she trudged inside to warm up some soup. Then she planned to tackle the front door.

CHAPTER 12
DECISION TIME

After another restless night in Judy's bed, tossing covers off and on as she alternated between hot and cold flashes, Claire made up her mind. She'd talk to Roger sometime this afternoon. But first she'd attend her Wednesday-morning exercise class. Facing the silent censorship of her classmates had become a personal challenge.

She made it through the class with Jill's support. She wished she'd had Ellen's too, but Ellen had had to switch her regular Thursday workday to Wednesday that week. After showering, Claire waited while Jill applied her makeup. Claire was looking forward to their lunch, a pure social occasion after all her tense confrontations with potential suspects.

"All done," Jill announced. "You still want to go out to lunch in this weather?"

The snow squall that had threatened the night before had blown in fast, spitting a couple of inches of snow on the ground before settling into a steady dusting of tiny flakes. But a light snowstorm wasn't going to stop Claire. "I deserve this lunch. If you want, I'll drive and bring you back here to get your car."

"Thanks. Even with snow tires, I'm still not confident on slippery roads. Let's go eat sushi at Jun. I love their lobster rolls."

While Claire negotiated streets swirling with Colorado's famous champagne powder, she half-listened to Jill bemoaning the lack of good Japanese restaurants in town—except Jun, of course. Upscale real estate agents brought their California clients there to show them Colorado Springs wasn't all white bread.

Once inside the restaurant, the waitress asked if they wanted the last unoccupied tatami table, where patrons sat on cushions on the raised floor with their feet dangling in a pit under the table.

Jill wrinkled her nose. "I'm too old to sit on the floor."

Claire had been looking forward to it, but demurred. She also let Jill choose which types of sushi they would share and order some hot sake.

As they waited for their food, Jill said, "What's going on with the murder investigation?"

"The police haven't done much." Claire summarized what she had accomplished and her conversation with Ellen, pausing when the waitress served the sake.

Jill's eyes had grown wide during the summation. "Jeez, Claire, I have to agree with Ellen. You're getting into dangerous stuff. You should let the police handle it."

"I can't just sit still and let them convict Roger of a crime he didn't commit."

"But you're making things worse, getting these drug guys mad at you." Jill's brows furrowed, giving her a troubled look. "You really need to stop."

Claire didn't feel like arguing with her friend. "I'll consider it, but right now we've got sake to drink." She poured the hot wine into their cups and took a long sip of the steamy, pungent brew.

Jill stared at Claire for a moment, as if appraising her, then raised her sake cup in salute. "I admire your spunk, though. I didn't think you had it in you."

Claire raised her cup to accept the compliment then grew serious. "You don't realize what you're capable of until something like this comes along and tests you."

A cloud passed over Jill's face. She leaned forward and peered at Claire. "Are you handling this okay?"

Claire nodded but felt her throat catch. "I think so."

"If you need anything, or someone to talk to—"

The waitress arrived with a huge platter brimming with sushi rolls stuffed with Oriental vegetables, salmon skin, smoked eel, and lobster.

After the waitress had left, Jill picked up a lobster roll between two chopsticks and waved it at Claire. "I'm here for you, is all I wanted to say."

"Thanks. I appreciate that."

Jill washed down the lobster with sake and pinched a vegetable roll. "What's your next step?"

"Huh?" The question caught Claire unaware. She couldn't divulge her plan to break into Condoleza's apartment, but she had no other cover story to tell. "I . . . I don't know."

"Yes, you do." Jill's lips curled. "You just don't want to tell me. Your face is an open book."

Claire felt her face redden. She had to change the topic fast. "Enough about me. Tell me what Paul thought of that 'Hot Anniversary Night' basket you ordered from me."

Jill swallowed. "It didn't have the desired effect."

"Oh, dear. I'm sorry. Not even the massage oil? Ylang ylang is supposed to be a very sensual scent."

Jill shook her head.

"So things haven't improved between you two?"

"No, they haven't." She pointed a chopstick at Claire. "What do you mean by improved? Did Ellen say something to you? She did, didn't she? I'll kill her."

Claire scrambled to recover. She had promised Ellen she wouldn't tell Jill she knew anything. "I assumed—"

"No." Jill's eyes narrowed. "You wouldn't assume, just from a basket order, that my marriage was falling apart. Ellen must have told you."

Claire realized she had blown it. "Don't be mad. Ellen cares about you, and so do I. She only told me that you asked about a divorce lawyer because she was trying to convince me to see one, too."

"Damn. Now I've lost my appetite." Jill threw down her chopsticks. "That's the problem, my appetite. Paul says I'm getting too fat. He says I disgust him."

"Oh, Jill. So that's why you're taking the exercise class?"

"It's not doing any good, though. You know me." Jill stared at her full plate then looked up. A tear rolled down her plump cheek. "I love to eat."

Claire tried to think of a soothing reply, but all she could come up with was, "I'm sorry."

Jill glanced at the chalkboard listing the daily specials. "Too bad there's no such thing as chocolate sushi. I could use some now."

Claire smiled politely at Jill's joke, but frankly, chocolate was the last thing her friend needed. "What can I do?"

"Be a friend. Tell me I look nice, like you did yesterday. It felt so good to hear something positive after all the negative comments I got from Paul and Enrique."

"Enrique?"

Jill looked embarrassed and fumbled in her purse for a tissue. "Boy, that slipped right out, didn't it?" She wiped the tear from her cheek and blew her nose.

Claire waited in silence.

When Jill had composed herself, she grinned sheepishly at Claire. "Enrique was quite a ladies' man, wasn't he? You've experienced that firsthand."

With a rueful wince, Claire nodded.

"With the problems Paul and I had been having, you know,

with him being disgusted with me and all . . ." She leaned toward Claire and whispered, "We haven't made love in a long time."

Jill leaned back. "I had heard about Enrique and thought maybe he and I . . ." She shrugged. "I needed someone to hold me and tell me I'm still desirable."

"So did you and Enrique . . . ?" Claire couldn't finish the question.

"He didn't say it directly, just kept putting me off, but I could tell. He was as disgusted with me as Paul."

Claire grimaced. "Ouch."

"He kept suggesting I talk to the gym's dietician." Jill made a sour face.

"Double ouch. So that's why you said those nasty things about him."

"He was an asshole." A smile played at the corner of Jill's mouth as she picked up her chopsticks again. "Can't say as I miss him."

An hour later, Claire stood on the front stoop of Dave Kessler's brick-fronted townhouse. It was situated in a prime development facing the Kissing Camels formation in the Garden of the Gods Park. She glanced up at the towering red sandstone rocks that the Ute Indians believed had been a magical place and whispered, "Wish me luck." She needed more than a rabbit's foot, maybe a whole bunny. Girding herself, she brushed snow off her shoulders and rang the doorbell.

Roger opened the door. He looked as if he hadn't showered that morning. He wore gray sweatpants and an old stretched-out Colorado Rockies T-shirt. His feet were bare, and his cheeks were unshaven.

When he made a move to close the door, Claire braced her hand against it. With a firmness that surprised her, she said,

"We need to talk. Face-to-face. Let me in." She pushed against the door.

Without a word, Roger turned aside to let her brush past him and walk down the hall into Dave's living room. The furnishings declared this was a man's place—all leather, burnished metal, and glass, with no softening feminine touches. It even smelled masculine, with its essence of grilled meat, gym socks, and stale beer. The young lady lawyer had lost interest in Dave a few months after his divorce from Ellen. Now he lived alone.

What a waste. Claire looked around but saw no sign of Ellen's ex-husband. "Where's Dave?"

"At work."

"Good." Claire took off her coat and wiped her sweaty palms on her jeans. Her fluttering heart and dry mouth gave her an extra reminder that the next few minutes would be crucial. She sat on the squeaky leather sofa and patted the matching chair next to her. "Sit."

Roger cast about as if looking for an escape route, then slumped into the chair with a sigh.

Determined to plead her case, Claire leaned forward and stared at him until he looked her in the eye. "I love you. You know that, don't you?"

Roger looked away and cleared his throat. "I don't think I do."

Claire reached for his hand. She caressed the familiar, rough skin on the back of his hand, tracing the veins whose pathways she knew so well. "I made a mistake, a horrible mistake. I realize that now and feel awful about it. But don't you see? I was so lonely for you."

"Lonely for me?" His expression skeptical, Roger tried to withdraw his hand. "You sure picked a weird way to show it."

Claire clutched his hand tighter, refusing to release it. "Yes, lonely for you. With Judy and Michael gone, I had hoped we could spend more time together, just the two of us, and rekindle the romance we had before the kids came along."

"C'mon, Claire. We're not young anymore."

"We're not dead yet, either. Remember how we'd lie in bed together Sunday mornings with the newspaper and breakfast plates scattered around us and talk about our future?"

A smile tugged at the corner of Roger's lips. "It wasn't all talk."

She returned the smile. "No, it wasn't. And I want that, too. Do you realize how seldom we've made love the last few months? Hell, the last couple of years."

Roger rubbed his forehead, as if trying to knead away a headache. "You've got to understand how exhausting my job is. I can't just rise to the occasion whenever you need stud service." He curled his lip in disgust.

Frustrated, Claire's voice rose. "You know that's not what I mean. I need you to love, to hold, to talk to, to plan our future with. Sex isn't what's important."

Roger frowned. "It sure seemed that way to me, with that young stud in our bed." He ground out the last two words.

Claire stared at her hands, still clenched around Roger's. How to choose the words? A tear slid down her cheek. She sniffed. "That was a cry for attention. A stupid cry, yes. He was giving me a massage. I didn't plan to have sex with—"

"You were in your underwear!"

She held up her hand. "I told you I had to take off my clothes for the massage. He said clothes would get in the way."

"You can't expect me to believe you were stupid enough to fall for that line." His nose wrinkled with disgust.

Claire's face flushed. *Yes, I was.* "I think I needed to believe him. It's just that he made me feel desirable, wanted, like a woman wants to feel. And he touched me."

Roger flinched.

"Not sexually. I mean like this, like I'm stroking your hand." She had to make him understand. "Do you remember the last time you touched me?"

Distress and confusion warred for control of Roger's expression. "I touch you."

Claire shook her head. "I don't mean just a quick hug or a peck on the cheek as you're rushing out the door. I mean *really* touch me, like you enjoy the feel of my skin, instead of just going through the motions."

Roger turned his face away and covered his eyes with his hand. His jaw worked as he tried to hide his emotions.

Gently, belying the tension gripping her, she placed her hand on his knee. "I didn't really want him. I wanted you. But you wouldn't have me. You were too busy building your career. Please, Roger, search your heart. Don't you feel anything for me anymore?" Tears streamed down her cheeks, unabated.

A tear inched its way out from under the hand covering Roger's eyes.

Claire felt a tiny spark of hope. She clutched his knee and waited.

Suddenly he groaned. "Of course I still feel something for you, Claire. That's why this hurts so much." His voice was raw with pain.

She sat on the arm of his chair and hugged him, burying his head in her shoulder. "I'm sorry. I'm so sorry." The dampness from his tears soaked into her blouse. When his shaking arms encircled her, her hope surged. He had not pushed her away. She gripped him tighter and rocked him gently in her arms, as she had rocked her children to sleep. This man was hers, her husband, her life mate, and she would never let him go. She kissed the middle of his bald spot and laid her cheek on the warm skin of his familiar brow.

When Roger raised his head, she shifted and settled into his lap. She placed her hand on his cheek and looked into his red-rimmed eyes. "Do you understand that you hurt me, too, by pushing me aside to focus on your work?"

He stared at her, then swiped his wet cheeks with the back of his hand, gently pushing her hand aside. "I do now. But I was working for both of us, to improve our lives. With more money, we could buy whatever we wanted, travel—"

"When would you have time to enjoy those things with your work schedule? And did you ask me if that's what I wanted?"

Roger shook his head. "I just assumed—"

"We have enough money now, Roger. The kids' education is paid for, and our house almost is. You don't need to push so hard." A thought struck her. "Or were you pushing for yourself? Do you really want to be a corporate power broker?"

Absently, Roger stroked her arm. "I thought I did. It's what I'm supposed to want, to be bigger, better."

"Is that your father talking?" Claire barely remembered Roger's executive father. Always working late at the office or jetting to corporate meetings, he missed many family gatherings. He'd pushed his son to follow in his footsteps. She didn't want Roger following him into an early grave from a massive heart attack.

"Maybe it's my father talking. But how can you blame him, or me? That's the mindset of the business world. You compete with your peers for the prize, the management positions that are listed in the annual reports. And if you don't make it, you lose."

He looked into her eyes. "But I didn't realize I could lose you."

Claire caressed his stubbled cheek. "You haven't lost me. And I hope I haven't lost you. But we need to work out some issues, maybe get some counseling, if we're going to salvage our marriage."

Roger cracked a bleak smile. "I don't think they offer marriage counseling in prison." He heaved a deep sigh. "I could very well be convicted, Claire. The police have a good case against me and no evidence for, or interest in, pursuing anyone else."

When Roger shifted his legs underneath her, she said, "Your sciatic nerve bothering you again?"

"It's been a long time since you sat in my lap." Roger grinned. "You've put on a few pounds since then."

"You!" Claire poked his round stomach. "Look who's talking."

Glad that Roger still had the ability to joke about something, she got up and resumed her seat on the sofa. But she held his hand again. She still needed to touch him, and though he probably wouldn't admit it, he needed her touch, too.

Claire noticed a wistful, faraway look had come into his eyes. He seemed to be resigned to his fate. She had to pull him out of the drowning suck-hole of his depression. She shook his hand to get his attention.

"Let me tell you what I've been doing. I hope to find something that will convince Detective Wilson he's got the wrong man." Claire told him about her meeting with Leon.

Roger stared at her, slack-jawed. "What the hell were you thinking?"

Annoyed at the implication—again—that she was stupid, Claire said, "I met him in the middle of the day, right by a gas station." The station was almost deserted, but Roger didn't have to know that. She went on to describe her meeting with Enrique's drug rival, leaving out Travis's come-on.

Roger shook his head. "This is terrible, Claire. You're putting yourself in danger, talking to these crooks."

Hoping to wipe the horrified look off Roger's face, Claire tried to joke. "Why would they bother hurting a middle-aged housewife? All they'd have to do is say 'boo,' and I'd run." She outlined her suspicions that either of them, or Condoleza, could have shot Enrique or arranged to have him killed.

Roger listened silently with a pained expression. "None of this is doing any good. I want you to stop."

"Stop? When I'm making such good progress?"

"Getting threatened by a drug kingpin who knows where you live is progress? No, I forbid it. We can hire Deb Burch to pick up where you left off. You've got to stop. You have no idea what you're doing."

Claire's back stiffened. Forbid it? No idea what she was doing? "I'm doing this out of love for you, to prove you didn't shoot Enrique. Deb's in L.A. We can't wait for her to return. You need to show Ned Peters that you're innocent before he puts you on long-term leave."

Roger leaned forward and gripped her hand. "I will not let you risk your life to save my job. It won't do me much good in prison anyway."

"Haven't you listened to anything I've said? I'm trying to clear you so you won't go to prison." Frustration welled up in Claire's throat.

Roger shook his head and slumped in his chair. "It's no use, Claire. You need to accept the idea of having a convict for a husband. The fact that I'm innocent doesn't seem to make a hell of a lot of difference."

Claire could see she was getting nowhere. He was too depressed to save himself. She had to lift his spirits. "Come home with me, then. Let me prove to you how much I still love you. I'll make your favorite dinner, lamb chops and baked potatoes."

Roger rubbed his chin for a moment, deep in thought. "Maybe you should get used to not having me around."

The dejection in his face made Claire want to cry again. "Damn it. You haven't been around much for years now. I'm tired of it, and I want you home."

Roger looked away. "I'm not sure I'm ready to come home. You broke my trust. That's damned hard to forgive."

About to blurt out a reply, Claire clamped her mouth shut. She could tell he needed to think about the things she'd said. Also, if he came home, she doubted he'd let her go ahead with her plan to break into Condoleza's apartment. She was determined to keep that appointment. Maybe she could find a clue, any clue, that would prove his innocence.

"I don't expect you to forgive me right away," she said. "I know that will take time. I just want the chance to earn your forgiveness."

Roger nodded, his sad eyes tearing at her heart. "I guess after twenty-six years, I owe you that."

"I can see tonight is too soon. I'll come again tomorrow. We can talk more then." Claire stood and put out her hand. "Will you walk me to the door?"

Roger took her hand. They walked down the hall in silence.

She put on her coat and opened the front door. She squeezed Roger's hand then kissed him full on the lips. "I'm not giving up on convincing you to come home."

Chapter 13
The Sleuth

That evening, under a brooding, starless sky, Claire pulled her car into the parking lot of the Faith Redeemer Baptist Church, its spire piercing the black night. The hulking church, with its tall, dark windows that stared down on her like damning eyes, sat two blocks from Condoleza's apartment building. Claire didn't want Condoleza, Travis, or one of their neighbors to recognize her car from her earlier visit.

She debated whether to park in the lot behind the church, where her BMW wouldn't be visible from the street, or under a blazing streetlight in front. The first provided more cover and the second more security. She chose the back of the church.

A glance at her watch showed nine o'clock. She had called the church earlier to ask about evening activities. The secretary had told her the Wednesday night Bible study class met from eight to ten. No one should notice an extra car in the lot for another hour.

Claire pulled on her black stretch gloves. Feeling foolish, she had dressed all in black, like an actor dressing up to play spy. She patted the pocket of her leather coat. The dental pick and screwdriver were there, along with a miniature flashlight.

She peered out the window. At least the snow had stopped. The lot contained about a dozen other cars, but no people. All the Bible study participants were inside the church. After stepping out of the car, she locked it and slipped the keys into a pocket. Turning her collar up against the chill wind—and to hide her face—she strode toward Condoleza's two-story garden apartment building.

"Spare a quarter?"

Claire jumped and stared at the darkened doorway of the dry cleaning store she had just passed.

A hunched, bearded figure in a sleeping bag held out a cupped hand. With his face in shadow, he seemed feral, almost inhuman.

After taking a deep breath to slow her racing heart, Claire said, "Sorry, I don't have any money on me."

She hurried on, wondering if the homeless man had gotten a good look at her or if he would try to follow. Her back crawled as she strained her ears to catch any sound of the man's approach. With her fists clenched, she prepared to run, but a glance back confirmed he hadn't moved. She decided to return to her car by a different route.

She turned a corner, entered an alley behind the apartment building, and clicked on her flashlight. She shuffled between snow-covered trashcans, mounds of discarded tires, and twisted pipes that cast garish shadows. A long-tailed, hairy creature scurried away from the flashlight's beam and across her shoes. A rat? She stifled a scream and stumbled into a battered bicycle. The bike lurched. She grabbed at it, but missed. It fell, clattering against a trash can.

She shut off the flashlight and stood stock-still, waiting for a reaction from the tenants. When she heard nothing, she released the breath she'd been holding. Leaning her hands on her knees, she sucked in deep breaths until her shakiness subsided. *Get a grip, Claire.*

She carefully righted the bicycle, switched her flashlight on, and continued down the alley. Finally, she reached a place where she could see the rear of Condoleza's apartment on the floor above her. A light shone out of one window.

Did that mean they were home? Or did they leave a light on when they went out? Maybe they weren't going dancing. Claire chewed on her lip and debated giving up on the whole venture.

The light came from the larger window, which she presumed belonged to the bedroom. Another light switched on in the small window, probably the bathroom. A shadow moved in front of the curtain. A toilet flushed. The idea that someone could be getting ready to go out gave her hope.

Claire waited fifteen minutes, stamping her feet and hugging herself to stay warm. Finally, both lights went out. She worked her way to the corner of the building and looked around to the street. Footsteps clattered on the balcony stairs above, accompanied by conversation. She recognized the boisterous male voice as belonging to Travis. She slipped into the shadows of the alley and crouched behind a trash can.

Soon Travis and Condoleza walked past the alley, the girl's spiked heels tapping a staccato beat on the sidewalk. She twirled and fell laughing into his arms. A whiff of flowery perfume teased Claire's nose.

The couple's footsteps stopped, and a car door opened. After two doors slammed shut, the car drove away. Claire forced herself to wait five more minutes.

At last, she crept to the side of the building and glanced up and down the street. Empty. Keeping her steps soft and noiseless, she circled to the front. She walked up the stairs and across the balcony past a half dozen apartments to Condoleza's door. Again, Claire glanced around. Again, she saw no one.

She licked her dry lips. After removing the dental pick and small flathead screwdriver from her pocket, she slid both into the deadbolt keyhole. As she had done on her kitchen door, she probed for the lock pins. Then she heard voices. Her heart leapt into her throat as she whirled around.

Two men, each carrying a six-pack of beer, strode across the parking lot toward the stairs.

Claire darted away from Condoleza's door. Realizing her haste could look suspicious, she checked her flight and walked deliberately toward the stairs, as if she were leaving one of the apartments. She stood aside to let the men pass and nodded when one said, "Evenin'."

Stiff-backed, she walked down the stairs and around the corner. Safely behind the building, she closed her eyes in relief and slid her hands into her pockets.

Oh, God. She'd left the tools in the keyhole. How could she have been so stupid?

She crossed her fingers, hoping the men didn't go to the end of the balcony and see the tools. After a few minutes of anxious waiting, she ascended the stairs again and crept to Condoleza's door. The pick and screwdriver still protruded from the keyhole.

Claire sent up a silent prayer of thanks.

Determined to avoid any more delays, she worked the dental pick furiously until she heard the click of the deadbolt sliding back. She shoved the door open, slipped inside, and shut it behind her. Leaning against the door, she swiped an ice-cold hand across her sweaty brow. So far, so good.

She flicked on her small flashlight and aimed it low to keep the beam from lighting the apartment windows. Starting her search at the bookcase under the TV, she looked for papers, photos, anything that might shed some light on the relationship between Enrique and Condoleza, on Travis or even Leon. The flashlight illuminated an open shoebox of photographs. She sat on the floor, clenched the flashlight between her teeth, and thumbed through the photos.

She found a picture of Leon sitting at a table cluttered with glasses and beer bottles. Flanked by Enrique and Condoleza, he had an arm draped over each. Claire flipped the photo over and read the date printed on the back. Four months ago.

Farther back, she found a picture of Travis, standing with two other men. She recognized one as Leon's driver. On the back was scrawled, "Someday I will kick Travis's ass. E."

Was it written by Enrique, or did Leon's driver's name start with "E"?

Below the first scrawl, in a different color ink, written with a different handwriting, it said: "I kicked yours first. T."

Was the second message written at the same time, in the spirit of friendly rivalry, or was it written after Travis killed Enrique? She pocketed the photo. Maybe the police could make something of it. But how would she explain having it in her possession? She shook her head. She'd figure that out later.

The remaining photos held nothing of interest. She replaced the shoebox and scanned the rest of the bookcase. No papers, only Spanish-language scandal magazines, a worn Spanish-English dictionary, and a few TV program guides.

She moved on to the kitchen. A stack of mail yielded only unpaid bills. Opening drawers, she found one stuffed with receipts. She rifled through them and saw one with a sizeable amount for a nine-millimeter handgun from a gun emporium in Woodland Park, Colorado. Dated approximately a year ago, the receipt was probably for Enrique's gun—the gun that had been used to kill him. Condoleza must have known Enrique owned it, maybe even where he kept it.

Claire lifted the lid of a cookie jar shaped like a sad-eyed bulldog. Inside, a stack of small plasticine envelopes filled with white powder lay partially covered by a handful of gingersnaps. *Cocaine?* She slammed the lid on the jar. No way was she going to touch that stuff.

Down the hall, she swept the flashlight's narrow beam across a disheveled bedroom. A dresser, end table, and queen-sized bed comprised the furnishings. A musty odor of sour sweat and dirty laundry hung in the air. Clothes, shoes, and newspapers littered the floor. Resisting the motherly urge to pick up the damp towel on the floor, she stepped over a few piles and made her way to the dresser.

She opened the top drawer. A thin journal peeked out from under a pile of women's thong panties. Claire pulled the book out and opened it. Tiny, cursive writing in Spanish covered its lined pages. A woman's handwriting, different from the men's scrawls on the back of the photos, so unless another woman occupied the apartment, virtually impossible, this was Condoleza's diary.

A date was written in the top left corner of the first page. Claire translated the date into October second, over four months ago.

She hoped her rusty high-school Spanish would be enough to translate the entries. She flipped through the pages until she found an entry for the current month, February, and sat on edge of the bed to study the text. The names of Enrique, Leon, and Travis appeared on the next few pages.

On one page, Enrique and Travis were mentioned in the same sentence. She studied the words. *Travis tiene envidia de Enrique.* *Envidia* looked a lot like "envious." Maybe Travis was envious of Enrique, of his success. Or jealous. She thought the same word could be used for either envy or jealousy in Spanish. Travis could be jealous of Enrique's relationship with Condoleza. Claire rubbed her aching forehead. If only she could remember more Spanish.

A rustling at the front door made her head jerk up. Glancing at her watch, she saw an hour had passed since Condoleza and Travis had left. *They couldn't be home already. Oh God!*

With her heart doing a clog dance against her chest wall, Claire shoved the journal in the dresser drawer. She ran to the window, opened it, and looked out. The drop to the alley below was straight down, with nothing to break her fall but metal trash cans. The familiar woozy tingle that signaled her fear of heights crept up her legs. Claire grabbed the window frame and closed her eyes. *No, can't do that.* She shut the window.

The front door creaked open. Condoleza said, "But I'm sure I locked it when we left."

"Be double damn sure next time. We got an investment to protect," Travis replied. "Get me some ice. My eye hurts."

"*Imbécil.* Why'd you have to pick a fight with that *hombre?*" Condoleza's heels clicked on the kitchen floor.

"The bastard was dissin' me. He asked for it."

An ice tray cracked, and ice clattered into the kitchen sink.

Frantically, Claire searched the bedroom for a hiding place. She tiptoed to the small closet. *Damn. Crammed full.*

"Here's your ice," Condoleza said. "So much for dancing. I'm going to bed."

Claire's gaze lit on the bed. She dropped to the floor, on the side away from the bedroom door, and looked under. The bed frame stood high enough off the floor for her to squeeze under. The light from the hallway exposed wadded-up tissues, dust balls, used condoms, and spider webs.

Condoleza's heels clicked down the hallway.

Claire had no choice. She scooted under the springs.

Condoleza flipped the switch, and light flooded the room.

Claire held her breath but could have sworn her heart thundered loud enough to be heard next door. The wood slats that held the springs above her grazed her breasts and nose. A jagged piece of the slat that should have been over her knees lay next to her legs. Her skin tingled as she imagined spiders crawling over her. She clenched her teeth.

Shoes hit the floor, then the bathroom door closed.

With a shudder, Claire swiped a spider web from her face and hoped the occupant had scurried away. *God, I hate spiders.*

The toilet flushed. Condoleza sat on the foot of the bed. The box springs sagged onto Claire's knees.

Travis walked into the room. "Hey, Leza, you ain't mad at me, are you?"

Claire turned her head toward his voice and caught a glimpse of two large bare feet stepping out of a pair of trousers dropped on the floor. The feet walked to where Condoleza's feet were being stripped of their stockings.

Condoleza sighed. "I was just starting to groove, and you had to pick a fight."

"Sorry, baby." His feet spread wider.

"Go away." Condoleza's tone was firm, tinged with anger.

Travis stumbled back then stepped forward again. "C'mon, I said I'm sorry. I'll take you out again. Let's kiss and make up."

After a moment, a faint smack signaled the end of a long kiss. "I'm still mad." But Condoleza's voice showed she was softening.

"I'll make it up to you. Love ya' real good, baby." The smacks and moans of serious necking followed.

Claire cringed. *How am I going to get out of here?*

A zipper slowly unzipped. His voice dropped lower. "Let's make our own music. Stand up and come to papa."

The springs lifted, and a slinky red dress pooled on the floor at the end of the bed. Condoleza's feet stepped out of the dress and kicked it aside. Then with toes curled, one foot caressed Travis's ankle.

Condoleza moaned.

A black lace bra fell on top of the dress.

Claire rolled her eyes. *Oh, God.*

The amorous couple toppled onto the bed.

The springs slammed onto Claire's chest, forcing the air out of her lungs with a loud "Ooof."

"What was that?" Condoleza asked.

The pressure lifted off Claire's chest. A second later, she

stared straight into a pair of furious brown eyes.

Travis grabbed Claire's arm and yanked hard, pulling her halfway out from under the bed.

Condoleza screamed.

The bed frame scraped Claire's cheek as her face emerged, but she barely felt it, frantically wondering if Travis would hurt her more—a lot more.

He kicked her. "Get out, bitch!"

She wormed the rest of her body out onto the floor then scrambled to her hands and knees. Blood roared in her ears, and stars whirled in front of her eyes.

Travis grabbed a handful of her hair and yanked her head up.

Her eyes focused. She stared as a switchblade snicked open an inch from her nose. Warm blood from her scratch trickled down her cheek. Cold sweat trickled down her back.

Travis forced her to a shaky stand then tilted her chin up with the cold, steel blade. His nostrils dilated like a raging bull's.

Claire trembled. *Is this it? Am I going to die here?*

"What the fuck were you doing under our bed? Who are you?" His eyes focused on her face. "Wait. I've seen you before. You're the bitch from the auto shop."

Condoleza shrieked again. She threw on a robe and yanked its belt tight. "She was here. She's the lady who brought Enrique's jacket." She lapsed into a frantic stream of Spanish, interspersed with hand-waving, finger-pointing, and more shrieks.

Claire stared at Travis, not daring to swallow with the knife under her chin. Her tongue was too thick to speak.

He stepped closer. Baring his teeth, he pressed the blade against her throat.

A drop of blood trickled down Claire's neck. A wave of nausea passed through her gut.

He waved the blade in front of her face. "What's your game?

Talk or I'll slice you."

Claire gulped. "I'm sorry."

The room swayed and tilted. She groped backward with her hand for the bed and plopped down on it. She tried to focus on something. Travis's black satin boxers swam in her vision before she clamped her eyes shut and dropped her head between her knees.

He laughed. "Damn lady's gonna faint."

Condoleza finally stopped shouting.

Travis clamped an iron grip on Claire's shoulder and shook her violently. "Don't you fade out on me. You got questions to answer."

Claire sucked in two deep breaths and opened her eyes. The room stopped swaying. Slowly, she raised her head and faced the young man glaring at her.

"I'm sorry," she repeated, her dry mouth making her speech hoarse. "I meant to be long gone before you came home. But you came back early, so I hid. I didn't mean to spy on or listen to . . . you know."

"So you're saying you ain't no pervert." Travis squinted at her.

Claire rubbed her damp hands on her jeans. "Yes."

"You're a thief. You're after our coke."

Claire shook her head. "I don't use it."

"But at the shop you talked like you wanted to buy some." Travis glanced at Condoleza. "This bitch don't make sense."

Condoleza came around to their side of the bed to study Claire's face. "Why'd you break into our apartment?"

"To look for—"

"Un momentito." Condoleza shuffled through some newspapers on the floor. "I know who you are. Here."

She pulled out a section, showed it to Travis, and tapped the front-page photo. "She's the wife of the man who shot Enrique."

"Roger didn't kill Enrique," Claire said.

Condoleza stabbed a finger in Claire's face. "You're one of Enrique's whores, those old ladies from the gym who couldn't keep their hands off him. I hate you. I hate all of you."

"Hey, you could make a man jealous with talk like that." Travis swelled his chest, causing his nipple ring to poke out.

Condoleza sniffed and swiped at a tear. "The bitches all thought they were better than him, but he was too good for them." She glanced at Travis. "So are you."

"That's better." He read from the paper. "Claire Hanover. Well, well, well." He tossed the paper aside and frowned at Claire. "What're you looking for?"

Claire's mind whirled. What could she tell him that wouldn't make him angry? He'd probably kill her if he knew she believed he might be the murderer. "I . . . I . . ."

"You a narc?"

Condoleza punched his arm. "*Imbécil*. She won't accept that her jealous husband killed Enrique and thinks one of us did it. Right?" Her face livid with rage, she poked Claire.

Claire nodded miserably.

Travis threw back his head and laughed. "*Imbécil?* She's the *imbécil*. Hiding under the bed of someone she thinks is a killer."

He leaned down and leered in her face. "Maybe I should prove you're right. Maybe I should slice you right now and toss you out the window into the garbage where you belong." He swung the knife under her nose in a slow, mesmerizing cobra death dance.

Frozen with fear, Claire stared at the knife.

Condoleza put a hand on his arm. "Wait. We don't need trouble. Leon will be angry if the cops find a body and start searching his building."

Rubbing her forehead, she paced the floor, then paused. A sly grin bloomed on her lips. "We are good American citizens, right? We should turn in this crook."

"Call the cops?" Travis's eyes flew open.

Claire felt equally puzzled.

"Sure." Condoleza stood with hands on her hips. "Listen to me. She broke into our apartment. This is a crime. If we turn her over to the cops, they will throw her in jail, where she cannot bother us."

Claire caught on. Jail was much better than death at the end of Travis's knife. She'd play Brer Rabbit and beg to stay out of the briar patch. "Please don't turn me in to the police. They're already mad at me for interfering in the investigation."

Detective Wilson's face, contorted with anger, loomed in her mind.

"Sweet." Travis leered at Claire. "Mrs. High Society gets her face in the paper again, but this time as a crook."

Maybe getting turned in to the police isn't such a good idea. "Or you could let me go. I'll pay you for your trouble, and I won't tell anyone what I found here."

His eyes narrowed. "What *did* you find?"

That was a mistake. Claire mentally kicked herself.

"Search her pockets," Travis said to Condoleza.

Condoleza found the photo and showed it to him.

Travis snorted, grabbed the photo by the corner, and threw it across the room. The photo twirled into a pile of trash heaped around a mostly empty trash can. "Damn. Missed again. Anyway, that picture don't mean nothing. Anything else?"

Condoleza shook her head.

Claire shook hers, too.

Travis stuck the knife under Claire's chin and spoke slowly. "Find anything interesting in the kitchen?"

If there was ever a situation where Claire needed to lie and lie well, this was it. She had to hide the fact that she'd seen the cocaine. Digging her fingernails into her palms, she told a half-truth. "A gun receipt."

"For Enrique's gun!" Condoleza shook Travis's arm. "The one her husband used to shoot him."

"Roger didn't—"

"Shut up!" Condoleza slapped Claire.

Claire accepted the pain gratefully because Condoleza's outburst had distracted Travis.

He motioned for Claire to stand. "Go to the front door. We don't want the pigs in here searching the place."

As they walked down the hall, he snickered. "Can't wait to see their faces." He called over his shoulder. "Get dressed, Leza, and call the cops. Tell 'em we nabbed a burglar."

CHAPTER 14
THE CROOK

Claire hunched on the end of a narrow metal bunk with a thin, soiled mattress. The bunk was bolted to the floor of the women's holding cell at the Gold Hill police station. She glanced at her watch—past midnight. But with the harsh, unshielded bulbs burning overhead, getting any rest was impossible.

She wasn't thinking about sleep, anyway. Her mind churned over what she should do next. Who she should call. She'd been too embarrassed to call Roger when she was brought in. Whatever made her think she could get away with breaking into Condoleza's apartment?

I'm an idiot, and now I'm a criminal to boot.

She faced the bars fronting the cell, leaned her chin on her hands, and stared at the gray-green stains on the floor. Wrinkling her nose in disgust, she wondered what had made those stains. The strong odor of industrial-strength cleanser that permeated the place was somehow reassuring.

Her head throbbed, and her cheek burned, although the scrape had stopped bleeding. She eased her fingers across her cheek and felt bumps of clotted blood. Her clothes were a mess, too. She picked a glob of dusty spider web off her pants leg. She itched to get home and shower, but she had no idea when that would be possible.

She refused to acknowledge the curious glances of the cell's other occupants, two surly-looking, stringy-haired teenage girls in patched and tattered jeans and jean jackets. The girls sat on a back bunk and whispered furtively to each other. They needn't have bothered. Claire had no interest in their conversation.

A loud clang announced the closing of a metal door. Heavy footsteps rang in the hallway. Claire glanced up as the footsteps stopped in front of her. A massive belly met her gaze. A uniform shirt gapped open between strained buttons, revealing a hairy belly button at Claire's eye level.

She looked up.

The guard's thick-lipped mouth sneered above two fat chins. He barked, "Claire Hanover."

Claire said, "Yes?"

"Stand two steps away from the door." The guard waited for her to comply, then opened the cell door. He waved her through. After locking the door, he walked her to the end of the hall.

They passed through a maze of locked doors and narrow hallways until the guard stopped in front of a scratched wooden door. He opened it, pushed her inside, and closed the door behind her.

The institutional gray room was bare except for a table and two chairs—and Detective Wilson. Wearing a rumpled trench coat and sitting slumped in his chair, he looked exhausted and angry.

Claire's heart sank. *Oh, God.*

He gestured at the other chair.

She slipped into the seat and sat stiffly, hands clasped in her lap.

"Imagine my surprise"—Wilson's voice dripped with sarcasm—"to be awakened close to midnight and told that the wife of my murder suspect had been arrested for breaking and entering."

Claire stared at her hands.

Wilson's voice rose. "And the apartment she broke into was leased by the man killed by her husband."

She had to say it. "Roger didn't kill Enrique."

Wilson slapped the table. "Your belief in your husband's innocence does not, I repeat, *does not* give you the right to break the law."

Claire flinched. "I understand. All I can say in my defense is that I was desperate."

"You better have been desperate to break into a drug dealer's apartment. You could've been killed! And we couldn't have done anything about it, because of the Make My Day law."

Claire's chin jerked up. She stared at the detective. "How did you know Travis was a dealer?"

Wilson looked at the ceiling, as if beseeching God for patience. "Why do you think they called me in? Your meddling upset a delicate drug interdiction operation. We had almost collected enough evidence to arrest him."

When he glared at her, Claire shrank back.

"Imagine how our officers felt to have a dealer watch them haul off a society dame. He stood there in his silk boxers smirking at them the whole time, because they didn't have enough on him and couldn't search the place."

Claire wanted to crawl into a hole and die quietly. "I'm sorry."

Wilson rubbed his forehead. "He'll have a field day with the story, bragging to every street hustler willing to listen about how he put one over on us. And what's worse, we can't go after him for awhile, because his lawyer will claim whatever new evidence we have was acquired illegally during your arrest."

Horrified, Claire realized the broad repercussions of her headstrong actions. "I didn't think—"

"Damn right you didn't think. I've spent the last hour trying to placate people on both sides."

"What do you mean, both sides?"

"Don't ask." With his last outburst, Wilson seemed to have blown off enough steam and sat fuming.

Claire wrapped her arms around her chest. Morose, self-chiding thoughts swirled in her head. She could never explain herself to Detective Wilson. "As soon as I can get hold of Dave Kessler, I'll be out of your hair."

Wilson chuckled.

Claire stared. *Why is he laughing?*

Wilson cracked a wry smile as the laugh subsided. His voice dripped with sarcasm. "That's what's so ironic. You're already out of my hair. For now, anyway. For some mysterious reason, Miss Martinez and Mr. Smith decided not to press charges. You're free to go, Mrs. Hanover."

Smith must be Travis's last name. Or a not very original alias. "Why would they do that?"

He shrugged. "Who knows? But I suggest you don't ask them. You should avoid any and all contact with them whatsoever." He peered at her, as if waiting for agreement.

"Don't worry." Claire shuddered. "I don't intend to see either of them again. But I discovered some things in the apartment. A photo—"

"Stop." Wilson held up a hand. "I can't use anything you found while snooping in their apartment. In fact, I don't even want to know. It could taint the investigation."

"But—"

"No."

Claire slumped in her chair. What good was it to find out stuff if he refused to listen? At least she could tell Dave Kessler. Maybe he could use the information in Roger's defense.

Wilson stood. "I said you were free to go. Usually a cab or two is loitering outside, even this late. If you don't see one, you can call a cab from the pay phone in the lobby. The guard will take you to get your personal effects."

He opened the door and faced Claire. "I plan to go home and go back to sleep. I suggest you do the same, Mrs. Hanover, and I hope I never see you or hear from you again." He walked out and let the door swing shut behind him with a loud thump.

Claire buried her head in her hands, too worn out to cry.

The door creaked open. The guard stood waiting.

With a sigh, Claire eased out of the chair and followed the guard. He led her to a desk where she retrieved her car keys, burgling tools, and flashlight. She remembered her car still sat parked at the Faith Redeemer Baptist Church. She wondered if it, and her purse inside, was still there. If it wasn't, she couldn't pay the cab driver. But that was the least of her worries.

Like an automaton, she plodded after the guard to the lobby. Before she knew it, she stood alone at the front entrance. Heeding Detective Wilson's advice, she stepped outside to look for a cab.

The street was quiet, with no car or foot traffic. Slick patches of melted snow refrozen into ice reflected the stark glare of a streetlight on the corner. Dark storm clouds raced overhead, blocking out starlight.

The somber scene echoed Claire's gloomy mood. Clutching her coat tight against her, she walked down the station steps to the street. She looked left, for a cab.

Nothing.

As she turned right, two pairs of rough hands grabbed her, and a gloved hand clamped over her mouth.

"Don't make no trouble now. The man needs to talk to you." The speaker and his companion lifted her off her feet and carried her down the street, away from the police station.

Claire glanced right and left, and her eyes grew wide. She recognized Leon's driver and bodyguard. She struggled, but she was trapped firmly in the grip of the large men flanking her. She tried to scream, but the hand over her mouth muffled the sound.

Where are the police when you need them, especially outside their own damn station?

She remembered what Leon had said when he spoke to her on the phone—"Don't talk to Travis or Condoleza again"—and the implied threat.

Claire's scalp and arms tingled as her hair rose to full alert.

They rounded the corner. With its engine running, the black limousine waited at the end of the block.

Oh, God. Furiously, she fought her captors again, but Leon's thugs easily overpowered her.

The driver's companion opened a back door of the limousine, and the two shoved her inside.

Howling, "Let me go! You can't do this to me," she landed on all fours on the car floor. The door slammed shut behind her, whacking her on her rump and heel. Sharp pains zinged up the nerves from both sites.

The door lock clicked.

Another loud click sounded from the back seat of the limo.

Her head whipped up. A wicked switchblade gleamed, reflecting rays from the streetlight overhead. She bit her lip to still the trembling.

Leon's large, black visage grinned at her from behind the weapon. "They not only *can* do this to you, Mrs. Hanover, they just did."

The two henchmen climbed in front, and the driver gunned the engine. The car shot forward.

The acceleration threw Claire against Leon's legs. Anxious to put distance between herself and the knife, she clambered onto her knees on the rear-facing seat, hands pressed against the side and ceiling of the car.

Deliberately, Leon turned the blade, scraped it under one of his fingernails, then wiped it on his pants leg. He waved the knife. "Sit down."

Staring at the blade, Claire slowly slid down until she was sitting in the corner farthest from Leon.

"Now put on your seat belt like a good girl. We wouldn't want you to get hurt if we make any sudden stops." Leon chuckled.

Claire didn't like the sound of that chuckle. Fingers trembling, she pulled the seat belt across her lap. She wondered what Leon planned to do. It took two tries to fasten the buckle.

He lowered the switchblade but kept it in his hand, tapping the side of the blade against his other palm.

Claire had no doubt he could use the knife with speed and deadly accuracy. She licked her dry lips.

Leon shook his head and clucked his tongue. "What are we gonna do with you?"

Claire had a suggestion—let her go—but she doubted he wanted to hear it. She glanced out the window, but she didn't recognize any landmarks in the dark. Where were they taking her?

A lighter flashed, and Leon held it to the end of his cigarette. He blew a large smoke ring.

The acrid smoke stung Claire's nose. She coughed.

"Bad habit, I know. But I ain't had a chance to break it yet." He took another drag. "Or a desire to."

After two more quick drags, Leon stubbed out the cigarette. "And I never do anything I don't have a desire to do."

Claire screwed up her courage to speak. "I hope you don't have a desire to kill me, Mr. . . ." She realized she didn't know his last name. "Leon."

He laughed. "Maybe, maybe not. But as I told you before, I don't 'desire' for you to mess in my business, either." He gave her a stern look.

"You said not to talk to Condoleza or Travis. I didn't plan to."

Leon rolled his eyes, but she plowed on. "I meant to be out

of the apartment long before they returned. They never should have known I was there, but they came home early."

"I know."

"So one of them told you. That's why you were waiting for me." Another realization hit her. "You knew Travis dropped the charges. That's how you knew when I'd be leaving the jail."

Leon fisted his hand and studied his fingernails. "I told him to drop the charges."

This admission jolted Claire. "Why?"

Leon waved his hand dismissively. "The last thing I need is Travis on a witness stand under oath."

He laughed again. "Travis didn't like it, no sir. He was enjoying his little game with the cops. Have to admit turning you in was a smart idea. The cops'll have to stay away from him awhile, and they were getting too close for my comfort."

"Turning me in wasn't his idea. It was Condoleza's."

"Really? In addition to being hot, the gal's got brains." Leon stroked his chin. "Well, well, well."

Claire put her own brain to work. "Since the outcome was positive for Travis, and for your business, maybe you can find it in your heart to let me go."

Leon dropped his hand and peered at her. "Did you tell the cops about the coke you found?"

"No." Claire's eyes widened. "Wait a minute. How did you know I found cocaine?"

"I didn't."

Damn. Her naiveté had gotten her in trouble again. Maybe she could use it for her benefit. "I didn't tell them Travis was a dealer, either. They already knew that."

"I know. Once this blows over, I'll probably have to work a deal to save his sorry ass again."

"You bribe the police?"

Leon shook his head.

Claire thought for a moment. Besides money, what else could Leon trade for the young man's hide? "Information. You must—"

Putting a finger to his lips, Leon smiled. "A smart businessman's got to find some way to eliminate the competition."

Claire realized he might be involved in the delicate drug interdiction operation Detective Wilson had mentioned. That would explain a lot. The notion also gave her some hope she could get out of this situation alive. "I won't tell a soul."

"No, you won't."

What's that supposed to mean?

Leon scowled. "Besides, it gives me satisfaction to get scumbags who hook kids on meth off the streets."

"But don't you do the same thing?"

"Hell, no. Cocaine's an expensive drug. We sell only to adults with dough. Got no kids working for me, neither. You gotta to be seventeen to work for Leon. I run a high-class business."

Amazed, Claire just stared at him. *A drug pusher with ethics?*

His face clouded over, as if reliving an ugly memory. "Meth's some nasty shit. Real nasty shit. Even nastier to make than take."

He shook off the reverie and refocused on her. "I admire your persistence, Mrs. Hanover, and the idea of hurting you doesn't give me great pleasure." He sighed and picked at another fingernail with his knife. "So I'm gonna tell you something to convince you to stop snooping around my business. But you gotta keep this in the strictest confidence."

"I will."

Leon pointed at her with the knife. "Swear it."

A cold trickle of sweat inched down Claire's back. "I swear I will not tell anyone what you are going to tell me. That's a promise."

"Good. Now, here's the shit. I know for a fact neither Condoleza or Travis killed Enrique. That's 'cause Condoleza was with me." Leon shifted in his seat and tilted his head toward the front of the car. "And Travis was with my two men up there during the time Enrique got shot."

"Then you and Condoleza were . . . involved, too?"

Leon nodded. "Enrique understood the relationship between Condoleza and me. The lady and me go way back. But Travis is different, new to my operation. Condoleza hadn't told him yet. I was being kind, giving him a little time to get used to the idea. So those two up front played pool with him while Condoleza and I had our . . . talk." Leon grinned. "I told you she's one hot little number."

Claire stared at Leon. He had no reason to invent this story for her benefit. And she had no reason to doubt him. The realization hit in the pit of her stomach. Her top two suspects had just been cleared. She'd been wasting her own, and Roger's, precious time. Tears threatened.

Leon watched her. Then, obviously coming to a decision, he closed the switchblade and tucked it in a pocket of his black denim vest. He leaned forward and tapped on the pane separating them from the two men up front. When the pane slid open, he said, "The church."

The driver nodded and slid the pane closed again.

Claire sniffed back her tears. "What church?"

"Faith Redeemer, where you left your car."

"You know everything, don't you?"

"It's my 'hood. People tell me what's going on, especially strange, fancy cars left in parking lots."

He pulled a bag of peeled baby carrots out of his pocket and popped one in his mouth. He held the bag out to her. "Carrot?"

Claire stared at the bag, then him.

He patted his paunch. "Doc says I have to lower my cholesterol. And my weight." He offered the bag again.

This time she took a carrot.

He took a couple more for himself then returned the bag to his pocket. "I've got a man watching your car. Otherwise, it would be gone by now."

"Why are you doing this for me?"

Leon reached over to pat her hand. "As I said before, I admire your loyalty to your husband. But I want you out of my hair for good this time."

"For good this time." Claire cracked a wry smile. "You know, Detective Wilson said pretty much the same thing."

Leon threw back his head and laughed.

The limousine pulled into the church lot and parked next to Claire's BMW. She saw the dark outline of a tall, thin man leaning against the back fence of the lot. When Leon's driver cut the ignition, the man doffed his hat at the limousine and walked away.

The bodyguard got out and tapped on Leon's window.

Leon rolled it down. "Let's see, the passenger side mirror, I think."

The bodyguard walked to Claire's car. He carried a tire iron.

Claire gaped. "What?"

The man raised the tire iron and smashed the side mirror of her car. Glass tinkled on the ground. He hit the mirror again. It fell off the car with a clunk.

Claire turned to Leon, her mouth hanging open.

"More subtle than busting your kneecaps."

"You wouldn't—"

Leon smirked and patted her hand again. "Just giving you a little reminder not to mess with me again."

Claire closed her mouth. Leon and his gang lived by a different set of rules from the ones her parents had taught her. She told herself to feel grateful they'd smashed her car mirror instead of some part of her body.

Leon leaned forward and touched her cheek, where Condoleza's bed frame had scraped the skin. "Better get this cleaned up when you get home."

Surprised he noticed or cared, Claire said, "I will. Thanks for your concern."

"Before you go, let me give you some advice."

Claire held up her hand. "Leon, I promise. I will not mess with you *ever* again."

He threw back his head and laughed. "I'm glad we understand each other so well, but that's not the advice I'm offering." He paused. "If I was you, I'd check out those gym ladies in Enrique's class."

Chapter 15
Gym Ladies

Thursday morning an insistent ringing woke Claire from a troubled sleep. Groggy, she checked the clock. Seven-thirty, less than six hours' sleep. She fumbled for the cordless phone she'd placed on the nightstand next to Judy's bed. "Hello?"

"Claire?"

"Deb?"

"Sounds like I disturbed your beauty sleep. Sorry. I flew in from L.A. late last night, and I'm due in court at nine. I wanted to check on your progress before I get tied up."

With a groan, Claire rubbed the sleep out of her eyes. "Last night was a doozy. I was set upon by rats, spiders, a homeless beggar, and a drug dealer wielding a switchblade. Then I was arrested, thrown in jail, kidnapped, and scolded like a misbehaving child by both a police detective and a drug boss. With a switchblade."

"Wow! A hot time in the old town."

"All my leads have gone cold." Frustration left a bitter taste in Claire's mouth. For the first time since she'd vowed to help Roger, she felt true despair. "And time's running out. Roger's already severely depressed, and he expects his boss to tell him to take leave tomorrow, the first step to firing him."

"Tell me everything. A fresh set of ears could help."

Claire briefed Deb on all that had happened since their last talk, on Monday. When she finished, Deb let out a long, low whistle. "What an adventure. I'd like to meet this Leon. Sounds like a cool dude."

Claire smiled, then winced. She touched the bandage on her cheek. Her scrape still stung. "Why in the world would you want to meet a drug boss?"

"He'd be interesting and a good contact in my business. Anyway, I agree with Leon. The women at the gym are your best bet."

Closing her eyes, Claire allowed herself a moment of self-pity, as an inner voice berated her for incompetence, inadequacy, stupidity, and false hopes. "That means I have to start all over again on new suspects."

"Tracing the relationships that existed between the gym ladies and Enrique Romero could lead to the one who killed him. One of those women may have fallen for him and flown into a rage when he dumped her."

"But how would she know he was at my house?"

"C'mon, you may have thought you were being discreet, but anyone could've seen you two leave the gym together."

"Sometimes you wield your honesty like a tomahawk, Deb."

She laughed. "Sorry about that."

"Okay, here's a harder question. What about the call to Roger's office? I didn't tell anyone at the gym where my husband works, not even Enrique. Only Ellen and Jill knew."

"You didn't have to tell anyone. Remember that charity photo of you two in the paper?"

"That was after Enrique—"

"Think back to the original article. Didn't you tell me Roger's company bought a table for that event?"

Claire closed her eyes and pictured the original group photo of the people at their table. "The caption. Yes, the photo caption named Roger's company. But—"

"Back issues of newspapers can be searched on-line. I do it all the time. I lay odds Enrique compared his class roster against the society pages, too."

"Ouch." Claire grimaced. *Is that why he came on to me?* "You mean, to select his next seduction target."

"All right, I'm tucking away my tomahawk. Let's get back to the gym ladies. Is today your regular class?"

"No. Enrique's class was Monday and Wednesday mornings."

"Would any of his class members be at the gym today?"

"Brenda would. She's the one who bought cocaine from him."

"Start with her."

Claire tried to roll onto her side, but her aching body resisted. "I'm exhausted."

"You need to find out something by tomorrow, right?"

"I know, I know. You've put my brain in gear, but the bod's still got the brakes on." With a groan, Claire pushed herself up into a sitting position. "I'll drag myself over there. But how do I talk to these women? I can't just ask them outright if they killed Enrique."

Deb laughed. "You've discovered investigating isn't easy. Here's what you do. Take advantage of women's natural tendency to gossip. Even better, if you find out one is mad at another, or dislikes her, you can feed off that."

"As far as I know, Brenda isn't involved enough with anyone in the class to have made enemies."

"But she was steamed at you for lying to her about needing to buy cocaine. Therefore, she has the potential to lose her cool. Get her emotional, so she doesn't think through what she's telling you. Same goes for the others. I should finish my testimony today, so I can drive down to help you tomorrow. In the meantime, here's some hints for what you need to do today."

Claire listened intently. After hanging up, she eased her stiff body out of bed. She adjusted the shower water as hot as she could tolerate and let the spray beat on her head and shoulders until she could rotate her neck without wincing. Maybe going to the gym would be good. She could work out the kinks in her sore muscles.

She peered in the mirror at the scrape on her cheek. She covered it with two small flesh-colored bandages, in place of the large gauze pad she had taped on the night before. As she dressed, she tried out and rejected a dozen stories for how she'd gotten the injury. She'd just have to gloss over it.

She arrived at the gym right after the ten o'clock aerobics class ended, and found Brenda dressing in the locker room—a red pantsuit this time, with red and gold matching jewelry. Claire looked down at her own jean shirt, khakis, and scuffed tennis shoes, and stifled a sigh.

"What happened to your cheek?" Brenda stared at Claire.

"It's just a little scrape." Claire plastered what she hoped was a disarming grin on her face. "Nothing important. I need to talk to you again. Can I buy you lunch?"

Brenda hesitated, looking ill at ease. "What's this about?"

"Don't worry. Not what we talked about last time. Do you want to eat in the health-food bar here or somewhere else?"

"Here." Brenda slung her gym bag over her shoulder. "I don't have much time."

Claire considered asking if Brenda had another appointment with Travis, then thought better of it. She led the way to a booth at the rear of the snack bar so they would have some privacy.

After they placed their orders, Brenda said, "Did you find out if Travis killed Enrique?"

Claire hesitated, not sure she should divulge what she knew.

"I helped you, Claire. Turnabout is fair play. I need to know what kind of person I'm dealing with."

She's right. I owe her. "I know for a fact that Travis didn't kill Enrique. I can't tell you how I know, but I think some woman who had an affair with Enrique in the past might have killed him. You know, a woman scorned . . ." Pausing for effect, Claire sipped her spring water.

With pursed lips, Brenda drew back. "You don't think *I* killed him!"

Claire shrugged. "I don't know."

"Not only no, but hell no. I never slept with the man." Eyes blazing, Brenda crossed her arms.

"So you didn't like him?"

"I don't like what you're insinuating. It was only business between us, nothing more."

Claire decided she'd better back down before Brenda left in a huff. "Okay, I believe you. But since you had a business relationship with Enrique, maybe you know which women from the gym have had liaisons with him."

"What do you plan to do with the names?"

"I'll ask each of them what they know about the others and what they thought of Enrique, to see if anyone showed jealousy toward his other women or excessive anger at him."

"Then what?"

"Then I'll take my findings to the police. Try to get them to investigate someone other than my husband."

Brenda snorted. "Good luck."

"I know Roger didn't kill Enrique." Claire leaned forward. "That means a murderer is running around loose, maybe to kill again. If I were you, I'd be scared. You might know something that would make you a target."

The waitress brought their lunch order.

Brenda took a forkful of teriyaki chicken salad. She chewed slowly then swallowed. "I never thought of it that way."

Slicing her grilled eggplant, Claire said, "Whoever shot Enrique should pay for the crime and needs to be taken off the streets. My innocent husband shouldn't go to jail in the killer's place."

Brenda raised a skeptical brow. "You're sure your husband

didn't kill him?"

"A hundred percent sure. I have evidence to back up Roger's story that he was framed, but it's not enough for the police."

Brenda studied Claire for a moment, then laid down her fork. "I'll tell you right off the bat that Enrique didn't discuss his affairs with me, so I can only tell you what I saw."

Now we're getting somewhere. "I understand. What did you see?"

"First, your friend Jill. She stopped Enrique to talk to him a few times after class, once making him late for an appointment with me. It looked as though she was flirting with him."

"Jill told me he turned her down."

"I can't say whether they actually got together or not. But if he turned her down, wouldn't she have a reason to be ticked off?" Brenda peered at Claire, then scooped another bite of salad into her mouth.

"You're right. She has to be on the list." Claire didn't believe Jill could kill anyone, but who knew who might be capable of murder deep down inside? "Anyone else?"

"About a year ago I saw Enrique leave the gym with a woman from the class, but she dropped out a few months ago. Someone said she moved. I don't remember her name." Brenda shrugged. "Then there's Karla Deavers."

"Karla?"

"The short, curly-haired redhead who stands in the front."

"I remember her." *Finally a useful name.* "She had an affair with Enrique?"

"I think so. A few months ago. I saw them talking and he had his arm around her, you know, possessive-like. Then I saw them walk into the gym together one morning."

"I'll try to catch Karla tomorrow after class."

"You can catch her today if you want." Brenda glanced at her watch. "She takes the eleven o'clock yoga class on Thursdays.

That class will be over in a few minutes."

"Great. Do you know of anyone else?"

Brenda thought for a moment. "Not with any certainty."

Claire signaled the waitress and asked for the bill, then said to Brenda, "Thanks, I really appreciate your help."

"You haven't said anything to the police about . . . you know?"

Claire looked directly into her companion's fearful eyes. "No, I haven't. And I don't intend to."

Relief flooded Brenda's face. "Thanks."

Claire glanced at the bill and pulled a twenty out of her purse. She studied Brenda. "Do you ever think of quitting?"

"Every day, Claire. Every day." Brenda drank the rest of her iced tea and stood. "Thanks for the lunch."

While she finished her grilled vegetables, Claire watched Brenda walk away. On the outside the successful-looking architect with the carefully coordinated outfits epitomized self-confidence and poise. But on the inside, she fought her desire for cocaine every day. Claire no longer envied her.

Could Brenda have killed Enrique? Brenda had sounded believable when she said she hadn't slept with Enrique. She was not a woman scorned. But did the tormented young architect have another motive?

Walking into the locker room to find Karla, Claire's thoughts turned to the redhead. Claire remembered the woman as being a talker, annoying her classmates with her constant prattle, usually juicy gossip about someone else. Maybe Claire could use that trait to her advantage.

Karla stood alone at the third row of lockers. The green sweater she wore complimented her bouncy red curls. Awkwardly, she straddled the bench with her short legs as she applied makeup in front of a small mirror on the wall.

Claire smiled. She'd often had to do the same thing when the space in front of the large, lighted mirror over the sinks became crowded. "They don't make it easy for you, do they?"

Karla glanced at her in the mirror. "The lighting sucks, too."

"Yeah, the shadows make me look even scarier than I usually do without makeup."

Karla snapped the cap on her lipstick and faced Claire. "What brings you here today? Aren't you in the Monday, Wednesday class?"

"Yes, but I'm here today because I need your help."

Karla's eyes went wide. "My help? Whatever for?"

"You know who I am, right? Claire Hanover."

"I know. Your husband shot—"

Holding up her hand to silence Karla, Claire glanced around, then whispered, "I'm convinced my husband didn't kill Enrique, and I'm looking for clues as to who might have."

Frowning, Karla stiffened.

Claire rushed on before Karla had a chance to refuse to help. "I'm new to the gym and haven't met many people. Since you seem to know everyone, I thought you might know some things about the other women in the class that could help me."

Karla raised a skeptical eyebrow. "Why should I help you?"

Claire realized she would have to play on Karla's love of gossip. "I hoped I could appeal to your sense of justice. I have proof that someone tried to frame Roger. And there's more."

Karla stopped piling things in her gym bag. "More?"

"Yes, more." Claire had set the hook. She leaned in close, winked, and whispered, "More than the police know, more than anyone here knows."

Karla's eyes narrowed. Her tongue flicked out to lick her lower lip. "Interesting."

"I'll tell you all about it over lunch, my treat. All I ask is that you be willing to tell me what you know."

As Karla wavered, Claire threw out a clincher. "Let's go someplace where we can talk in private. How about the Cliff

House in Manitou Springs? Do you like Continental food?"

"I never turn down a meal at the Cliff House."

Karla's eyes glittered, either from anticipating a luxurious meal at one of the most exclusive restaurants in town or a sumptuous serving of gossip. Claire couldn't tell which and didn't care.

Half an hour later, Claire sipped a glass of Chardonnay and surveyed the elegant dining room. Waiters glided between tables covered with cream-colored damask linens that matched the walls, on which hung oil paintings of local scenes—the Garden of the Gods, Manitou Springs, the Rocky Mountains. The clink of silver on china and ice in crystal goblets punctuated quiet conversations at other tables.

She leaned across the table to speak softly to Karla, as if sharing a monumental secret. Claire described the phone call from a mysterious woman to Roger's office, leaving out the Hispanic accent.

Karla's eyes grew wider as she gulped her wine.

"I'm looking for the woman who made that call. From another source, I got the impression that many of the women at the gym either bought cocaine from Enrique or"—Claire raised an eyebrow—"had affairs with him."

"I didn't realize someone already took over Enrique's coke dealings. I'll have to check out the auto shop."

Surprised, Claire said, "Were you one of Enrique's customers?"

"Heavens, no. I wouldn't touch the stuff. I just like to know who's buying."

To hide her disgust at Karla's malicious curiosity, Claire patted her mouth with her napkin. "Do you know who used to buy from Enrique?"

Karla speared a chunk of bleu cheese out of her salad. "I know Brenda did, and Patti, that woman with a limp, who usually stands in the third row."

"I know who you mean. Isn't she Hispanic?" *Maybe this Patti was the one who called Roger.* Claire refilled Karla's wine glass and splashed a few drops into her own.

"Yeah." Karla grinned slyly. "I bet you didn't know this. Brenda owed Enrique a boatload of money."

Claire almost dropped the wine bottle. "How do you know?"

"I overheard them talking in the health bar, week before last. I'm short enough that they must not have seen me in the booth behind them. Enrique told Brenda she had to increase her weekly payments." Karla leaned forward. "He was talking thousands of dollars."

Shocked, Claire gaped. "Thousands?"

"Yep, and he said he'd only give her a gram a week until her debt was wiped out."

"Do drug dealers make a habit of lending buyers money?"

Karla shrugged. "How the hell should I know?"

Claire shook her head in disbelief. "What did Brenda say?"

"She got mad, said she couldn't hide payments that big from her husband. She begged Enrique to accept less."

"Did he?"

"No. He said her husband was her problem."

"Wow." This revelation changed Claire's whole perception of Brenda. And Enrique.

The waiter brought their entrees.

Claire gave the waiter her salad even though she'd only eaten two bites. She hoped Karla was too interested in gossip to notice. Still full from lunch with Brenda, Claire nibbled a bit of her tilapia fillet, then pushed the rest under the rice pilaf.

Karla dug into her raspberry-glazed duck and closed her eyes in rapture. "This is delicious."

"I'm glad you like it. Now, which women have had affairs with Enrique that you know about?"

"Patti, who I mentioned before, and . . ."

"And who?"

With a tilt of her head, Karla studied Claire. "I'm surprised you don't know."

Still puzzled, Claire shook her head.

"Your friend, Ellen."

Claire's mouth fell open. "Ellen?"

"I know for a fact that she and Enrique got it on. It started about a year ago and lasted a few months. I saw them leave the gym together lots of times and even saw him lean over and kiss her when they were in her car." Karla stabbed her fork in the air. "And it was not a casual peck on the cheek."

Claire's mind raced. If Ellen had been seeing Enrique, why would she push Claire into getting a massage? "You said their affair lasted a few months. They broke it off?"

"Enrique moved on to someone else."

"Who?"

Karla drank some wine then smiled over the top of the glass. "Me."

So, Claire had confirmation of Brenda's story. "You?"

"The affair was fun while it lasted, but I had no illusions." Karla waved her hand dismissively. "When I got tired of him, I ended it. Then he moved on to you."

"Well, yes." Embarrassed, Claire shifted in her chair. "But we never, you know, made love. He was giving me a massage when he was killed. That's all."

Karla winked. "Whatever you say."

Chapter 16
Unhappy Divorce

On the way to Ellen's house, Claire drove through slush puddles steaming in the glittering winter sunshine. Claire steamed inside. Karla's wink hinted that she was spreading rumors. *Did you hear that Enrique was making love to Claire when he was killed?* What a malicious gossipmonger! Claire could imagine what people thought. She hated being viewed as a sordid adulteress, but her denials would only fuel the rumors.

She had to squelch her anger and focus. Questions whirled. The list of suspects included Brenda, Patti, Karla, Jill, and now Ellen. But Claire couldn't believe Jill or Ellen would hurt her like this. It had to be one of the others. How could she narrow down the list? First she had to quiz Ellen.

After dropping off Karla at her car, Claire had called Ellen and said they needed to talk. Like the good friend she was, Ellen had told her to come right over. Or was she a good friend? Did a good friend murder a man in your bed and frame your husband?

Realizing her hands were clamped tight on the steering wheel, Claire flexed her fingers to release the tension. She considered the other women. She knew nothing about Patti and would have to talk to her. Claire could confirm Brenda's debt to Enrique by calling Leon. She could also ask him about other women who bought drugs from Enrique. Did she dare? She clenched her teeth. *I must.*

Time was running out. Tomorrow was Friday. She had nothing solid to offer Detective Wilson or Roger's boss. Roger's whole self-image was wrapped up in his career. If he lost his job, Claire had no idea what he'd do. Hate her? Of course. Sink so far into depression he'd consider suicide? She refused to face the possibility.

She pulled into Ellen's curved driveway. The long shadows of slim poplars lining the drive swept over the car like dark fingers reaching out for her. Claire shuddered. Resolutely, she stepped out of the car and pushed the doorbell.

Ellen threw the door open wide and hugged Claire. "I'm glad you called me."

Claire stiffened, unable to respond to the hug.

Ellen stepped back, peered at Claire's face, and touched the bandage on Claire's cheek. "What's this?"

"It's a long story."

"I'm all ears. Come in."

Ellen ushered Claire down the hall and into her sunny, steel-plated kitchen. At least Claire thought of it as steel-plated because all the appliances, including the pricey Sub-Zero refrigerator, were fronted with the burnished gray metal.

A stainless steel teapot, two cups, and a plate of almond biscotti lay on the blue glass table. Claire groaned inwardly. *Not more food.* She slid onto one of the cushioned window seats lining two sides of the table.

Ellen slid onto the other and poured Claire a cup of tea. "Here, drink some of this, then tell me all about it. Did Roger hit you?"

Claire choked on her tea. "Of course not!" She touched the bandage on her cheek. "I did this to myself. An accident. But this little scrape isn't what I needed to talk about."

"Oh?"

"I've been interviewing women at the gym, trying to get information on those who have had affairs with Enrique or bought cocaine from him."

Ellen sat back and peered at Claire. "Why?"

"I'm looking for suspects." Claire shifted uncomfortably in her seat. "Someone who had a reason to kill Enrique."

Ellen pursed her lips but said nothing.

"So far, I've discovered that Brenda and Patti bought cocaine from Enrique. But you already knew about Brenda."

"Why would anyone kill her own drug supplier?"

"If she owed Enrique money, she might. But, more importantly, Karla and Patti had affairs with Enrique. And Jill approached Enrique, but he turned her down."

Ellen nodded. "That hurt Jill. A lot."

"Did Jill really love Enrique?"

"Of course not. After her husband rejected her, she just needed a man, any man, to find her attractive. I wish Enrique hadn't pushed her away. Her self-esteem hit rock bottom."

"Are you sure they never got together?"

Ellen laughed her hard, humorless laugh. "I'm sure. Jill cried her eyes out to me afterward. Took two pints of fudge-swirl Häagen-Dazs to cheer her up. Too bad we didn't have one of your 'Cornucopia of Chocolate' baskets to dig into."

A sudden realization struck Claire, and she sucked in a breath. "Oh, God."

"What?"

"When you said basket, I remembered that the baby basket I haven't finished is due today. What time is it?"

"Just after three-thirty."

"The shower starts at five-thirty. I've got to fly. But first, what did you say to Jill?"

"I told her Enrique wasn't worth her tears, and neither was her husband. She didn't like that." Ellen raised her cup to her lips.

"Why not?"

"She still loves Paul. She can't admit that she'd rather direct her anger at someone who doesn't matter, like Enrique. I decided it was healthier for her to hate him than to turn her hate against herself, and left it at that."

Claire gripped her teacup. "Then there's you."

Carefully, Ellen set down her cup. "Me?"

"Karla told me you had an affair with Enrique before she did."

Ellen frowned. "Little Miss Copper-top Blabbermouth."

"Well?"

"Well what? Did I have an affair with Enrique?" Ellen's eyes blazed defiantly. "Yes."

"Why?"

"Why not?" Ellen shrugged. "He's a hunk. I wanted him. He made me feel good. I don't mean just in the physical way, though that was damn good. I mean about myself. Here I was, forty-eight, and a young stud wanted me, a washed-out divorcée. I was flying high for awhile."

Claire felt aghast. *Could this be the Ellen I know?* "Then what?"

"Then I got tired of him. Tired of always lending him money that he never paid back."

"So you ended the affair?"

Ellen's eyes grew wide. "Of course. What, you think he broke my heart and I killed him?"

Claire studied her friend, trying to determine if she was lying, but Ellen looked composed, except for a blooming flush of anger. "No, no, it's not that—"

"Damn right it's that." Ellen pushed herself up from the table and paced the length of the kitchen. Hands on her hips, she stared at Claire. "I know you, Claire, and I know when you're lying. I can't believe you'd think that of me, think that I'm capable of murder."

"I'm desperate. If Roger loses his job tomorrow, that could

send him over the edge. He's already so depressed. And if he's convicted . . ." Claire's eyes teared up. She choked down a sob and forced herself to continue. "I'll do anything to save him, even investigate my friends. I talked to Jill, too."

Ellen clenched her hands. "This is ridiculous. You know she and I were at the Broadmoor that day. Why aren't you chasing someone besides your two best friends? Like those drug dealers?"

"Leon and Travis?"

"Listen to you. You're on a first-name basis with drug dealers!"

Claire pulled on Ellen's hand. "Sit. Hear me out. This is difficult enough without you flying off the handle."

"You'd fly off the handle, too, if your best friend accused you of murder." Ellen plopped on the window seat, crossed her arms, and glared at Claire.

"I'm not accusing you of murder. I'm trying to find out as much as possible about Enrique's life to see who might have wanted him dead."

"And you think I wanted him dead?"

Frustrated, Claire crossed her arms, mimicking Ellen. "Maybe. Maybe lots of women did. That's my point. If Enrique had a history of breaking hearts—"

"He didn't break my heart. And Jill got over him. After our ice cream confessional, she never mentioned him again."

"What about Karla?"

"What about her?"

"Her fling with Enrique came right after yours, so I thought you might know something about it."

Ellen grabbed a biscotti, and it snapped in her hand. She dropped the pieces on her napkin. "That bitch."

"But didn't you break it off with Enrique?"

"Damn right I did."

"Then why are you mad at Karla?"

"She put out the story that she took Enrique from me. That little gossipmonger enhanced her reputation at the expense of mine. By the time I found out what she was saying about me, it was too late to repair the damage."

Claire knew Ellen hated being portrayed as the jilted lover, even if she really was. Her divorce was a good example. Ellen probably had more trouble forgiving Dave for chopping up her image than for his infidelity. "Karla told me she ended her affair with Enrique."

Ellen laughed. "She would tell you that."

"I don't understand."

Ellen leaned forward. "Enrique broke up with her. He told me so himself. Said she was getting too demanding. It's just like her to lie and say ending it was her idea."

Who was lying here? Karla or Ellen or Enrique or some combination? Claire's head pounded. Her own inexperience in lying handicapped her ability to figure out when someone else was. And she didn't have time to spare right now.

"That's one reason I thought Enrique's interest in you was so great," Ellen said. "Once Enrique and you were an item, I could get back at Karla. I could tell everyone what Enrique told me, that he dumped her, and you would be the proof."

Claire gasped. "You tried to set me up with Enrique so you could get back at Karla?"

"No, no, no." Ellen covered Claire's hand with her own. "My first thought was for you. You needed a fling, an ego boost. Roger's lack of attention was really depressing you. Getting revenge on Karla was just gravy."

Claire shook her head. The surreal situation confused her. She bit into a biscotti while she tried to clear her jumbled thoughts. Ellen, Jill, and Karla all could have been rejected by Enrique and wanted revenge. "What about Patti?"

"If she bought cocaine from Enrique, she didn't have an affair with him."

"Karla told me she did."

Ellen waved her hand. "What does Karla know? She's just spreading rumors again. Enrique told me he never had affairs with customers. It could hurt his business when the fling ended."

"Could Patti have been angry at Enrique for something else?"

"You'd have to ask her." Ellen toyed with the biscotti pieces on her napkin. "You seem so sure someone at the gym killed him. Why not one of his drug-dealing buddies?"

"I can't tell you how I know," Claire replied, "because I'm sworn to secrecy, but I'm sure neither Leon nor Travis did it."

"Who the hell did, then?"

Claire drove home as fast as she dared. As she pulled into her street, the sun slipped behind the Front Range, tinting the snow-laden flanks of Pikes Peak orange and mauve. But Claire had no time to enjoy the spectacle. She rushed inside, clambered down the stairs to the basement workroom, and madly stuffed tissue paper and baby gifts into the basket. She wrapped the whole construction in a large sheet of cellophane, then went to work on the final bow. In her haste, she bungled the large bow twice. She cursed her awkward fingers as she glanced at the clock.

Almost five.

Sweating more from anxiety than her labors, she carried the basket up the stairs at a half-run. She threw on her coat, hopped in her car, blew the hair out of her eyes, and drove at breakneck speed to the hostess's home.

She arrived at five twenty-five. A few cars were parked on the street out front. Praying that the guest of honor hadn't arrived yet, Claire grabbed the basket and trotted toward the door.

The hostess flung open the door. "Thank goodness you're here. Come in the kitchen."

As she led Claire into the kitchen, she kept up a running monologue. "I was so worried. The shower starts in five minutes, you know. At least Samantha's not here yet. I called your house awhile ago, but you weren't there . . ."

Trying to control her heavy breathing, Claire stood with the weighty basket in her aching arms and her eyebrows raised in a question.

The hostess finally noticed her dilemma. "Oh, put it there." She pointed to the kitchen table.

Claire placed the basket on the table and plumped the bow. "Sorry I'm late. It won't happen again. I've had an awful week, as I'm sure you understand."

With her pen poised over her checkbook, the hostess's eyes grew wide. "Oh, yes. You poor thing. I can't wait to hear all about it. Was it just awful? A lot of blood?" She shuddered with what Claire could tell was delicious anticipation.

She was in no mood to give the woman a lurid tale to tell her guests. "I don't want to keep you any longer from your party guests. If you'll just give me the check, I'll be on my way. Thanks for your concern, though." Claire held out her hand.

The woman's mouth drooped with disappointment, but she had the good grace to realize the subject was closed. She handed the check to Claire and led her to the door.

Claire turned to shake the hostess's hand. "Good luck with the shower. I hope you'll think of me again when you need a gift basket. And thanks for your understanding."

The hostess started to reply, but a shower guest calling to her from the driveway diverted her.

Claire took the opportunity to beat a hasty retreat. She drove a few blocks then stopped to collect her thoughts. Thinking Deb Burch probably had finished her session in court, Claire picked up her cell phone and called Deb's home in Denver. When the answering machine picked up, Claire left a message.

She desperately needed help. She had uncovered five possible suspects among the women in Enrique's class, two of them her best friends. After talking to four, she was no closer to discovering who had killed Enrique than when she started. She knew nothing about the fifth woman. And she had no guarantee she hadn't missed someone. Damn. She couldn't offer any hope to Roger.

Roger. I have to talk him into coming home. If he kept his distance, she would never convince him she hadn't been having an affair with Enrique, and that she still desperately loved the man with whom she'd shared the last twenty-six years.

She put the car in gear and headed for Dave Kessler's townhouse. When she saw Dave's silver Volvo gleaming in his driveway, she smiled. The car was the same model as Ellen's red one. The couple had bought the cars together before their marital troubles began.

Dave opened the door, a glass of what looked like his usual single-malt scotch in his hand. His rumpled shirt was open at the collar and his loosened tie lay askew below the neckline. "Hi, Claire. Roger's not here right now." He didn't ask her to come in.

"Where is he?"

"He's picking up some Chinese takeout."

"I need to talk to him." She stepped forward, but Dave's arm blocked the doorway. Remembering he was now single, she wondered if he had a woman visitor. "Am I interrupting something? Do you have company?"

Dropping his arm, Dave frowned and shook his head. His brusque manner suggested he still blamed her for Roger's predicament.

"Then I'll wait." She stepped over the threshold.

He stared at her face as she walked past. "What happened to you?"

Claire fingered the bandage on her cheek. She didn't want to talk about her arrest the night before. Dave would insist on a long, detailed description and would probably get angry with her. "Nothing important, just a scratch. I got careless." The truth, though not the whole truth, so help her God.

Dave walked to the dining room, picked up a bottle, and poured more scotch into his glass. "I suppose I should offer you a drink." He said it reluctantly, as if he hoped she would decline and leave.

Claire smiled politely. "A glass of white wine would be nice."

"I have a bottle in the fridge." He left to fetch the wine.

With butterflies tickling the inside of her stomach, Claire sat on the sofa and rehearsed what she would say to Roger. First, she'd ask him to come home. No, first she should tell him about the gym ladies. No, that was negative news. What positive news could she give him?

An annoying clicking sound intruded on her thoughts. She looked down and realized she'd been snapping her purse open and shut. She laid the purse on the glass-topped coffee table and clutched her hands in her lap.

Dave returned and handed her a glass of wine.

Claire took a large sip.

He settled in the chair next to the sofa and studied her as if waiting for her to make the next move in a chess game.

Nervous under his scrutiny, Claire glanced around the room and noticed an open file folder and papers scattered next to Dave's chair. "Is that Roger's case?"

"Yes. Before he left, we discussed what the next few steps should be. I'm preparing to hand over his file to the criminal lawyer who'll represent him at the trial."

Oh, God, the trial. Claire clanked her wineglass hard on the coffee table. The glass wobbled. She steadied it. "Sorry, I'm feeling anxious tonight."

"You should be." Dave scowled at her. "After what you did to Roger."

Claire bristled. "I didn't sleep with the man, didn't even intend to."

"I find that hard to believe, given that he was found on your bed."

She winced as she realized he must have read that sordid little detail in the police report. Would she never live that down? "Enrique was standing next to bed when he was shot and fell on me."

"C'mon, Claire. I wasn't born yesterday." Dave's face held a look of extreme distaste.

Claire had had enough. "You have no right to judge me after what you did to Ellen. A full-scale affair behind her back."

Dave raised his glass in salute. "Touché. Can't say I'm very proud of that."

"I'm not proud of what I did, either." She drew a shaky hand across her brow. "But Roger should come home. We need to be together to work this out."

"Unfortunately, I agree."

Astonished, Claire wasn't sure she'd heard him correctly. She peered at him. "You agree?"

"Roger's my best friend. I don't want what happened to Ellen and me to happen to you and Roger. I've been encouraging him to give you a chance." A wry grin played at the edge of Dave's lip. "Surprised, aren't you?"

"Yes, frankly. I thought you were mad at me."

"I am, but then I started thinking of Roger. If he loses his job *and* you, he'll have nothing. He's already scraping bottom. The fool still loves you. I don't want him to end up like Ellen."

Claire wasn't sure what he meant. "Ellen? You mean hating you for your affair?"

"Not just hating me. She can't derive pleasure from anything anymore. All her energies are concentrated on getting even with me."

"I agree. She's negative about everything, especially men."

Dave drained his scotch and stared into the glass. "I realized soon after she threw me out that I'd made a horrible mistake. I was an old fool. Brittany made me feel young again, but once I became available and we didn't have to sneak around anymore, she lost interest. She didn't love me. She loved the intrigue, the illicitness of the affair."

"Did you ask Ellen to take you back?"

He nodded and started to speak, but his voice came out as a raw croak. He closed his eyes, as if willing away the emotion. "She wouldn't have me. Even after I begged her forgiveness. Said I'd ruined her life, which I had."

"Oh, Dave." Claire reached over and covered his hand with hers. "I'm so sorry. For both of you."

He withdrew his hand and focused an intense gaze on Claire. "So am I. I'll never forgive myself for what I did to Ellen. Never. That's why I've urged Roger to give you another chance."

As Claire digested Dave's revelation, the front door opened. With a large brown bag in his arms, Roger stood in the doorway and stared at her.

Chapter 17
Homecoming

Claire thought she saw a flicker of desire in Roger's eyes—not sexual, but a cry for comfort—before he turned to close the door. The sight bolstered her courage.

Dave walked over to Roger. "I'll take this into the kitchen."

As Dave left with the bag of food, Roger cleared his throat and stepped into the living room. He sank into the chair Dave had vacated and said, "What happened to your face?"

Claire couldn't help but smile. "I scratched it on a bed frame."

Angry eyes glittering, he sneered. "Whose bed frame?"

Her smile died. "I guess I deserved that. You look tired."

"I'm not sleeping well." Licking his lips, he picked up Dave's glass, then put it down.

Yes, a drink might help. Claire recognized the familiar shoulder hunch that came when he was tense. "Why don't you fix yourself a scotch?"

"Good idea." Roger moved to the dining room.

She chose a neutral subject to ease him into conversation. "Dave told me you were picking up Chinese food tonight. Your usual twice-cooked pork?"

"You know me too well." The side of his mouth twitched as he returned to the chair, a generous glass of scotch, neat, in his hand. He took a large gulp then closed his eyes as he held it in his mouth before swallowing.

When he reopened his eyes, he said, "Okay, tell me how you got the scratch."

Knowing full well he'd lose his temper, she laced her fingers together in her lap and launched into the story of breaking into Condoleza's apartment.

Roger's jaw dropped. "Dammit, Claire, what possessed you to do such a stupid thing?"

"I was trying to find evidence to exonerate you. Detective Wilson wasn't doing anything, and Deb wasn't available."

"Didn't I tell you to stop?" Roger's face grew splotchy red.

Claire tried a wry smile. "You should know by now that I don't always do what you tell me to."

"I don't believe this. You're lucky no one saw you."

"Um, not that lucky." She described being collared by Travis.

"You could've been killed!"

She shook her head. "As Leon said, Travis is too smart to do that."

"Leon? The drug boss? What makes you think you can believe a word he says?"

Claire opened her mouth to defend Leon, then shut it. Why defend Leon to Roger? She rubbed her forehead to clear her thoughts. "Let me tell this story in sequence, or we'll both get confused. Obviously, Travis didn't kill me. He did something much smarter. He had me arrested for breaking and entering."

Roger choked on his scotch. "Breaking and entering? Now we're *both* going to jail."

"That's not true. You aren't a criminal. You didn't kill Enrique." Furious at his negativity, she spoke louder than she intended. She took a deep breath to calm herself. "Technically, though, I'm a criminal. What I did is against the law, but I won't be prosecuted."

Roger's eyes widened. "What the hell?"

"Drink your scotch and let me finish the story."

He eyed the glass. "With all the surprises you're throwing at me, maybe I'd better stay sober."

Claire laughed, but when she realized Roger wasn't laughing with her, she stifled it. She resumed her story, telling how Leon had forced Travis to drop the charges. When she reached the part where Leon's henchmen had muscled her into his car, Roger gripped the arms of his chair until his knuckles turned white. He opened his mouth, but Claire silenced him with an outstretched palm.

As she told him about the church parking lot, she shifted in her seat, nervous about how he would react to the damage to the BMW. "Leon's bodyguard smashed the mirror on the passenger side of my BMW . . . a warning," she said. Tempted to cringe, she waited.

"Christ almighty." Roger leapt out of the chair. He paced back and forth, running his fingers through his hair. "Think what he could have done to you."

His reaction was much better than Claire had hoped for. *Better not mention the switchblade,* she thought.

"That guy's dangerous," Roger continued. "We need to get him arrested, get him off the streets." He whirled and pointed a finger at her. "You're calling the police right now."

Claire crossed her arms. "I'll do no such thing. I don't think the police want Leon arrested. And besides, I promised him I wouldn't mess with him."

"Promised him? How can you make promises to a drug kingpin?"

"How can I break a promise to him? Please stop shouting and sit down."

He sank into the chair.

"I trust Leon," Claire continued. "His code of ethics is different than ours, but he has one. He smashed the car mirror, not me. And he helped me. He suggested I investigate the women in Enrique's class at the gym." She described her meetings with Brenda, Karla, and Ellen.

Looking confused, Roger said, "I can understand being suspicious of a cocaine addict, but how could you think Ellen or Jill killed anybody? They're your friends."

"And you're my husband. I'll do whatever it takes to clear your name."

Roger peered at her. "Any more surprises?"

"That's it."

"Good." He picked up his glass and tossed back the rest of his scotch. "I don't think I could take any more."

Claire reached for his hand and traced a finger over his knuckles while she sought the right words. Gazing into his eyes, she said, "Dave told me he didn't want us to wind up like him and Ellen."

Roger flinched and tried to pull his hand out of her grasp. "I'm surprised he told you that."

"You shouldn't be. He's your friend. He wants what's best for you."

"How does he know what's best for me? How does anyone know, you and me included?"

"We don't, not for sure. But throwing away our marriage over one mistake—" When Roger opened his mouth, Claire held up a hand. "Yes, I know I made a huge mistake, with horrible consequences, but still, it was *one* mistake."

"One? He was the first?"

She deliberately misconstrued the question. "I've had massages before. And that's all that was going on—a massage."

"I'm not a hundred percent convinced of that."

"After twenty-six years, you should know when I'm telling the truth." She leveled a steady gaze at him.

He stared back, then slowly nodded. "I believe you."

"Giving up on our marriage can't be the right thing to do, not without giving it a chance to start healing first." Claire paused and screwed up her courage. "You promised you would give me the chance to earn your forgiveness."

"You should get used to me not being around."

"You're *not* going to prison, so I don't need to get used to anything. Come home with me. I miss you, and we need each other."

He leaned forward and traced his finger along the bandage on her cheek. "I guess I'll have to come home, if only to keep an eye on you. You need protection, someone to keep you out of any more scrapes." A smile twitched at the edge of his lips.

Claire saw hope in that smile. She rubbed her cheek against the familiar strong warmth of his palm and felt an answering warmth grow in her belly.

Dave cleared his throat behind her. "Now that's what I like to see. A cozy little tête-à-tête."

Claire turned and saw him grinning at them. "Roger's coming home with me."

"Good. I was getting tired of him moping around here."

Roger returned Dave's smile with a sheepish grin. "Can I eat my dinner first?"

Claire tailed Roger as they drove their two cars home. When they turned onto their street, she spied an unfamiliar vehicle parked in front of their home. Someone stepped out of the strange car as Roger pulled into the far bay of the garage.

Claire followed Roger's car up the drive, entered her side of the garage, and cut the engine. As she got out, a voice called, "Mr. and Mrs. Hanover?"

Roger stepped out of the garage. "Who are you?"

The man held out his hand, offering to shake Roger's. "Marvin Bradshaw, reporter for the *Gazette*. I've already met your wife." He smiled and nodded at Claire.

She bristled. "It was not a friendly meeting."

Roger ignored the reporter's outstretched hand. "What're

you doing here at this hour?"

"I've been waiting quite some time to see you." Bradshaw's gaze flicked from Roger to Claire and back, assessing them. "I thought I'd give you a chance to tell your side before I file my story for tomorrow's paper."

"What story?" Roger frowned.

Bradshaw grinned and rocked back on his heels. "The one about your wife's arrest for breaking and entering."

"Those charges were dropped!" Claire shouted.

Roger grabbed her hand. "Shush."

He spoke to the reporter in a low, ominous voice. "You aren't welcome here. Leave."

"I'm just doing my job, Mr. Hanover. If I don't get a statement from you, I'll have to go with what my other sources said."

Oh, God, what will he write? Claire's head pounded. "Roger, maybe we should talk to him."

Roger's face reddened. "We're not letting this guy blackmail us."

Bradshaw glanced at Claire, as if looking for an ally. "But—"

"If you aren't off my property in three seconds," Roger said, clenching his fists, "I'll throw you off myself. One."

Bradshaw stood his ground. "You wouldn't do that."

Roger stepped forward, forcing Bradshaw to stumble back. "Watch me. Two."

After a last beseeching glance at Claire, Bradshaw's shoulders slumped, and he walked down the driveway.

"Three!" Roger shouted.

Bradshaw's steps quickened. When he reached his car, he yanked open the door, climbed in, and roared off.

Claire ran her hand across Roger's ramrod, angry back. "Thank you. He's been a real pest. This is the first time he's come to the house, though."

"He'd better not return."

Claire's lips curled. "I doubt he will after your performance. C'mon, let's go in."

Once inside, she hung up her coat while Roger carried his bag up the stairs. When she reached the landing, she saw him standing stock-still at the threshold of the master bedroom. Reaching past him, she flicked on the light.

A tranquil, domestic scene awaited them, complete with a fresh spray of miniature roses Claire had bunched in a small vase on the nightstand. She placed a tentative hand on Roger's arm. "What do you think?"

His gaze traveled around the room, then returned to the spot where she had stood when he'd last entered the room. He cleared his throat, but his voice still came out hoarse. "I still see you there, covered with blood and staring at me in terror. I was so afraid for you, Claire. My gut wrenched when I thought you were hurt."

She squeezed his arm.

He stared at her. "When I realized you were afraid of me, you have no idea how desolate I felt."

Fiercely, Claire hugged him.

His arms slowly encircled her.

She nuzzled her face against his chest and breathed in his familiar scent, a combination of musky maleness and his favorite shaving cologne. She lifted her head. "I'm not afraid of you now."

He stroked her hair. "I'm glad."

When he bent his head, Claire pursed her lips, expecting a kiss.

"It's late." He grazed her cheek with his lips as he released her. "We need to get ready for bed."

Disappointed but determined to let him set the pace, she pulled away. "I guess you're right."

As she brushed her teeth and combed her hair in the master

bathroom, she waited for Roger to join her at his sink, but he didn't appear. She heard him moving about the bedroom, taking things out of his bag and putting them away.

She changed into the blue silk nightgown Roger had given her for their anniversary two years ago. It was one of his favorites. Feeling as awkward as if it were their wedding night, she stepped into the bedroom. Her restless hands flitted about, smoothing her gown, until she locked them together in a tight clasp before her.

Roger's gaze softened. "You look beautiful. I won't be long." He walked into the bathroom.

Claire climbed into the bed, pulling the covers up tight over her shoulders. She shivered but not from the cold. Resolutely, she pushed gory memories from her mind. Enrique's death would no longer keep her from her bed. Determined to take this step to restoring normalcy to her life, she focused on how she should act with Roger.

He returned a few minutes later, lay down, and rolled on his side to turn off the light on his nightstand. He didn't face her but lay silently with his back toward her.

She inched over and spooned her body against his, her breasts brushing against his back through their bedclothes. His warmth seeped into her. She cleared her throat. "Roger . . ."

He moved away and flopped on his back with a sigh. "I can't do this. It's too soon."

"We don't need to make love. I just want to hold you."

"I don't mean that." He threw back the covers. "I can't sleep in this bed. I'm going to Michael's room."

As Claire listened to his bare feet pad down the hall, a crazy thought popped into her head. Why had she chosen Judy's bed, while Roger chose to sleep in Michael's bed?

Do we find solace in retreating to a time of innocent childhood?

She debated if she should go to Judy's room, but she was

here now and had to get used to sleeping in this bed sometime. She lay rigid, arms by her side, and stared at the dark ceiling.

Maybe he'll return.

Tears rolled down her cheeks, soaking her pillow.

CHAPTER 18
DEATH THREAT

Claire grunted and fought. She struggled to push something heavy off her body, but her hands couldn't grab hold, getting tangled in the sheets. Panic welled up as the weight crushed her chest, making it hard to breathe.

Her eyes flew open, and she gasped for air. Frantically, she glanced around. The early-morning sun streamed in the bedroom window, highlighting the yellows in the new bed linens.

She clutched her chest. *Oh, God. It was all a nightmare.*

She swept a quaking hand over her damp forehead and took a deep breath to slow her racing heart. Below, a chair slid on the kitchen floor. Her heart pounded again. What was that?

Then she remembered Roger was home. He must have awakened and gone downstairs. She got out of bed, splashed cold water on her face, and threw on a robe.

When she walked into the kitchen, she inhaled the rich aroma of fresh-brewed French roast coffee. She noticed Roger had already poured himself a bowl of cereal. "You should have wakened me. I wanted to make you breakfast."

The words sounded strained to her. The whole situation felt awkward. Normally his getting out of bed would have awakened her.

Roger looked up from the newspaper. He seemed uneasy, too, his eyes reluctant to focus on hers. "I didn't want to disturb you, but I almost did when I had a hard time figuring out the newfangled pot that grinds the beans." He cracked a goofy, unnatural smile.

That pot was over a year old. Claire realized she had made coffee for him every morning since then. She returned his smile, trying to put them both at ease. "I guess it's about time you learned how to use it."

She poured herself a cup and sat across from Roger, who returned to reading the paper. At first, she felt shunned, isolated by the wall of newsprint. Then she chided herself for being self-ish. If he needed solitude now, she could give it to him. She sipped her coffee and watched him read, back home where he belonged.

Finally, he glanced at her. "Sorry about last night."

"I understand. For most of the week, I've been sleeping in Judy's bed. Even so, I had a nightmare last night."

With a look of concern, he laid down his spoon. "About the murder?"

A memory of Enrique's bloody body lying across hers popped unbidden into her mind and she shuddered. "I don't want to talk about it. How did you sleep?"

He folded the paper. "Not well. I had a lot on my mind. Ned told me to come back into the office today. Probably so he can do the equivalent of firing me."

"Don't go, then."

Roger ran his hand through his already mussed hair. "What do you mean, don't go? I can't just blow him off, even if my whole career is flushing down the toilet."

Claire cringed. "I'm sorry."

"Might as well throw myself in the toilet, too." He blinked hard a few times and picked at the newspaper. "I don't have much of a life left. My marriage and career are in shambles." His other hand lay on the table, clenched tight.

She covered the hand with hers and tucked her fingers inside the fist. "I'm here. We'll get through this together."

Roger didn't look convinced.

"Did Ned set a time for you to come in?"

"I assumed he meant at the start of the day." His tone conveyed puzzlement with her question.

"Then wait." Claire got up and paced the kitchen. "I have aerobics class today, so I can find out more about the women who had affairs with Enrique. And Deb should be able to come down from Denver. We three can go see Detective Wilson with the new evidence I've found. She can help us convince him to expand the investigation."

"What new evidence?"

"About Brenda, Patti, Karla, Jill, and Ellen." Claire ticked the names off on her fingertips.

Roger shook his head. "You have suspicions, Claire, not evidence."

"Then I'll dig up more information today." She faced him with her hands on her hips, trying to sound more positive than she felt. "Don't go into the office until after I get home."

"I don't think what you're doing is going to make a whit of—"

"Just wait until I get home." She glanced at the clock. "I've got to hurry if I'm going to make it to class."

She headed for the kitchen door then whirled to face Roger. "Promise?"

Morosely, he shrugged. "Unless Ned calls—"

"No, promise."

"Okay, okay. Go get dressed."

When Claire arrived at Graham's Gym, she caught a glimpse of a young Hispanic woman who looked like Condoleza from the back. The woman was towing a mop bucket into the pool area. As she disappeared through the door, Claire shook her head. *I'm getting paranoid.* Condoleza couldn't work at the gym. Enrique wouldn't have wanted her around.

Claire entered her usual row of lockers and found Ellen and Jill preparing for class. They glanced at her then averted their eyes. Ellen slammed her locker door shut and scooted out of the row, heading for the toilet stalls.

Frowning, Claire stuffed her gym bag into a locker. "Ellen's still miffed at me, I suppose."

With a wounded look in her eyes, Jill peered at Claire. "She told me you think one of the women in the class killed Enrique. She said you even included the two of us on your list. Is that true?"

Claire placed her hand on Jill's arm. "As I told Ellen, the more women I have on the list, the better case I can make to Detective Wilson. He needs to investigate Enrique's life. Then maybe he can find the person who really killed Enrique."

"I can understand you wanting to defend Roger," Jill whispered, with a glance around the crowded locker room, "but how can you accuse Ellen and me of murder? We're your best friends."

Claire sat on the bench and pulled Jill down beside her. She knew what she was about to say was lame, but she hoped her friend would buy it. "I'm not accusing you two of murder. I'm compiling a list of people who had a reason to want Enrique dead. You told me yourself that you didn't miss him."

Jill drew back, her eyes flashing with anger. "That's a long way from wanting to kill him."

"I know. Maybe no one on my list killed him. Maybe it's someone totally different. But the list will show that Enrique had enemies, and those enemies should be checked out."

"Did you even think about the consequences of your actions? Karla's told most everyone what you've been doing. If you thought you were persona non grata before, just see how these women treat you now."

Having to find another gym was a minor sacrifice, thought Claire. "I'll deal with whatever comes," she said. "I'm determined to take this information to the police, no matter what anyone else thinks or whose feelings get hurt. Sorry, Jill, but that's how I feel."

Claire glanced at the clock. She stood. "Class starts in a few minutes. You coming?"

Her expression dark and brooding, Jill bent down to lace her shoes. "You go ahead."

Claire went alone to class and stood in the last row. The room fell silent as the others studiously avoided her gaze or glared at her. The woman next to her wrinkled her nose in distaste and moved to the other end. When Brenda entered, she nodded solemnly at Claire but took a position in the first row.

A moment later, Ellen and Jill walked in and stood beside Claire. Grateful they didn't avoid her, Claire smiled at them. Neither returned the smile. Claire felt like the lowest chicken in the barnyard's pecking order.

During the class, a couple of women bumped her at different times, one almost knocking her off her feet, but neither offered an apology. Claire felt sure the actions were deliberate, but chose not to make an issue of it.

Toward the end of the class, as they stretched their legs, Jill whispered, "What's your next move?"

"I need to talk to Patti, the one with the limp." Claire spied the woman at the other end of the second row. "I want to catch her after class. Do you know anything about her?"

Jill followed Claire's gaze. "No. Why do you need to talk to her? She didn't have an affair with Enrique."

"But she was a customer."

"Customer? What do you mean?"

On the other side of Jill, behind her back, Ellen caught Claire's attention. She pursed her lips and shook her head.

Jill didn't know about Enrique's drug dealing and Ellen didn't want her to know, Claire realized. Maybe Ellen believed that Jill would feel even worse if she knew that Enrique had dealt drugs, too.

Claire glanced at Jill, who waited for an answer. "Enrique was a massage therapist remember?" Awkwardly, Claire looked away as she lifted her arms overhead, avoiding Jill's puzzled gaze.

At the end of class, Claire hurried toward the locker room but got stuck behind two wide, slow-moving chatters. She darted from side to side until she could move around them. She wanted to shower and dress quickly so she could invite Patti to lunch. Claire only hoped she could penetrate the fog of hostility in the class and convince Patti to talk to her.

Once Claire arrived at her locker, she shucked off her shoes and reached for her lock. A sheet of paper folded like an accordion stuck out from one of vents in the top of the door, as if it had been pushed through.

Claire glanced around the locker room.

Karla stood watching, her eyes narrowed in speculation. When Claire caught her gaze, the redhead turned away and grabbed a towel from her locker.

Claire extracted the paper and opened it.

In large type, the note read: STOP SNOOPING AND DON'T TELL THE COPS ABOUT THIS NOTE OR YOU WILL DIE NEXT. I'M WATCHING YOU.

Oh, God. Claire's hands shook. She stared in horror as the sheet dropped to the ground. The room swayed, and she felt as if she was losing her grip on reality, tumbling to her doom like the climber in the Garden of the Gods.

Ellen rounded the corner of the lockers, saw Claire, and stopped. "What?"

Jill peeked around Ellen's shoulder.

"Read that." Claire put her hand against a locker to steady herself and pointed at the note.

Ellen picked up the paper and held it where Jill could see it, too. "Sweet Jesus."

Jill gasped and held a hand to her mouth.

"Where'd this come from?" Ellen asked.

"It was stuck in the top of the door." Claire nodded at her locker. She looked for Karla, but the woman was gone.

Glancing around the locker room, Ellen whispered, "Some woman from the class left this note."

Claire gulped and nodded.

"Not necessarily." Jill crowded in close. "It could have been a staff person who snuck in while we were in class."

A scary thought popped into Claire's mind. *Oh, God. What if that woman I saw was Condoleza?*

"Or someone in Leon's gang," Claire managed to add.

"What are you going to do?" Jill asked.

"Take it to the police, I guess."

A look of horror crossed Jill's face. "You can't do that! Read the note. You'll be killed." She snatched the paper from Ellen and shoved it in front of Claire's nose.

Claire grabbed the note. "But this is proof that Roger's not the killer." And that she was getting close to ferreting out the real murderer.

"And whoever the real murderer is, she or he is after you." Ellen glanced over her shoulder toward the rest of the locker room. "Someone could be watching. If you head for the police, you may not make it."

Jill nodded solemnly. "The risk is very real, Claire."

Claire stared at the paper clutched in her hand. The sounds of women showering, blow-drying their hair, and gossiping swirled around her. Any of them could be the murderer, including one of the two women standing before her, waiting for her decision.

A locker door slammed, the bang not unlike a gunshot.

Claire flinched. Then she shoved the note and the contents of her locker into her gym bag. "I have to think about what I want to do."

As she shrugged on her coat and looped the strap of the gym bag over her shoulder, she pushed from her mind all thoughts of talking to Patti. Survival was paramount now. She grabbed her purse and keys. "I'm leaving."

Ellen and Jill stared at her, then each other.

Jill was the first to recover. "Are you just going to go home?"

"I don't know. Maybe I'll drive around and think awhile, but first I've got to get out of here."

With her mouth set in a grim line, Ellen grabbed her coat. "C'mon, Jill. We'll escort her out. You get behind her on the left, and I'll take the right. Stay close."

Jill hesitated, then threw on her coat and moved next to Claire. "Ready."

Tears sprang to Claire's eyes. Like the climber's buddies who broke his fall, these two were here to support her. "Thanks, guys, but I hate to put you in danger, too."

"We're not the target." Ellen whispered as she pulled Claire toward the locker room door. "You are. Hopefully, having all these witnesses will make the killer think twice. He or she can't shoot everyone in the gym."

"But when we get outside—"

"You have the two of us."

Claire hurried down the hallway, with Ellen and Jill forming a human wall behind her. As they burst through the gym doors into the parking lot at a half trot, Claire's skin crawled. She chided herself for overreacting, but she kept envisioning an unseen gun sight following her progress.

Ellen and Jill each looped an arm in hers and zigzagged through the cars to her BMW, with frequent glances over their shoulders. A stiff winter breeze ruffled their sweat-dampened hair and blasted through their open coats, but neither complained.

By the time they reached her car, Claire's teeth were chattering, from both fear and the February cold.

Ellen looked around as Claire unlocked the car and slid into the driver's seat. "No one followed us."

Jill reached in and squeezed Claire's hand. "Let us know what you decide, please." Her pinched face indicated great concern.

Mutely, Claire nodded.

Ellen peered at her. "And watch your back." She stepped away and closed the car door.

As Claire drove off, she glanced in her rearview mirror. Ellen and Jill stood side by side, their expressions grim as they clutched their coats closed.

Claire put some distance between herself and the gym, switching between I-25 and the city streets. Frequent checks in the rearview mirror assured her that no car followed. Finally, she stopped at a gas station to fill up and call Deb Burch. Deb didn't answer her office phone, so Claire tried Deb's cell phone number.

"I'm glad you called, Claire. I'm on my way down from Denver. I just crested Monument Hill and should see the Air Force Academy soon."

Claire told Deb about the death threat and her dash out of the gym. "I'm scared, but I think I should go to the police. Do you agree?"

"Definitely. You've got to take the note to Detective Wilson right away. This is direct evidence that someone other than

Roger is involved. Plus, the CSPD might be able to pull prints off it."

"Oh, no. Ellen, Jill, and I all touched it."

"Where is it now?"

"In my gym bag."

"Okay. Don't touch it again. Take your bag to Wilson and let him remove the note."

Claire huddled against the car with her back toward the dinging gas pump. The chill wind blowing against her thin, damp leggings made her teeth chatter. "What then? I can't keep driving around the city in my sweaty gym clothes."

"The note could be an empty threat. I'm sure those women at the gym don't want the police finding out they bought drugs from Enrique, or slept with him. The note may not even be from the killer."

"But what if it is?"

"We'll ask the police if they can provide you with some protection."

"Oh, God. Roger's home. The killer may go there looking for me and find him instead."

"Roger's okay. The killer wants to frame him, not kill him. But just in case, tell him to leave the house and meet us downtown at the police station. I should be there in twenty minutes. We can talk to Detective Wilson together. Are you sure no one followed you?"

Claire glanced around the gas station. "I see only one car here, a young mother with two kids in the back seat."

"Good. Sit tight for a few minutes, then head for the station. We should arrive about the same time."

After Claire hung up, she called home. Roger didn't answer. She left a message asking him to call her cell phone.

Apprehensive, she called his work number. "Has Roger come into the office today?" she asked his secretary.

"Not yet. Mr. Peters told me he wanted to see him, though, so I called your house."

"When?"

"About an hour ago. Roger said he'd come right in."

"He must be on his way," Claire said calmly, hiding her dismay. "When he arrives, tell him to call my cell phone before he talks to Mr. Peters. It's vital that I talk to Roger right away."

"I'll tell him."

Claire paced beside the car as she debated whether to drive to Roger's office and stop him at the door. But if the killer had lost her, he or she could be following Roger's car after watching him leave the house. She halted her pacing mid-turn.

She had to warn him! No. Whomever wrote the death threat was after her, not Roger. He'd call her when the secretary gave him the message, wouldn't he? She tried his cell phone but got the message that indicated the phone was turned off.

Where is he?

She climbed in the car, fired up the heater, and pulled out of the gas station.

When her cell phone rang a few minutes later, she grabbed for it, knocking it onto the car floor. Hastily, she pulled over to the side of the road and scooped up the phone. "Hello."

"Claire, it's Deb. I'm at the police station."

"I'm almost there, but I'm worried about Roger. I'm sure he's on his way into the office to talk to his boss. I've left messages everywhere, asking him to call me, but—"

"Leave your cell phone on, but get down here."

"Maybe I should go to Roger's office first."

"Claire, the best way for you to help him is to show the note to the police."

CHAPTER 19
TEAMWORK

As Claire approached the police station, Deb waved from the corner. Her coal-black ponytail tossed in the wind, and her ski jacket was zipped up tight. She walked over as Claire parked her car in the lot across from the station. After Claire had climbed out of the car, Deb gave her a big bear hug, engulfing Claire in the padded jacket.

She reveled in Deb's hug, then stood back to get a good look at her friend. "God, I'm glad to see you. It's been too long."

Deb gazed at her with merry eyes, outlined with laugh lines. "Yes it has. I wish I could've come down earlier, but I'm amazed at the progress you've made without me. You go, girl." Playfully, she punched Claire in the arm.

Flashes of light blue on Deb's hand caught Claire's eye. "Any new rings?"

Deb pointed to a twisted silver ring inlaid with turquoise stones on her middle finger, one of four on that hand. "This one from my sister. And these are from my aunt." She flipped one of the blue beaded earrings dangling from her ears. "Wish I could make 'em myself, but I don't have the patience."

"Your sleuthing talents more than compensate." Claire patted her gym bag. "I've got the note in here."

"Let's move." Deb linked arms with Claire and escorted her across the street.

After they had checked in at the front desk, Claire said to Deb, "I'm not sure what kind of reception we'll get from Detective Wilson. The last time I saw him, he said he hoped he'd never see me or hear from me again. And he doesn't like private investigators mucking around in his cases, as he put it."

Deb patted Claire's arm. "You let me handle Detective Wilson."

As Claire and Deb entered the detectives' bullpen, Wilson stood and glowered at them from behind his desk. Then he forced a polite smile. "Why, if it isn't Mrs. Hanover again. Who did you bring with you?"

Deb stuck out her hand. "Deb Burch, Detective Wilson. I'm a friend of Claire's. She has some important new evidence in her husband's case. Understandably, she felt unsure about your reaction, so I came along to provide moral support."

"I hope this evidence wasn't obtained illegally." Wilson glared down his nose at Claire.

"No." Claire unzipped her gym bag and pointed to the death-threat note inside with a shaky hand. "I found this in my locker at the gym when I left class this morning."

Wilson raised a skeptical eyebrow at Claire, but opened his desk drawer and took out a pair of overlarge tweezers. He extracted the note from the gym bag and sat down to read it.

Deb glanced at Claire and pointed to Wilson's visitor's chair. While Claire sat, Deb pulled over a chair for herself. "Claire's been investigating women at the gym who had affairs or business dealings with Enrique Romero. She thinks this note may have come from one of them."

"Or from Mrs. Hanover herself." He dropped the paper on his desk and stared at Claire. "The basement door story wasn't good enough, so you produced this."

"I did not!"

Deb laid a restraining hand on Claire's arm then craned her neck to look at the death threat. She wet her finger and dabbed her spit on the last word, smearing the ink. "This was printed on an inexpensive ink-jet printer."

Wilson narrowed his eyes. "So?"

Deb turned to Claire. "What kind of printer do you have on your home computer?"

"Laser."

"You can't get the ink to smear like that from a laser printer." Deb crossed her arms and grinned at Wilson.

Claire leaned forward. "Detective Wilson, I wouldn't be stupid enough to make this up, especially after our last meeting. This death threat is real. And there's more."

Wilson rubbed his chin. "Go ahead."

Claire told him about Karla and Ellen's affairs with Enrique, his rebuff of Jill, and Patti, the Hispanic cocaine buyer who limped. She felt as though she was unburdening herself, laying the evidence at Wilson's feet. If he took over her lines of investigation, she could focus on taking care of Roger, stop taking risks, and leave the whole case in Wilson's hands.

He took notes and nodded thoughtfully during her tale. He pulled a plastic bag out of his desk drawer and put the death threat in the bag. As he sealed and labeled the bag, he asked, "Who's touched this?"

"Me, Ellen, and Jill," Claire answered.

Wilson looked at Deb. "And Miss Finger-licker here."

He wrote the four names on the bag. "It probably won't do much good, with all of you handling this, but I'll have the note analyzed for fingerprints. If whoever produced this has any brains, we won't find any prints other than yours."

He peered at Deb. "What's your occupation, Miss Burch?"

Deb pulled out a card and handed it to him.

Wilson read it, pursed his lips, then said to Claire, "So this is your P.I. friend."

Claire sank a little lower in her chair. "Yes."

"I told you, I don't work with private investigators." Glowering, he tossed the card on his desk.

"I'm only here as Claire's friend," Deb said. "I won't interfere in your case."

"Mrs. Hanover has done enough of that herself."

Simmering, Claire said, "Look. I came here even though I knew you'd be angry, because I thought this note was important. And, frankly, it scared me. Can we get back to discussing it instead of past history?"

"As long as you two understand my position."

In a conciliatory tone, Deb said, "We understand. Now, can you reach any conclusions about the note?"

Wilson leaned back in his chair. "I see at least four possibilities. First, that the note is a serious threat from someone ready to carry it out. It could have come from a person at the gym or one of Enrique Romero's gang members."

"Leon's already threatened you, right?" Deb glanced at Claire.

"What's this?" Wilson sat up. Surprise, then worry, crossed his features. "Have you been talking to Romero's drug boss?"

"His bodyguards kidnapped me right in front of the police station after you released me Wednesday night."

"What the hell! What did he do to you, and why don't I know about it?"

Claire told him the story, then finished with, "You said you never wanted to see or hear from me again."

Wilson gritted his teeth. "Maybe I deserved that. But the audacity, right in front of the station." Ruefully, he shook his head.

"I got the impression Leon was providing some service to the police," Claire said. "You mentioned a drug interdiction operation. Leon alluded to it, too."

Agitated, Wilson rubbed his forehead. "That doesn't excuse these kinds of actions. He's gone too far, snatching you and leaving this." He tapped the plastic bag.

Claire shook her head. "Leaving a note isn't his style."

"It's a way of showing he can get to you, even in a women's locker room."

"True," Deb said, frowning at Claire. "Travis or Leon could have coerced one of their customers at the gym into leaving the note."

"Or Condoleza. I saw the back of a cleaning woman who looked like her in the pool area. At the time, I didn't think she could possibly work there, but maybe she does. Or maybe the whole getup with the mop was a disguise."

"I'll check on that." Wilson jotted a note.

"What about the two women who bought drugs?" Deb asked. "Did one of them follow you into class or leave before you?"

Claire thought for a moment. "One came into the classroom after me, and just about everyone made it into the locker room before me."

"Two women?" Wilson glanced down at his notes. "You only mentioned one—"

"I won't name the other woman. Sorry, but I gave her my word. If *you* discover she's the killer during *your* investigation, that's not my fault."

"Claire . . ." Deb looked at Claire's face, then shrugged.

"You said there were four possibilities," Claire said to Wilson. "What are the other three?"

"One of these women on your list could have stashed the note in your locker. Not as a serious threat, but to keep you from coming to me and exposing her sordid relationship with Enrique."

Deb nodded. "Claire and I already discussed that."

"Then, as I already said, the third possibility is you constructed the note to try to save your husband's skin." He glanced at Deb. "Using some computer other than your own."

Claire opened her mouth to speak, but Deb squeezed her arm.

"And fourth, your husband or one of your concerned friends is trying convince you to stop your snooping."

"In the fourth case," Deb added, "that concerned person would have to think Claire was putting herself in danger."

"But not necessarily from a killer on the loose," Wilson said. "She's been meeting with drug dealers, for Christ's sake." He turned to Claire. "Where's your husband been this morning?"

She winced. "I don't know. Roger was at home, but he got a call to come in to the office over an hour ago. I haven't been able to reach him." She glanced at the cell phone in her hand. "I'm worried about him."

Wilson quirked an eyebrow. "Why?"

"I told him to wait before talking to his boss. I wanted to find more evidence that someone else killed Enrique first, to prevent his boss from putting him on long-term leave, which is the same as firing him. But I'm afraid he may be talking to his boss right now. Or he's already been told not to return to work.

"I'm also afraid that whomever wrote the note could have gone to our house, looking for me, and . . ." Claire choked on the lump in her throat and couldn't continue.

Deb handed Claire a tissue. "Detective Wilson, I know Claire very well. We go all the way back to college, and I can swear on the Bible that she would not fabricate this note."

"I'll decide that for myself."

Deb leaned toward Wilson. "Even if you keep open the possibility that her husband or a friend wrote the note, if Mr. Romero's killer wrote it, then Claire's life is in danger. She needs protection." Deb pulled out her wallet, opened it, and handed Wilson a folded paper. "I've got a concealed weapons permit and training in defensive techniques. If you can't assign anyone to protect Claire, I'll do it."

Wilson whistled. "A baby Glock. I'm sure you paid a bundle for that." He handed the permit to Deb then addressed Claire. "Where do you plan to go from here?"

"Roger's office."

"I'll check out these women from the gym this afternoon, and contact you if I find out anything. In the meantime, you'll cover her?" He looked at Deb.

"That was my plan."

Wilson tapped his pencil on his notepad. "As we discussed, a lot of people could've planted the death threat, Mrs. Hanover. What I'm getting at is, you should tell no one, not even your husband, that you brought it to me."

"Okay."

"I suggest you go home and lock the doors. Don't do anything stupid."

After Claire had unlocked her car, Deb plopped into the passenger seat. "That went well."

"C'mon. He nearly ripped my head off when we walked in, then he accused me or Roger of fabricating the death threat."

"Just what I expected him to do." Deb smiled. "But he reopened the case, didn't he? He's going to investigate the women at the gym. We couldn't ask for more."

"I suppose." Claire still felt like grumbling. "I didn't like his last comment, though. Does he really expect me to do something stupid?"

Deb laughed. "Last time he saw you, you'd just been pulled out from under a drug dealer's bed."

Claire grinned sheepishly. "I've got to admit that was stupid."

She drove out of the lot, leaving Deb's car there for the time being, and headed for Roger's office building. After a short elevator ride, she strode through the subdued, gray-and-maroon lobby of the corporate suite with Deb in tow. Without hesitation

Claire walked straight to the secretary's desk outside Roger's office. "Is Roger in?"

"Oh, hello, Mrs. Hanover." The secretary's eyes widened in surprise. "Roger came in a while ago, met with Ned, then left."

Claire's heart sank. "When did he leave?"

"About an hour ago."

"Did he indicate how the meeting with Ned went?"

The secretary shook her head. "Roger didn't come back to his office after the meeting, just left the building."

Claire took out her cell phone and tried calling Roger's cell phone and their home phone, again with no luck. Desperately, she wracked her brain, trying to figure out where he might have gone, but an image of Roger's agonized face clouded her thinking. She shook her head to clear it.

"Is Ned in?" she asked the secretary.

"He left for a lunch meeting right after he talked to Roger."

"So no one can tell me what went on during their meeting."

The secretary pursed her lips. "Sorry."

"I bet Roger's on his way home," Deb said. "Why don't we head there ourselves?"

Claire drove to her house, her stomach in a knot over what Roger must be going through. She felt even worse when she opened the garage door. His car wasn't there. "Where is he?"

"Let's have some lunch while we wait for him," Deb said. "But first, I'm going to check the perimeter."

Claire looked at her watch. One-fifteen. With her stomach in knots, she didn't think she could eat anything, but realized Deb probably felt hungry.

Deb returned. "Nothing. You have a security system, right?"

Claire pointed to the box by the door into the house. The light showed it was still armed and un-tripped.

"Good," Deb said. "We can assume whomever threatened you isn't here."

Claire disarmed the security system, pointed Deb toward the kitchen, and quickly changed out of her gym clothes into a pair of jeans and a sweatshirt. When she returned, Deb had placed sandwich fixings on the counter.

As Deb spread mayonnaise on a slice of rye bread, she said, "Let's review the suspects from the gym. It'll help keep your mind off Roger, and we might discover something useful." She put down the bread and pulled a PDA out of her pocket. "Give me the names again."

"Sure. Brenda Johnston, Karla Deavers, Patti . . . I don't know her last name . . . and my friends, Jill Edstrom and Ellen Kessler."

"Your evidence against Patti is pretty thin." Deb's rings flashed as she typed the names, then she put the PDA aside to stack ham and Swiss on the bread. "You just suspect she bought cocaine from Enrique, and she happens to be Hispanic."

"Karla said Patti had an affair with Enrique, but Ellen said she didn't."

"We need confirmation of her buying drugs, and her affair."

Too anxious to sit, Claire paced the kitchen. "I planned to talk to Patti today, but then I found the death threat in my locker's vent."

"We'll get back to her." Deb typed a note into the PDA. "Now, Brenda's situation is interesting. I've never known a drug dealer to lend money to his clients before. Could Karla have made up the story?"

"I could be wrong, but my impression is that she'd pass on gossip, maybe even embellish it a little, but she wouldn't outright lie."

Deb bit into her sandwich and chewed slowly. "Karla's an interesting character. Apparently she and Ellen had this competitive thing going."

"And they kept contradicting each other. Each said she ended her affair with Enrique and that Enrique ended it with the other one." Claire held out her hands, palms up. "I don't know who to believe."

Deb licked her fingers then tapped the PDA. "We need another source, someone who may know about Enrique's affairs but doesn't have a personal interest. Also, someone who can confirm this loan to Brenda. I'm thinking Leon."

Claire shook her head. "That's not a good idea. Remember the warning he gave me last time we talked?"

"If he's an informant, maybe Wilson can ask him these questions. Let's move on to Jill and Ellen. Since they're your friends, you probably don't think they're capable of murder. Right?"

"Right." An image of Ellen, with feet planted in a wide stance and hands clutching a pistol, floated into her mind. *No, no, it couldn't be.*

Deb wiped her mouth with a napkin. "So you could've missed some clue about one of them. As I remember, Ellen gave you the coupon for the massage from Enrique, conveniently setting up the rendezvous. She also gave herself an alibi by claiming she and Jill were having lunch together when Enrique was killed. Did Jill confirm that?"

Claire reviewed her recent conversations with Jill in her mind. "I don't think she did."

Deb reached for the phone book. "Where did Ellen say they ate lunch?"

"The Broadmoor Hotel."

"Which one of their restaurants?"

"She didn't say, but it wasn't Charles Court, because it's only open for dinner, and the Lake Terrace only serves breakfast and brunch. And they wouldn't have gone in the Tavern or the Golden Bee Pub."

"What about the Golf Club dining rooms?"

"Maybe, but Ellen likes Café Julie best for lunches. I bet

they ate there."

"And with the Broadmoor being a fancy-schmancy five-star resort, I bet they made a reservation." Deb flipped through the phone book then punched a number into the phone.

She winked at Claire. "Hello, my name is Ellen Kessler. I need to verify a charge on my credit card, and my memory is getting so bad. Do you have a reservation for lunch at one of your restaurants on . . ." She gave the date Enrique had been shot. "It would be under my name or my friend, Jill Edstrom."

Deb waited a moment, then said, "Thank you very much. You've been so helpful. I'm sure I'll be back again." She hung up the phone and rubbed her hands together. "Interesting."

"What?"

"They didn't eat at Café Julie. They were at the Lake Terrace."

"But—"

"Their reservation was at ten-thirty, for brunch, not lunch."

Claire stared at Deb as a sudden chill pimpled her arms. "Ohmigod. That means—"

"They weren't lunching together when Enrique was murdered." Deb crossed her arms and leaned back on her stool.

Horrified, Claire tried to resist the possibility worming into her mind that one of her friends hated Enrique enough to kill him.

"So one of them could have high-tailed it over here and shot Enrique," Deb continued. "And with Ellen setting up the massage, she's my number-one suspect."

Claire pictured the murder weapon. "But she would have to have known he carried a gun."

"Good thinking." Deb swallowed the last bite of her sandwich. "If I was the killer, I'd bring my own gun to do the job. But if I saw Enrique's gym bag in your hall and knew he kept his gun there, I'd use his instead. Then the cops couldn't trace the ballistics to my gun and me."

Claire shuddered. "That's cold-blooded."

"Just smart. Look, you've already talked to Ellen about the lunch meeting." Deb stood. "I think a pow-wow with Jill is in order."

"But what about Roger?" Reluctantly, Claire rose to put away the lunch fixings.

"Leave him a note to call your cell phone when he gets home." Deb shrugged on her coat.

"I should phone Jill to tell her we're coming."

"Surprising her is better. She won't be able to prepare. She could very well have been in on the plot with Ellen."

CHAPTER 20
NOTHING STUPID

On the way to Jill's house, Deb laid out a plan. Claire was to do most of the talking while Deb observed Jill's body language. She briefed Claire on the questions to ask.

Slick with sweat, Claire's hands slipped on the steering wheel as she turned onto Jill's street. "I'm really nervous."

"Don't worry." Deb patted the pistol hidden under her jacket. "I'm prepared if Jill comes after you."

That wasn't exactly what Claire had been worrying about, but she added it to her growing list of anxieties.

She pulled into Jill's driveway under the ice-cold shadow of a towering blue spruce, and cut the engine.

Deb gave her a thumbs-up. "Let's go."

With Deb following, Claire walked to Jill's porch and rang the doorbell. They waited, with their breaths puffing little clouds.

The door opened, but the woman standing in the hallway wasn't Jill.

Claire clutched her chest and gasped. "Condoleza."

Condoleza's eyes widened, then narrowed in fury. "You! Why are you here?"

"I could ask you the same question."

"I work here."

Thoroughly confused, Claire blinked, hoping to clear her whirling brain. "Doing what?"

"Mrs. Edstrom is one of my cleaning customers. Why did you follow me here? I thought Leon told you to buzz off." She dismissed Claire and Deb with her hand.

"We're not going anywhere," Deb said.

Claire tried to make sense of the situation. "I didn't follow you here. I'm a friend of Jill's. I came to see her, not you."

Deb peered at Condoleza. "Is she Enrique's—"

"Shush." Condoleza glanced over her shoulder. "Don't say anything to Mrs. Edstrom about me and Enrique."

"How did you wind up working for Jill?" Claire asked.

"When Enrique heard her tell someone she needed a new cleaning woman, he asked another lady at the gym whose house I clean to recommend me."

Claire remembered the worker she'd spotted at the gym. "Do you clean at the gym, too?"

Condoleza looked puzzled. "No. Why do you ask that?"

Staring at the woman, Claire wondered if Condoleza was lying. Or maybe she'd only visited the gym to plant the death threat, and the mop bucket was a prop. "I just—"

"Condoleza? Who's at the door?" Jill's voice came down the hall, followed soon after by footsteps clunking on the hardwood floor.

"A lady says she's a friend of yours," Condoleza shouted back.

"Why the big secret about you and Enrique?" Deb asked.

Condoleza glanced down the hall, fists clenched, then whispered, "She would not like it. I need this job. If you make me lose it, I'll go to Leon."

Claire turned to Deb.

With eyebrows raised, Deb shrugged.

Jill arrived at the door. "Claire, what a surprise. I assumed you'd be holed up in your house after"—she shot a curious glance at Deb—"you know, what happened at the gym."

"I'd just drive myself crazy with worry at home."

"Did you go to the police?"

"Claire's been with me since she left the gym," Deb said before Claire could reply. "I called to tell her I was in town and got the whole story."

"I'm sorry," Claire said. "I should have introduced you two. Jill, this is Deb Burch. We roomed together in college. She's down here from Denver. I thought I'd bring her around to meet you."

"It's not a great time, since Condoleza's in the middle of . . ." Jill looked at Condoleza, who stood wringing her hands. "What's wrong?"

Condoleza backed away. "Nothing. Nothing at all. I will finish the kitchen." She scurried down the hall.

With a puzzled frown, Jill watched her go. "What got into her? I'm sorry. I was going to introduce you. She's my cleaning lady."

"We've met," Claire said. *Damn.*

"When?"

"Just now at the door," Deb said as she sidled past Claire into the hallway and looked around. "Claire told me about your beautiful home, Jill. I really like the frame around this mirror. Hand-tooled, isn't it?"

"Thanks. An artist in Manitou Springs made it."

Deb traced a finger along the carved wood. "I'd love to see what you've done with the rest of the house. Can I get a tour?"

"All of Condoleza's stuff is out right now. Perhaps another time."

"But I won't be in town for long." Deb patted Jill's arm. "Don't worry. I'll ignore the cleaning supplies and look at your decorating. I really like this wallpaper." She walked farther down the hall.

With a reluctant sigh, Jill held the door open for Claire.

"Thanks." Claire stepped inside. "It was getting chilly out there."

Jill led them through the main floor of her house.

Deb kept up a running commentary. When they reached the dining room, a large pot with black-and-white geometric designs sat on the sideboard. As she stepped closer to examine it, she said, "This is a lovely example of a Ute Corn Ceremonial pot."

"Yes. I bought it at the Pow Wow three years ago."

"Excellent workmanship. Probably made by one of the Cloud sisters." Deb reached to pick up the pot. "May I?"

Jill nodded.

After turning the pot over to study the bottom, Deb carefully replaced it. "I was right. It's signed by Beverly Cloud. You have good taste."

Jill glowed with pride. "How do you know so much—"

"Deb's a Ute Indian herself." Claire could see that Deb's magic was working on Jill.

When they entered the kitchen, lemon wax and ammonia fumes permeated the air. Condoleza swept up her cleaning supplies and trotted upstairs.

"I don't know what's gotten into her," Jill said. "It's like you two have the plague."

"Has she been here all day?"

"Since I got back from the gym." Jill's brows knitted together. "What's that got to do with how she's reacting?"

So Condoleza could have been at the gym this morning. Claire tried to shrug off the question. "I thought she may have been tired and our visit was an added bother to her."

Deb said, "Could I trouble you for a glass of water?"

When Jill went to the cupboard, Deb signaled Claire to sit at the kitchen counter then joined her. After sipping her water, Deb said, "Jill, Claire tells me you're quite a connoisseur of the local restaurants. I'd like to take Claire and Roger out for brunch tomorrow before I leave. What do you think of the Broadmoor?"

"You can't beat the Lake Terrace for brunch, especially the Sunday buffet." Jill licked her lips. "I love their crepes. You can choose any of a dozen fillings, like blueberries, whipped cream cheese, or even chocolate chips."

"When was the last time you ate brunch there?"

"Last week with Ellen."

"Is the service quick? I have to get on the road pretty early in the afternoon."

"The service at the Broadmoor is always impeccable."

"Give me an idea," Deb said. "How long were you and Ellen there?"

Jill shrugged. "We probably finished eating in an hour, but we stayed and talked awhile."

"They didn't try to rush you out of there after you paid?"

"Heavens no. We only chatted a few minutes, anyway."

"That should work out great. We'll have a nice brunch, and I won't be late starting my trip home to Denver." Deb raised her water glass. "Thanks for the tip."

"You're welcome." Jill scratched her head, as if confused.

Not wanting Jill to draw any conclusions from Deb's questions, Claire groped for a new topic. "I'm grateful Deb's here, because she can provide me with some protection."

"Because of the death threat, you mean?"

Claire nodded.

"How can Deb protect you?"

"She's a private investigator, so she has a concealed weapons permit and is a crack shot."

Deb pulled aside her jacket, exposing the semiautomatic pistol in its worn leather case attached to her belt.

Jill's eyes widened, and she took a step back.

"Lots of people carry concealed these days, especially in Colorado Springs." Deb let her coat fall back in place. "You'd be surprised at the number of people who've applied for permits. You ever know anyone to carry a gun?"

Jill shook her head.

"The police told me Enrique owned a gun," Claire added, watching Jill closely. "That's what was used to shoot him."

"Really?" Jill seemed genuinely surprised. "How did Roger get Enrique's gun?"

"He found it on the floor of our hall."

"So Enrique dropped his gun there?"

"No, the killer did, after he or she shot Enrique. Then Roger picked it up when he heard me screaming and came upstairs to investigate." Claire glanced at Deb.

Nonchalantly sipping her glass of water, Deb kept her gaze focused on Jill's face.

Jill looked distressed. "I admire your loyalty to Roger, Claire, but you have to consider the possibility his story is just that. A story." She glanced at Deb, as if for support.

Deb remained mute.

Jill returned her gaze to Claire. "I think this death threat is a sure sign you need to stop and let the police handle things their way. I don't want you to get hurt."

Deb put down her glass and stood.

"Thanks for your concern, Jill." Understanding Deb's signal, Claire gathered up her purse. "We need to get going. I'm glad you two could meet."

Deb held out a hand to Jill. "I loved seeing your house, and thanks for the brunch recommendation."

Looking distracted, Jill shook Deb's hand. "You're welcome." She followed them to the door and let them out.

As Claire walked with Deb to the car, she waved to Jill.

Before Jill shut the door, a thoughtful expression passed over her face, as if she were trying to puzzle out what this visit had been about. Claire replayed the visit in her own mind. "Jill seemed to be telling the truth."

Deb opened the passenger-side car door. "Either that, or she's a better actress than you."

"I'm not sure about Condoleza, though. I thought I saw her at the gym this morning."

"She *was* awfully jumpy."

As she slid onto her seat, Claire saw a light blinking on the cell phone lying between the two front seats. "Damn, I forgot to bring my phone inside. I hope that message's from Roger." She punched the right buttons and held the phone to her ear, almost afraid to listen.

Roger's voice was listless, flat. "The spineless bastard did it. Might as well have fired me. Didn't have the faith in me to stand up to the board." Suddenly, the phone went silent.

Oh, God. Claire put her hand to her mouth and stared out the window, fighting tears. She felt Deb's hand on her shoulder.

"Was it Roger?"

"He sounded terrible."

Deb squeezed Claire's shoulder then reached for her seat belt. "Let's return to your house. If he's not there, we'll set a plan in motion to find him."

Half-blinded by unshed tears, Claire started the car and backed out of Jill's driveway.

After leaving Jill's house, Claire headed north. She planned to take the shortcut through the tourist haven of historic Old Colorado City on her way home. A black limousine passed her then pulled into her lane a couple of cars ahead before the traffic stopped for a red light.

"That looks like Leon's limo," Claire said.

Deb leaned forward. "Follow it. If it's him, we can ask him the questions we came up with earlier."

Claire stared at Deb. "Are you crazy?"

Deb stayed focused on the limousine. "Nope. Opportunistic.

I never pass up a chance to find out something about a case. And if that's Leon, this opportunity just dropped in our lap."

"But I want to find Roger, not talk to Leon."

"I'll ring your house to see if Roger's there." Deb picked up Claire's cell phone, punched in the number, and waited. After a long pause, she hung up. "No answer. We'll keep this with us. When Roger gets home and sees your note, he'll call."

Claire wasn't so sure, but she couldn't talk to him if she had no idea where he was.

The light turned green. Claire hesitated.

"Follow that limo and step on it." Deb chuckled. "I've always wanted to say that."

"This is serious." Claire didn't see anything funny in the situation. "And it sure fits the definition of doing something stupid." She prayed the limousine belonged to someone else.

Deb shook her head. "In my book, this is a smart move. Remember, we have questions for Leon."

Claire followed the long, black car onto Colorado Avenue. An eclectic mix of eateries, antique shops, art galleries, clothing boutiques, and Colorado souvenir shops lined the now-quiet street, awaiting the summer vacation crowds. Normally Claire would pop into the Rocky Mountain Chocolate Factory for sinfully rich truffles, or La Baguette for a fresh loaf of crusty French bread, but she was on a mission now. The limousine turned onto a side street and stopped in the parking lot behind a southern-style barbecue restaurant.

Claire parked her car on the other side of the lot.

As Deb put her hand on the door latch, Claire said, "I wouldn't do that. If Leon is in the limo, I bet they know we've been following them. And they won't let us approach until we've been frisked."

"Gee, I haven't had a date in awhile." Deb cracked a smile, then grew serious. "But if they frisk us, they'll find my gun."

"Why don't you put it in the glove compartment?"

"But then you won't have any protection. Leon could have been the one who wrote the death threat. Do you trust this guy?"

"In an odd way, I guess I do. He's the one who told me to investigate the gym ladies. And he cleared Travis and Condoleza."

Deb looked skeptical. "He could be covering for them."

"I don't think so. He wouldn't have waited so long to tell me if that's the case. He's got a different set of morals, but he seems to stick by them."

One of the limousine's doors opened and a large, bald-headed white man stepped out.

Claire grabbed Deb's arm. "That's Leon's bodyguard. I recognize him. Hide the gun."

"I hope I can trust your judgment." Deb unclipped the leather gun case from her belt and slipped it under her seat.

"Don't worry. If someone comes after me, Leon's driver and bodyguard are armed."

"That's what I'm afraid of." Deb shifted in her seat to get a better look at the approaching man crunching across the icy parking lot. "I suppose we just wait for him to come to us?"

"That's right." When the bodyguard was close enough, Claire rolled down her window. "Hello. I'd like to talk to Leon again."

The bodyguard leaned over and peered through the car window at Deb. "Who are you?"

Deb pulled out her wallet, extracted a card, and handed it to him. "Deb Burch, an old friend of Claire's and a P.I. I'm helping with her investigation."

He read the card. "Stay here." He crunched back to the limousine.

Claire chewed her lip as she wondered what Leon's reaction would be to Deb's occupation.

The bodyguard handed the card through the back window of the limousine, said a few words, nodded, then returned. "Mr. Leon has asked you to join him in the restaurant."

Claire exhaled in relief.

"You know the drill."

Claire stepped out of the car and placed her hands on the hood.

With a raised eyebrow, Deb assumed the same position on the opposite side of the car.

The bodyguard frisked the two women, checked Claire's purse, then said to Deb, "Where's your purse?"

"I don't carry one. Just my wallet." She held it up then stashed it back in her coat pocket.

"Walk on over to the restaurant."

Claire and Deb preceded the bodyguard, stepping gingerly over frozen puddles on the asphalt. When they passed the limousine, the solemn driver nodded at Claire.

The bodyguard directed them through the restaurant's back door. The tantalizing odors of fried chicken and wood-smoked pork surged through the open kitchen door. The guard pointed left into a small private dining room.

A couple of tables-for-two lined the far wall. In the middle stood a round table for six, covered with a plastic, red-checked tablecloth. Deb took a seat facing the door, and Claire sat next to her.

Trailing a cloud of cigarette smoke, Leon entered the room with an arm around the hostess. When the chubby, gray-haired woman whispered the punch line for some joke, Leon guffawed. He dismissed the hostess with a friendly pat on the rear and walked over to the table. "Mrs. Hanover, we meet again." He held out his hand.

Claire shook it. "This is my friend, Deb Burch."

Leon grinned, showing polished white teeth. "Nice to

meetcha', Miss Burch. It's not every day I get to meet an Indian P.I." He shot a look at his two men, who laughed obediently.

Leon studied Deb. "I can see you don't like your back to the door, just like me, but this is my table, so I'll have to ask you to move." He pulled out a chair on the opposite side, with its back facing the door.

Deb stood and changed her seat.

Claire rose to do the same.

Leon waved his hand. "You can sit next to me, Mrs. Hanover." He walked around the table and took Deb's original seat.

The bodyguard and driver sat at one of the tables-for-two, where they had a good view of the door.

When the server brought water, Leon said, "The usual," then turned to Claire. "What did you want to ask me?"

She waited for the server to leave. "First, do you know where Condoleza was this morning?"

Leon shook his head. "I ain't that woman's keeper."

Claire decided to change the subject. "I followed your advice and have been investigating the women at the gym. Deb and I have some questions, and we thought of you. I mean, we thought maybe you could answer them. The questions, I mean."

Leon smiled at her obvious edginess, then inclined his head, indicating she could proceed.

Claire glanced at Deb for support. "First, there's Brenda, a tall brunette in her thirties."

Leon nodded. "Cool bitch. Always smart-looking."

"I know she owed Enrique thousands of dollars and was making weekly payments, but I don't know the exact amount or if she had trouble coming up with the money."

Leon leaned back and puffed on his cigarette. "You think she knocked off Enrique so she wouldn't have to pay off the loan?"

Claire spread her hands wide. "Maybe."

Leon shook his head. "Enrique didn't have the cash to loan her. He couldn't hold onto more than a couple hundred at a time. Always spending to impress the ladies."

"Then why was he asking for payment?"

"He was working for me in another capacity. See, I run a little personal financing business on the side. The lady owed that money to me." He pointed to his chest. "And she knew it."

"Maybe she thought by killing him—"

"Don't make no sense for her to kill Enrique. She's owed me before and paid it off. Besides, she's made a payment since Enrique was shot. Travis is collecting on that loan now." Leon nudged Claire. "One of your favorite people, Mrs. Hanover."

Claire smiled, relaxing a little. "I found out that another woman bought drugs—"

"Ah, ah, ah." Leon wagged his finger at her. "We don't use that word. Products. My business is selling products to people who need 'em."

"Right. Products." Inwardly, Claire cringed. "The woman's first name is Patti. She's Hispanic and has a limp. I don't know her last name."

"I do."

Claire waited, then realized Leon wasn't going to offer the name. "At first, I assumed she owed Enrique money, like Brenda, but that doesn't seem to be a strong enough motive now. Do you know if either Patti or Brenda had another reason to kill Enrique?"

Leon thought for a moment, but as he started to speak, the hostess returned with a helper. Both carried steaming trays laden with barbecued ribs, corn on the cob, biscuits, and coleslaw. Leon waited for the bustling women to place the food on the table, then waved at the platters. "Help yourself."

He grabbed a rib and ripped off a huge bite. His lips curled in contentment. "Best ribs west of Louisiana. Go on, have some."

Claire took a rib. "I thought you were on a diet, Leon."

He laughed. "Sure am, but I can't never resist these. I'll skip dessert."

Claire ate a bite of her rib and swiped at barbecue sauce dribbling down her chin. Her stomach grumbled, and she remembered she hadn't eaten lunch. "These are delicious."

"Tell your friends. I got a little investment in this place." Leon took another bite then dropped the rib on his plate and wiped his mouth. "Now, to answer your question, I don't know why either of those ladies would have a problem with Enrique. That's what I like about those gym lady customers. No problems."

"Who else at the gym bought 'products' from Enrique?" Deb asked.

"So the P.I.'s got a tongue." Leon turned to Claire. "Seems you're doing all the work."

Deb winked at Claire. "I said pretty much the same thing. I told her she had a lot of chutzpah to see you the first time, and she should come work for me."

Leon stabbed a thumb in Claire's direction and laughed. "Yup, this lady's got balls."

Claire blushed.

"Back to my question," Deb said.

Leon took a bite of biscuit and swiped flaky crumbs from his fingers. "I ain't telling you who all my customers are, but I will tell you this. We checked 'em all out ourselves, and we'd sure be surprised if one of them shot Enrique. Now, a lovers' spat, that's different. You know, a woman scorned?"

Deb looked at Claire. "He's got a point."

"Did Patti have an affair with Enrique?" Claire asked.

Leon shook his head. "Enrique liked to boast about his ladies.

He didn't mention her." He winked. "Last one he told me about was you. Said he thought you'd be next."

Claire grimaced and rubbed her forehead.

A loud gasp at the doorway made her look up.

Condoleza stood with eyes blazing and a wavering finger pointed at Claire. "What's *she* doing here?"

CHAPTER 21
FAILURE AND REDEMPTION

"The lady's lunching with me, Leza. Join us." Leon smiled and waved toward the empty chair on his left.

Still pointing at Claire, Condoleza marched to the table. "She made me lose a customer."

Claire hadn't had time to recover from the shock of Condoleza's appearance when this new surprise hit. "Jill fired you?"

"Mrs. Edstrom told me to leave and not come back."

"I'm sorry, Condoleza. We didn't say anything to Jill about you. I don't know why she did that."

Still standing, a red-faced Condoleza faced Leon. "She's lying."

Leon patted his mouth with his napkin. "No, she's not."

"What?" Condoleza stamped her foot. "You take her side over mine? I don't believe this."

Leon grabbed her wrist. "Sit, Leza. I'm not siding with her. I just know she ain't any good at lying."

Open-mouthed, Condoleza dropped into the chair next to Leon.

He draped an arm around her shoulders. "Calm down, and tell me the story."

"After they left, Mrs. Edstrom said she knew the whole story, and I better tell my side. I told her I never said anything bad about her to Enrique. It wasn't my fault he turned her down. That's when she yelled *vete!*"

Leon raised an eyebrow at Claire.

Claire shook her head. "We didn't say a word to Jill about Condoleza's relationship with Enrique."

Deb leaned forward. "Condoleza, you got real jumpy when we showed up at Mrs. Edstrom's. She probably noticed, even though we tried to distract her. She fooled you. She made you think she knew something, and you incriminated yourself."

A tear ran down Condoleza's cheek. Chin quivering, she whispered, "I am not a fool."

Leon handed her a paper napkin. " 'Course not."

Claire's heart went out to the young woman, but Claire also sympathized with Jill. "I can understand why Jill would be mad. She was very hurt when Enrique refused her advances. Did she pay you for your work today?" Claire reached for her purse.

Condoleza blew her nose in the napkin and shook her head.

Leon stayed Claire's hand and pulled a roll of bills out of his jacket pocket. He peeled off two hundreds and pressed them into Condoleza's hand. "You're better off without that Edstrom lady."

He signaled his bodyguard. "Take Claire and her friend to their car while I calm Leza here."

Claire rose to leave. "Again, I'm sorry, Condoleza. If I can do anything . . ."

Leon shook his head and pulled Condoleza to his side. "Your business is done here today."

Back at the car, Deb gazed speculatively at the restaurant. "Leon's awfully protective of Condoleza. I wonder . . ."

Claire unlocked the car doors. "Wonder what?"

"He's the one who provided an alibi for Condoleza. Maybe that was to protect her, too. Or, if Enrique Romero hurt Condoleza somehow, maybe Leon or one of his goons knocked him off."

"But why would they kill him in my bedroom?"

"Leon's smart. By setting it up to look like Roger caught you two in the act, Enrique's drug dealings aren't relevant to the investigation, so the police stay out of Leon's business."

After sliding into her seat, Claire waited for Deb to do the same. "If Leon had Enrique killed, why is he being so helpful to me?"

"To stay informed. To keep track of what you and the police are doing. When he realizes you won't give up and go away, he has Condoleza plant the death threat."

"I see what you mean, but I feel like I'm going backward. Instead of narrowing the list of suspects, we're widening it."

Deb patted her hand. "Don't worry. Anytime we find out more information, we're making progress, even if we don't know yet how it all fits together."

Claire checked her watch. "Right now I'm worried more about Roger. It's after three, and I still haven't heard from him."

"Back to your house, then. That's the most likely place we'll find him."

Roger was severely depressed, and Ned telling him not to come back to work could push him over the edge of some cliff. But Claire didn't voice her private fears, afraid Deb would think she was overreacting. Claire chewed on her lip as she drove home.

When they arrived, she cut the engine and leapt out of her car. Roger's car wasn't in the garage, but the security system was off. Maybe he'd gotten drunk and someone had brought him home. Despite's Deb's warning that she wanted to check out the house first, Claire ran inside. When she didn't see Roger in the kitchen or living room, she ran upstairs and searched the bedrooms.

Breathless, she returned to the front hall, where Deb stood waiting. Claire couldn't keep the fear out of her voice. "He's not here." A sob caught in her throat.

Deb hugged her. "I'm sure he'll turn up."

"You haven't seen how depressed he's been." Tears welled out of Claire's eyes. Ashamed of her lack of control, she walked to the kitchen to get a tissue.

Deb followed.

Claire blew her nose and wiped her eyes.

The front door flew open with a crash.

Roger stumbled in.

"Oh, God." Relief washing over her, Claire ran to him and threw her arms around him. He reeked of cigarette smoke. "I've been so worried. Where have you been?"

"Had shom drinks at Cleat's."

The peaty tang of scotch assaulted Claire's nose. She pulled back and looked at Roger's bloodshot and unfocused eyes. "You went there after talking to Ned?"

"Yesh." Roger spread his hands apart. "I'm kaput. Finished. All washed up."

Defeat thudded in the pit of Claire's stomach. She reached up to smooth Roger's ruffled hair, aching with the need to comfort him. "Why'd you go to the office? You promised you'd wait."

"He told me to. Can't say no to the bossh."

"Why didn't you call me?"

Roger looked irritated. "I *did* call you, right after Ned called me. You didn't answer."

"That must have been when I was in aerobics class. Why didn't you leave a message or call after you got to the office? I told your secretary to have you call me."

"No time. Ned was waiting. I left a message later, though."

"That message scared me." Claire glanced behind her.

Deb stood in the kitchen doorway, sympathy showing in her eyes.

Claire faced Roger again. "Deb and I found out a few things

that could help prove—"

"Too late. Too late." Roger waved his hand as if swatting at a pesky fly. The movement threw him off balance. He stepped forward, stumbling against Claire.

"You need to sleep this off. Let's get you upstairs." She led Roger to the staircase. With one arm around him and the other bracing against the rail, she guided him up the steps, into the master bedroom, and onto the bed.

By the time she removed his shoes, he was snoring.

She covered him with an afghan. In repose, the lines in his face faded, reminding her of his younger self, the one she couldn't keep her hands off of. She smiled as she remembered when they had first locked eyes at a fraternity party at the University of Colorado. She, the shy freshman, planning to major in French and fine arts, fell hard for the outgoing business major in his last year, whose wind-tousled hair smelled of the freshly mown grass of the rugby field.

Amazingly, he fell for her, too.

She caressed his cheek. She'd seen Roger eyeing his middle-aged paunch in the mirror with a dissatisfied frown. But he didn't see his backside, which was firm and dimpled and made her gut clench. She whispered, "Honey, you still turn me on," kissed him gently on the forehead, then backed out of the room.

She leaned against the wall and sniffed back tears. She'd failed him. Utterly. Because of her, he lost his job, and his self-esteem along with it. And soon he might lose his freedom. With shoulders slumped in defeat, she walked downstairs and into the kitchen.

Deb looked up from her PDA. "Is he going to be okay?"

"Yes. I'm relieved he made it home in one piece, but . . ." The lump in her throat was too large to continue. Claire sat on a stool, leaned her elbows on the counter, and held her throbbing head. She took a moment to compose herself, then looked at Deb. "I've failed him."

"The fat lady hasn't sung yet. Don't give up." Deb poured a cup of coffee and handed it to Claire. "Here. I made us some coffee."

Claire rubbed her forehead and took a sip. "All my sleuthing was for nothing."

"There's still hope. If we can prove Roger's innocence, maybe his boss can be convinced to take him back."

"I doubt Ned wants us to be associated with the firm anymore. We're too scandalous." Bitter resentment lashed Claire. At the injustice of Roger's situation and, especially, the futility of her own actions. "Damn, I feel so powerless."

"Maybe you're pushing yourself too hard." Deb's brow furrowed.

Maybe it was time to let the professionals take over, Claire thought. It wouldn't be hard for Detective Wilson and Deb to do a better job than she had so far.

The doorbell rang.

Detective Wilson stood on the stoop, along with another man. The short, scruffy-haired guy didn't look like a cop, not even a plainclothes cop trying to look like an easy mark. Wilson waved his hand at the man. "This taxi driver is looking to get paid."

Confused, Claire stared at Wilson. "You rode here in a taxi and want me to pay?"

Wilson rolled his eyes. "Apparently, he dropped off someone else. Said a bartender from Cleat's called him."

"Oh, Roger. He probably used up his cash at the bar. I'll get my purse." Claire paid the driver and led Wilson to the kitchen.

He took a stool. "I came by to discuss the results of my investigations. Also, I've arranged for the patrol officer in your area to drive by as often as he can. So, have you been sitting tight here since we talked?"

"Not quite." Claire glanced at Deb, who grinned.

Wilson frowned. "I thought I told you not to do anything stupid."

Deb pushed a mug of coffee across the counter at Wilson. "She didn't. Don't get your shorts in a bind."

Wilson glowered at Deb. "And you were supposed to protect her."

She thrust her hand on her hip and stared back. "I'm doing okay, so far. Listen to what she has to say."

Before Wilson could extend the argument, Claire told him about the encounters she and Deb had with Jill and Leon.

After a skeptical glance, Wilson fished out his pocket notebook and began writing. When Claire finished her story, he put down his pen. "I guess, short of locking you up, there's no way to keep you from sticking your nose in a hot oven. I have to admit, what you found out is helpful, but your visits with Leon make me real nervous."

Deb mimed a sweet face. "It was my idea."

"Listen." Wilson pointed a finger at Deb. "The only reason I'm putting up with you is that a colleague of mine in the Denver P.D. vouches for you. You need to keep Mrs. Hanover out of trouble, not lead her into it."

"Sorry." Deb looked contrite. "I won't do it again."

Wilson peered at Claire. "Promise me you won't talk to Leon again."

"I promise." Relieved, Claire had no qualms about making the promise. "What did you find out about the women at the gym?"

Wilson flipped a few pages and read from his notes. "Karla has an alibi. She went shopping with a friend the morning Romero was shot, and the friend vouched for her. Plus, she had credit receipts with time and date.

"I also talked to Patti. She doesn't have a solid alibi, but she doesn't have a good motive either." Wilson raised his head. "I tend to agree with your friend, Leon. This case has always looked like a crime of passion to me, making your husband the prime suspect."

When Claire opened her mouth to speak, Wilson held up his hand. "I'm open to other possibilities. Back to Patti. She denied having an affair with Romero, and I found no evidence that she did."

"What about her Hispanic accent?"

"Her limp is more important." Wilson stared at Claire. "Think back to when you heard someone running down the stairs after Romero was shot. Was the cadence uneven, like someone favored one leg?"

Claire closed her eyes to focus. She shut out the memory of Enrique's blood-soaked body, and tuned her mind to what she'd heard. The steps had been even and . . . "Light."

"What?"

Claire opened her eyes. "The steps were even and light, steps a woman would make."

"Did the person hit every step?"

"I don't remember. Why is that important?"

"A fleeing man would be more likely to skip steps than a woman would, especially a small one."

"C'mon, Claire, I'm going to run down the stairs," Deb said. "Maybe that'll help you remember. Go listen from the bedroom."

Deb led them into the hall then glanced up. "Hope you don't mind disturbing your husband's rest."

Claire walked to the stairs. "He's dead to the world." She flinched. "Ouch. I didn't mean to say that."

Deb followed Claire to the top of the stairs, waited for Claire to get ready, then ran down.

Claire met Wilson and Deb at the bottom. "The steps I heard that day were light, like Deb's. There were lots of them, too, as though the person hit every step. That's another clue the killer wasn't Roger."

Deb looked at Wilson. "Of the female suspects we've checked out so far, we've narrowed it down to—"

"Condoleza Martinez, Jill Edstrom, and Ellen Kessler." Wilson paced the hall. "Which of these women knew where your husband worked?"

"Jill and Ellen did, for sure," Claire replied. "I don't think Condoleza knew, but Jill could've told her, or Ellen could've told Enrique, who passed it on to Condoleza."

"Leon vouched for Condoleza," Wilson said. "He had a liaison with her while his men kept Travis occupied."

"He's probably protecting her." Deb leaned against the banister. "And his two goons will say whatever he tells them to."

Wilson nodded. "Makes sense, but I'm inclined to give Leon the benefit of the doubt." He flipped forward in his notebook. "And you said Mrs. Edstrom confirmed she and Mrs. Kessler ate brunch, not lunch, at the Broadmoor that day."

"True," Deb said. "Why would she say that if she had something to hide?"

"Maybe she didn't. That leaves Mrs. Kessler."

"At one point I thought it could be Ellen," Claire said, "but deep down I can't believe she'd kill someone, let alone hurt Roger and me like this."

Deb placed her hand on Claire's shoulder. "Murderers don't wear signs around their necks, especially the ones who kill in a fit of rage or jealousy. They probably surprise even themselves."

"But Ellen said she left Enrique. Why would she be jealous?"

"Maybe she lied when she said she ended the affair. Maybe Karla was right and he ended it."

"Then why would she encourage me to see him?"

"To set you up," Deb said. "Or, more precisely, to set your husband up. Remember the phone call to Roger's office? Ellen knew you were meeting Enrique. She could have faked an accent."

"Oh, God." Claire's head whirled with the implications. "Ellen knew Roger and I had problems. She said she thought I needed a fling. Ellen can be manipulative. In fact, another reason she pushed Enrique on me was to get back at Karla. But I can't believe she'd be that scheming. We're not just talking about a crime of passion here."

"Murder one," Deb said. "Planning ahead in cold blood."

Claire shuddered.

Upstairs, a toilet flushed. Claire wondered if she should check on Roger.

Deb said, "Ellen's our best suspect, Claire. We've got to find out if she's the one."

"How do we find out?"

"I've been thinking about that while you two've been talking," Wilson said. "There's no physical evidence to help us. We'll have to extract a confession."

Deb looked at Claire.

Wilson studied Claire, also.

She felt like a squirming germ on a microscope slide. "Why are you two staring at me?"

"We could wire her," Wilson began.

"And school her in what to say," Deb added.

"But . . ." Claire reviewed her conversation with Ellen the day before. "I've already talked to Ellen, practically accused her of the murder. Except for getting mad at me, she acted cool and had a logical explanation for every move of hers that looked suspicious."

"That was before we found out about the brunch," Deb said, "before she lost her alibi. If you tell her you know she wasn't at the Broadmoor during the time Enrique was killed, that might unnerve her."

A groan at the top of the stairs made Claire look up.

Roger stood at the rail, gripping it so tightly his knuckles showed white. "No."

Deb and Wilson stared at him.

"No," Roger repeated, then shakily descended the stairs. He blinked to focus his bleary eyes on Wilson. "I don't want Claire put in any more danger."

Roger gripped Claire's arm, stumbled off the last step, then grabbed the banister to steady himself. "You've done enough. You convinced Wilson to investigate other people. He can move on from here. And Deb can help him, if you want."

Claire nodded. *That's what I was thinking. It's time for the professionals to take over.*

Deb glanced from Roger to Claire. "If Ellen's the one, we already know how cagey she can be. She'd refuse to talk to Detective Wilson and I'm a stranger."

Claire sighed and said, "The only person she might let her guard down with is me. Or Jill."

Roger jiggled her arm. "You're not listening. I said no."

She gently removed Roger's hand from her arm as newfound determination surged through her. "I have to do this. If Ellen is guilty and doesn't confess, you'll go to jail. You're still charged with the crime, and the physical evidence points to you."

"She could shoot you," Roger said.

Claire shook her head. "I don't think she'd kill me."

"Don't forget about the death threat," Deb said.

Roger's eyes grew wide. "What death threat?"

"Your wife received a note at the gym this morning, telling her to stop snooping or face death herself." Wilson turned to Claire. "Ellen Kessler is your friend, but that note shows desperation. If she's Romero's murderer and you corner her, she may try to kill you."

"It's too dangerous." Roger shook his head, then held his

forehead, wincing in pain.

"We can fit Claire with a bulletproof vest and a wire she can wear under a sweater," Wilson said. "My men and I will listen to the conversation close by and will intervene at the first sign of trouble." Wilson's eyes narrowed on Claire. "But if you do this, you have to go in with full knowledge of the risks. Don't assume you're safe because she's a friend."

"Claire," Roger said, "I'd rather take my chances fighting this charge on my own. If you got hurt or killed, I couldn't live with myself."

He led her away from Deb and Wilson and said quietly, "I almost couldn't live with myself after Ned basically fired me."

"That's what I was afraid of," she whispered.

He gripped her hand. "But while I downed those damn scotches, I kept thinking of you. How I'd miss growing old with you. How hurt you'd be."

Claire looked into his bloodshot eyes. Love for him flooded her heart. So did resolve. "I got you into this mess. I couldn't live with myself if I didn't get you out of it."

"No, Claire."

She licked her lips. "Remember the three-legged stool?" The minister had explained the concept in his sermon when he married them, and she and Roger had based their relationship on it.

Roger said, "Love, trust, and respect, the three legs of a good marriage."

"Without any one, the stool topples," Claire said. "I knocked out trust, and we need to repair that leg, but I'm asking you to hold onto respect. Respect my right to make this decision."

He stared at her, then squeezed his eyes shut. His chin dropped in defeat.

Claire glanced at Wilson. "I'll do it."

Chapter 22
Confrontation

Saturday morning, Claire sat in an unmarked white police van parked three driveways away from Ellen's house. A curve blocked the view of the van from the house. Claire licked her lips in nervous anticipation. She watched and listened while Wilson and the two other policemen in the van made final checks on the recording equipment. Her empty stomach roiled. She hadn't been able to eat anything for breakfast.

Wearing a serious frown, Detective Wilson studied her.

"What is it?" Claire asked.

"I'm just checking to make sure none of the equipment's poking out." He patted her damp hand. "Try not to worry. She'll pick up on your nervousness."

Claire tried to crack a smile. "Now that was a real helpful comment."

Wilson peered at her. "You can still back out."

"I'm in." Claire gritted her teeth. "This is for Roger."

"You know we'll be there in a flash if you need us." Wilson paused, as if giving her one last chance to refuse. "Ready?"

Claire nodded, though Mickey Hart of the Grateful Dead was pounding out one of his famous drum solos in her heart. She climbed out of the van and sucked in her breath as an icy wind blasted her face. She shot a thumbs-up sign and a weak smile that she didn't really feel at her personal support team, Deb and Roger, who sat in Deb's car, parked behind the van.

Claire nodded at Deb's return thumbs-up. With her hands

tucked under her armpits, she walked to her car, parked behind theirs. She let out a long, slow breath to calm her nerves, then drove around the curve and into Ellen's driveway.

She walked to Ellen's front porch and took a moment to steady her trembling hands. A rustle in a copse of scrub oak in the front yard startled her.

A six-point buck stared at her from the midst of the barren trees, warily protecting his harem of three does. Through the bare branches, the bright mid-morning sun cast long rays, dappling his proud back. Apparently satisfied that Claire posed no threat, the mule deer bent his head to nibble at the dried grass.

Unlike the buck, Claire knew that the danger she faced was yet to come. She patted her knobby, loose sweater and felt the form-fitting Kevlar bulletproof vest underneath. Running her hand over her hair, she reassured herself that the miniature radio receiver in her right ear was covered. Her fingers searched for the thin, wireless microphone hidden under her collar.

"Test."

Wilson's voice answered from the earpiece. "All clear. We're right with you. Go in when you're ready."

Claire shivered, only partly from the cold. She glanced down the street. She couldn't see the van, but she drew strength from knowing it was there. She squared her shoulders and rang the doorbell.

When Ellen opened the door, her face registered surprise. "I didn't expect to see you this morning. When I called Dave about some legal paperwork last night, he told me Roger had gone home with you. Why aren't you with him?"

"The reunion didn't go well. I need to talk to you. May I come in?"

Ellen's expression changed to concern. She ushered Claire inside and locked the door. "I was afraid this might happen."

"What might happen?"

"That your hopes of getting back with Roger wouldn't pan out." Ellen put her arm around Claire's shoulder.

Claire flinched, then willed herself to act calm as Ellen led her down the hall. When they entered the kitchen, the lingering smell of fried bacon made Claire's stomach twist into a knot and threaten to beat its way up her throat. She gulped down the taste of bile.

Ellen didn't seem to notice Claire's reaction. "Come have some tea and tell me all about it."

As she settled onto a padded bench beside the kitchen table, Claire realized that talking about her relationship with Roger might lower Ellen's defenses. "Roger's been sleeping in Michael's room."

Ellen turned from the stove where she had lit a fire under the teakettle. "Uh-oh."

Awkwardly, Claire pressed on. "He couldn't sleep in the master bedroom. He said it brought back memories of seeing me covered in blood. And screaming."

Ellen's brow furrowed. "That would be enough to turn most men off." She carried teacups and teabags to the table.

"Roger said what really upset him was that I was afraid of him."

"The toad! In that situation, anyone would be afraid of him. Enrique had just been shot, and Roger had a gun in his hand. What did he expect?"

"For me to trust him not to shoot his wife of twenty-six years. I'm sure Roger wasn't exactly turning away from me last night. He was trying to avoid the memory of the killing, don't you think?" Claire desperately hoped so.

Ellen put the teakettle on the table, slid onto the bench across from Claire, and covered Claire's clenched hands with one of her own. "You want that to be the reason, don't you?"

Claire nodded miserably.

Ellen poured tea. "Then you should believe that's the reason, unless he says otherwise."

Claire cupped her ice-cold hands around her warm teacup. "So you really think he didn't reject me?"

"He's your husband. You know him better than I do." Ellen peered at her. "Looks like you haven't gotten much sleep lately."

"I haven't."

"What can I do to help?"

Oh, God, here's my opening. Claire released the fragile cup before she cracked it. "You can help me figure out something. Remember you told me you and Jill had lunch at the Broadmoor the day Enrique was killed?"

"Yes."

"Deb and I called the hotel." Claire tried to gauge Ellen's reaction, but her friend's expression was unreadable. "They said your reservation was for the Lake Terrace at ten-thirty, not lunch at Café Julie." Claire took a deep breath. "Jill told me you had *brunch* that day."

Ellen waved her hand, as if brushing away an annoying insect. "So?"

"So . . ." Claire squirmed in her seat, but kept her gaze trained on Ellen's face. "That means you could have finished in time for one of you to, you know, come to my house afterward."

Ellen's jaw dropped. "Are you serious? You aren't just collecting evidence about Enrique's affairs. You really think one of us killed him." Her eyes narrowed.

Instinctively, Claire drew back. "Yes, I do. And whomever did wrote that death threat."

Ellen's hands slapped the table. "How could you think Jill or I would want to harm you?"

"Maybe I was getting too close. Maybe one of you was desperate to stop me, not necessarily by killing me, but by scaring me off."

"We both escorted you out to your car, remember?"

Claire took a quick sip of tea to wet her desert-dry throat. "You could have been acting."

Ellen leapt up from the table and strode to the other side of the kitchen. "I don't believe this."

"I'm having a hard time believing it too, but all the clues point to you."

With an incredulous expression, Ellen clutched her chest. "Me?"

Claire's heart ached as she watched the devastating effect her accusation was having on her friend. "You said you met Jill for lunch, but she told me you met for brunch. She wouldn't give up that alibi so easily if she shot Enrique."

"It was a slip of the tongue, Claire." Ellen turned away and gazed out the window. When she faced Claire again, a tear rolled down her cheek. In an anguished whisper, she said, "How could you think I'd kill someone? Or that I'd frame your husband and hurt you in the process?"

For the first time that morning, Claire felt a twinge of doubt. Ellen truly looked stricken. Claire hesitated, debating what to say next.

Detective Wilson's voice sounded in her ear. "Good. She's emotional and more likely to make mistakes. Keep pressing."

Claire stood and approached Ellen. "Maybe it wasn't the real you. Maybe something snapped when Enrique rejected you."

"I told you, he didn't reject me."

"And Karla told me he did. Ellen, if you shot Enrique, you need help."

"Damn you!" Ellen shouted. "I am not crazy, and I did not shoot Enrique!"

"Ellen." Jill's voice called from beyond the sliding-glass door on the deck. "Let me in."

Claire felt a surge of panic. How had Jill made it past the

police van?

Then Claire remembered the shortcut through backyards that the two friends often used to visit each other.

To let Wilson know what was happening, she said, "Jill sure picked a bad time to visit."

Ellen glanced at the clock. "I asked her to come over this morning, so we could talk about you."

"Me?"

"We're your friends, Claire. We were trying to figure out how to support you."

And here I am, stabbing you in the back. "I'm sorry, Ellen."

"I can't leave Jill standing out in the cold." Ellen grabbed a tissue, wiped her eyes, and moved to the door.

With her back to the door, Claire whispered into her collar, "How do we protect Jill?"

"It's a complication, but we'll deal with it," Wilson replied. "Don't give up. Keep pushing Ellen."

Chewing on her lip, Claire faced her friends. The situation was spinning out of control, and she didn't know what to do. How could she extract a confession from Ellen with Jill here?

As they walked side by side into the kitchen, Jill peered at Ellen. "You look upset. Have you been crying?"

Ellen waved her hand in Claire's direction. "Claire accused me of killing Enrique."

Jill frowned. "Claire said she was making a list of people who had a reason to want Enrique dead, but—"

"No, that's not it. You told her we had brunch that day, not lunch, so now she thinks I was making up an alibi."

"We made a reservation, Ellen. Anyone could've checked it." Jill glared at Claire. "And you did, didn't you?"

"Yes." Unsettled by Jill's anger, Claire struck back. "You told me about the brunch because you realized I'd find out anyway, didn't you? And by telling me, you made me suspect Ellen."

Jill jammed her fists on her hips. "Don't you dare blame me for this. You're the one hurting Ellen, not me."

Claire's thoughts raced, along with her heart. Her previous conversations with Jill came rushing back. Jill had called Enrique an egotistical moron, and he'd refused her advances. Not only that, he'd insulted her, a fatal blow to her already battered self-esteem. A doorknob turned in Claire's mind, and a door opened to another possibility.

She stepped toward Jill. "You were protecting yourself, weren't you? You knew that I knew how badly Enrique treated you. You hated him. He called you fat, didn't he?"

Jill's face flushed. "I'm a lot more attractive than some of the other women he slept with, like that horse-faced Karla. But he refused me. He *rejected* me!"

Claire stared at Jill's reddened face. *Oh, God. Ellen didn't kill Enrique, Jill did!*

"He hurt you," Claire continued. "Deeply. And you wanted to hurt him back."

"Of course I did. Lots of women did. He deserved to have his pretty face cut." Chest heaving, Jill slashed her hand through the air.

Slack-jawed, Ellen stared at Jill.

Jill seemed to realize her reaction looked suspicious. Quickly, she dropped her arm.

Ellen put a hand to her head, as if to stop it from whirling. "I thought you were depressed about Enrique. Where'd this rage come from?"

"I could only keep it bottled up for so long, Ellen. Night after night that rat's rejection, and Paul's, tormented me so much I couldn't sleep. Paul wanted to put me back on Prozac, but I'm sick of drugs. They don't solve anything."

Jill paced, clenching and unclenching her fists. "Drugs don't stop your husband from cheating on you while you try to keep your plastic smile from cracking. While you play the perfect wife, hoping he'll stay with you, hoping you won't have to find a job and support yourself when you've never worked a day in your life. Then, when you turn to someone else for comfort, pills don't stop the slimebag from rejecting you."

She stopped, sides heaving, then stared wild-eyed at Claire. "I told you Ellen and I talked for a while after we ate," she said. "Didn't I?"

Claire wiped her clammy hands on her jeans and nodded.

"So neither one of us had time to get to your house."

Before Claire could form a reply, Ellen said, "But we left before noon—"

"Stop!" Jill glared at Ellen. "Shut up, Ellen!"

"Because I wanted to pick up some groceries." Ellen finished.

"So you left before noon." Claire studied Jill. The maniacal glint in her eyes reminded Claire of a fragile glass figurine, ready to crack if someone slid it off its perch.

Jill's chin thrust out. "That doesn't prove anything."

With sympathy, Claire said, "No one's saying you're a cold-blooded killer. Enrique wounded you, and to protect yourself, you struck back." *And you couldn't target your husband, so your tortured mind focused on someone else.*

Jill shook her head, hunching her shoulders like a cornered animal.

Claire glanced at Ellen. An unspoken message of horror passed between them.

"Jill . . ." Ellen held out her hand.

Jill backed away, against the kitchen counter, still shaking her head. "No, no, I didn't do it."

"Yes, you did." Claire felt even more certain now. "And you planned it beforehand." She made an educated guess. "To avoid leaving fingerprints, you wore gloves. Didn't you?"

Jill started to nod her head, then stopped herself. Her glance darted from Claire to Ellen and back.

"I'll help you get through this, Jill," Claire said. "Ellen will, too. We're your friends."

Jill's mad stare burned into Claire. "You couldn't let up, could you? That death threat should have stopped you, but you kept pushing."

Claire replayed Jill's words in her mind. All Jill had admitted to so far was the death threat. Claire had to find some way to get Jill to confess directly to the killing. She tensed, almost holding her breath. "You shot Enrique, didn't you?"

"That asshole was the scum of the earth." Jill ground out the words. "He preyed on innocent women."

"So you killed him."

Jill's eyes blazed. "Yes, I killed him. And I'd do it again. He deserved to die, especially after what he did to me."

Ellen held her hand over her mouth. Tears trickled down her cheek.

"But why frame Roger?" Claire asked.

Nervously, Jill licked her lips. "I had to pin it on someone. I thought I was doing you a favor. Ellen said you were unhappy in your marriage, that Roger was ignoring you, but you'd never leave on your own. So I made it easy for you."

"How'd you know Enrique would be at my house?"

Jill grinned an unnaturally wide grin. "Ellen told me the day before. So I changed our lunch to brunch and—"

"That's right," Ellen gasped.

"And I left the table to call Roger at his office." Jill's voice took on an Hispanic accent. "I couldn't mimic your voice, Claire, so I disguised mine. I've been listening to Condoleza for months."

"And you counted on Enrique carrying a gun?" Claire found this hard to believe.

"I brought my own, but when I saw his gym bag in your hall,

I decided using his was better." Beads of sweat stood out on Jill's forehead. She jerked her head back and forth, scanning the kitchen counter.

Is she trying to escape? "How'd you know about his gun?"

"I saw it in his open bag one day and asked him about it. He told me he always carried his gun in there. Probably because of his drug dealing."

"I thought you didn't know about that." Ellen's wide-eyed stare conveyed her surprise.

Jill whirled on Ellen. "I'm not stupid! All those secret meetings, sometimes two or three an hour. Even Enrique couldn't be servicing that many women. It had to be drugs."

"Then, after you shot Enrique, you dropped the gun in the hall and ran out the basement door." Claire hoped Wilson was getting all this.

Jill slid farther from Ellen, along the kitchen counter, her fingernails scrabbling along the edge. "I heard Roger drive up. I didn't realize I'd be cutting it so close. By sheer luck he was dumb enough to pick up the gun."

Breathing heavily, Jill glanced at Ellen. "And lucky for me, Ellen's nervous about break-ins and showed me where she keeps her gun." Jill slid open the drawer next to her.

Ellen screamed, "Watch out, Claire!"

Jill yanked a small snub-nosed thirty-eight revolver out of the drawer. She aimed the barrel at Claire. Glancing sideways at Ellen, Jill held up her hand. "Don't move."

Claire backed up until she felt the edge of the kitchen table. Her chest ached as she fought the urge to scream, but she had the foresight to say, "Jill's got a gun."

Ellen looked puzzled. "I can see that. Put it down, Jill."

Claire heard "Shit!" in her ear, then the loud clang of the van door being thrown open.

Sweat trickled down the sides of Jill's plump face. "I won't put it down." She aimed the revolver at Claire's head.

With a sinking feeling, Claire realized the bulletproof vest wouldn't protect her against a headshot. She raised her trembling hands, stared at the gun barrel, and groped for words to stall Jill until the police arrived. "Stop and think, Jill. What good will shooting me do?"

"I can't go to prison. I just can't." Jill's hand shook. She brought up her other hand to steady the gun.

Ellen inched toward Jill.

Keeping her gaze locked with Jill's, Claire said, "Get out, Ellen. Now. She'll go for you next."

Claire tensed her legs, making ready to spring at Jill. Jill would shoot her no matter what, but maybe she could save Ellen.

Jill cocked the hammer. "Sorry, Claire."

"No!" Ellen leapt forward, lunging for the gun.

Jill squeezed the trigger.

The loud report made Claire instinctively duck.

The bullet ripped through Ellen's shoulder, then shattered the clock on the wall behind Claire.

With a groan, Ellen sagged against the counter. She fell face-up on the floor, her eyes rolling back in her head. Bright red blood flowed out of the exit wound and smeared the tiles.

Her reason conquered by raw anguish, Claire screamed.

Jill's cry mingled with Claire's, rising in a high-pitched keen. Tears streamed down her cheeks. She aimed at Claire again.

Propelled by guilt and rage, Claire lunged for Jill's gun hand. She shoved it up in the air and held on.

Jill's shot seemed to echo down the hallway. The bullet ripped into the kitchen ceiling, showering plaster flakes.

Clawing and kicking, Jill fought Claire like a goaded bear, trying to free her hand.

Claire's arms throbbed, but she bit her lip and kept her hands clamped on Jill's.

The front door crashed open. In a blur, Wilson rushed in, followed by his two officers, all with guns drawn.

Wilson dove into the women, knocking them down. He batted the pistol out of Jill's hand then pinned her face down on the floor.

Gasping for breath, Claire struggled to her hands and knees.

One of the officers knelt beside Jill. He pulled her arms behind her then snapped handcuffs on her wrists.

Jill thrashed and whimpered. Her eyes rolled back in her head, white and unseeing.

The other officer pulled out his radio. "Send an ambulance." He knelt beside Ellen's unconscious body and felt for a pulse in her neck as he recited the address.

Sobbing, Claire reached for Ellen. She saw her friend's ashen face and the spreading pool of blood. *Oh, God. She tried to save me. And after I accused her of murder.*

"Don't die, Ellen," Claire whispered. "Please don't die."

Wilson called out, "All clear."

Deb ran into the kitchen. She quickly grabbed two kitchen towels off the stove handle, knelt beside Ellen, and pressed one towel on the seeping entrance wound below Ellen's collarbone. She slipped her hand with the other towel under Ellen's shoulder.

Eyes tearing, Claire asked, "Will she live?"

Deb looked over, sympathy in her gaze. "I think so." But she kept her hands tight against both sides of the wound.

Suddenly, Claire was pulled to her feet.

Roger engulfed her in a bear hug.

"When the cops leapt out of the van, we followed." Deb nodded toward Roger. "He's a little slower than the rest of us."

"I've never felt so scared," Roger whispered in Claire's ear.

"We heard the gunshot right before we reached the front

door, but it was locked." Deb nodded toward the cop on the radio. "This guy shot the lock."

Dawning realization hit Claire. "I thought that was the echo of Jill's shot."

"That's when Wilson rushed in to play the hero," Deb said.

Wilson grinned. "Looked to me like you could have brought her down yourself, Mrs. Hanover." He began reciting the Miranda rights to Jill.

Roger leaned back and held Claire's face in both hands. "I thought she'd shot you. God, I feared I'd lost you." He hugged her again.

"I thought so, too, when she aimed at my head." Claire started to shake, and her knees buckled.

"Sit her on the bench," Deb said.

Roger lowered Claire to the bench by the kitchen table and sat beside her, keeping a protective arm around her shoulders.

She took a deep breath. The dizziness passed for a moment.

"Adrenaline shock," Deb said. "Perfectly normal."

With his face scrunched with worry, Roger peered at Claire. "You okay?"

Even though she wasn't sure, Claire said, "I'm fine."

He squeezed her shoulder and raised her chin so that she could look directly into his eyes. "I love you, Claire." He kissed her, a kiss filled with promises renewed, then ever so gently pulled away.

Claire smiled. "I love you, too." Then the room spun and went black.

CHAPTER 23
NEW BEGINNINGS

As Claire paced the lobby of the hospital, she glanced at her watch. "It's been two hours since Ellen got out of surgery. How long does it take to come out of the anesthesia?"

Roger glanced up from the *Newsweek* he'd been thumbing through. "I don't know. Sit down." He scooped up the lopsided pile of magazines he'd already scanned, clearing the seat cushion beside him. "The doctor said the surgery on her shoulder was successful, didn't he? The important thing is, she's alive."

Deb returned from the front desk. "They said Ellen's awake and we can see her. They warned she'll be groggy, though."

"Let's go." Claire grabbed the gift basket she'd thrown together, piled with potpourri, flavored waters, chocolates, and romance paperbacks. She headed for the elevators, then an attack of the jitters swept over her. She rubbed her sweaty palms on her sleeves. "Oh, God. Ellen probably hates me after all the terrible accusations I made. How am I going to apologize?"

Roger put his arm around her. "Just be yourself and tell her the truth."

"That's good advice, Mr. Hanover." Marvin Bradshaw, the *Gazette* reporter, walked up behind Roger. He peered around Roger's shoulder at Claire. "I understand you caught Enrique Romero's real killer, Mrs. Hanover."

Roger wheeled on the reporter. "You again. Get away from—"

"Roger, wait. He's just doing his job."

Bradshaw tilted his head at Claire, his gaze showing surprise.

"I appreciate your understanding. I'd like to get the whole story for our readers. A front-page headline would be a good way to clear your name, Mr. Hanover." While he spoke, he pulled a pad of paper and a pen out of his jacket pocket.

Roger glowered at Bradshaw.

Claire shook Roger's arm to get his attention. "He's right."

"He's right?" Roger stared at her.

"You were all over the front page when the police arrested you. The only way to erase that impression in people's minds is to get the proof of your innocence on the front page, too."

She turned to Bradshaw. "I need to visit my friend now, but we'll talk to you after that. Can you wait?"

"For this story, sure."

Deb pushed the elevator button. The three of them filed onto the elevator, leaving Bradshaw scribbling notes.

When they arrived at the door to Ellen's hospital room, Claire stopped and pulled a tissue from her purse. Nervously, she crumpled it until she had a wad clenched tight in her fist.

Roger gave her a little nudge. "Go on."

Deb smiled. "We'll wait here."

Gingerly, Claire stepped into Ellen's room. The odor of antiseptic and alcohol crinkled her nose.

Ellen lay on a raised hospital bed, an I.V. tube snaking down to her arm from a clear bag suspended on a rack next to the bed. Her disheveled hair lay spread out on the pillow behind her. Without her makeup, and with her skin so pale, she looked older. The word "frail" popped into Claire's mind, one she'd never used to describe Ellen before.

When Ellen saw her, she held out her good arm, the one with the I.V.

Claire put the basket on the bed-stand then gave Ellen a gentle hug, careful not to jostle her bandaged shoulder. "Oh, Ellen, I'm so sorry." Tears streamed down her cheeks. "Damn, I wasn't going to cry."

Ellen's lips curled. "Getting shot was my own dumb fault. I shouldn't have jumped in front of Jill. How was I to know you were wearing a bulletproof vest?"

"Who told you about the vest?"

"Detective Wilson, when I first woke up. I was too groggy to give him much of a statement, so he's coming back."

She glanced at the gift basket. "Is that one of your 'Hospital Hedonist' baskets? It's almost worth getting shot for one of those."

"It can't even begin to make up for what you did for me, and . . ." Claire swallowed. "I owe you an apology."

"For what?"

"For accusing you of killing Enrique, for even believing you could do such a thing."

A faraway, sad look came into Ellen's eyes. "I wouldn't have thought Jill could do such a thing, either."

"Neither would I." Claire clasped Ellen's hand. "Contrary to what Wilson said, you saved my life. Jill was aiming at my head."

"I still can't believe she was ready to shoot you. You are, or were, one of her best friends."

"Jill's reasoning was twisted. How could she think that killing a man in my bedroom was doing me a favor?"

Ellen pursed her lips. "Maybe she thought that. Or maybe she just said it. She could have been jealous of you, you know."

"Jealous?"

"Yes. Enrique didn't want her, but he wanted you. Maybe killing him in front of you was a form of revenge."

"Oh, God, that's too awful to imagine. I don't want to believe that of her."

With a sigh, Ellen said, "Neither do I." Feebly, she patted Claire's arm. "I've been doing some thinking. You were on the right trail. You knew the killer was Jill or me. If you hadn't come to my place to accuse me, Jill wouldn't have confessed. So you did the right thing."

"Still, I'll never forgive myself for thinking you were a murderer."

"Well, I forgive you. But you owe me big time." Ellen held a finger to her chin. Her eyes twinkled. "A day of shopping should do it. That is, once I get out of here."

"First we'll look for a new kitchen clock." Claire warmed to the topic. She loved shopping, especially with Ellen. "Then we'll go to your favorite shop, the Silent Woman. I see a new silk flower arrangement."

Roger walked in with Deb. He grinned at Ellen. "The silent woman? That doesn't sound like you."

Ellen let out a weak laugh, then said, "It doesn't, does it?"

"And I'll throw in lunch at the Ritz Grill," Claire said. "You can't let me off that easy."

Ellen winked at Roger. "That's me. Easy."

"Until then, I'll come by every day to see you." Claire frowned. "Are you in much pain?"

"They've got me doped up pretty well. I've seen some pretty colors and had some interesting dreams. Maybe I should contact Travis when I get out."

"Good God, I hope you're kidding." Noting Ellen's sly grin, Claire smiled.

Deb rounded the bed to stand on Ellen's other side. She scanned the dressing on Ellen's shoulder. "Looks like they patched you up well. What did the docs say?"

"No permanent damage. The wound should heal in a few weeks, then I start physical therapy."

Roger grasped Ellen's hand. "I'll be forever in your debt. If not for you, Claire may not have been here today." He put his other arm around Claire.

Ellen looked from one to the other and her face softened.

"You two have made up, haven't you?"

Claire gazed into Roger's eyes. "We've started."

Roger nodded then glanced down at Ellen. "You call me, you hear, anytime you need anything. A man's help around the house, whatever. I'll patch up your kitchen ceiling for you."

The sound of a throat clearing made Claire turn toward the door.

With a sheepish expression on his face, Dave Kessler stood there. He held a vase that contained a dozen long-stemmed red roses. "I'd like to take that job, if I may."

He carried the roses to the bed-stand then looked down at Ellen. Finally, he said softly, "How are you?"

Ellen swallowed hard. "I've been better."

An awkward silence followed.

"Looks like it's time for us to go." Claire signaled Deb with a nod toward the door.

Roger clasped Dave's hand. "Take care of her. She's a special woman."

"I know." Dave glanced at Ellen. "I know."

Claire bent down to hug Ellen and whispered in her ear, "Give him a chance. He still loves you."

Then Claire left, pushing Roger out in front of her.

Deb waited for them in the hall. "Was that Ellen's ex-husband?"

Claire glanced back in the room and saw Dave leaning down to grasp Ellen's hand. "Hopefully not ex much longer. C'mon, let's give them some privacy."

As they walked down the corridor toward the elevator, Detective Wilson approached. "Looks like you came from Ellen Kessler's room. Is she lucid?"

Claire placed her hand on his arm to stop him. "Yes, but she has a very important visitor. Can you give them a few minutes alone?"

"Sure." He looked at Roger. "The D.A. is filing the papers to drop all charges against you. You're a free man."

"Congratulations, Roger." Deb clapped him on the back.

"It's all due to Claire," he said.

Excited, Claire hugged him. "Now you can go to Ned and get your job back."

An expression of distaste passed over Roger's face. "We didn't part on good terms. Some things came out in that meeting that probably should've been said a long time ago. Other things shouldn't have been said at all." He smiled at Claire. "I've been thinking about what you said last week about not pushing so hard. I think I'll take some time off before I start looking for another job, and spend it getting reacquainted with my wife."

Claire smiled back as a warm glow suffused her. "I'd like that."

ABOUT THE AUTHOR

Beth Groundwater lives with her husband, two teenagers, and dog in Colorado Springs. Her first forays into fiction writing at age ten were short stories about a boy named Freddie whose adventures included burrowing to an underground mole city in a giant screwmobile. As an adult, Beth still lives vicariously through her characters and has published six short stories, including one in *Wild Blue Yonder,* the in-flight magazine for Frontier Airlines. Between writing spurts, she chauffeurs her children to their busy social engagements while bemoaning the lack of her own, defends her meager garden from marauding mule deer and rabbits, makes gift baskets for friends, and tries to avoid getting black and blue on Colorado's black and blue ski slopes. She's currently working on her fourth mystery manuscript, so look for more novels from this promising author. Please visit her website at www.bethgroundwater.com.

MYSTERY

GROUNDWATER, BETH
A REAL BASKET CASE

$25.95